## 'You know m

'For my pains.' [...] reassured himself [...] marily shot, the burglar sank gratefully on to the Holland covers that swathed a vast and lumpen sofa. Allegra could only stare in incredulity at the impudence of the creature.

Not that she would really expect anything else of Aunt Lydia's notoriously eccentric acquaintance. Only. . .he seemed very young to be another of Lydia's — well, *amours*.

'Am I Lydia's latest lover, you would ask if you were not so gently nurtured? No, my lady, I'm not.'

**Dear Reader**

We welcome back both Louisa Gray, with an intriguing Regency, and Sarah Westleigh, who has moved to Tudor times to explore the death threats to Elizabeth, both gripping reads.

We introduce a new American author, Kate Kingsley, where Danielle is ostracised by New Orleans and ends on the high seas, and have a second Patricia Potter story for you, set in New Mexico 1846, where Tristan Hampton has a hidden enemy.

June is bursting out with goodies indeed!

*The Editor*

**Louisa Gray** attended, for an incompetent at games, a disconcertingly sporty boarding school in Wales. She read Italian at university but left after a year, a decision she has never regretted. Her interest in history stems from her own family background, and she has a weakness for Chopin, violets and her very patient Italian fiancé, who was the model for her first historical hero. She lives in the West Country with her dog Cressy.

**Recent titles by the same author:**

THE MANSINI SECRET

# BEAU'S STRATAGEM

## Louisa Gray

# MILLS & BOON

MILLS & BOON LIMITED
ETON HOUSE, 18–24 PARADISE ROAD
RICHMOND, SURREY, TW9 1SR

# For my mother, with love

*First published in Great Britain 1994*
*by Mills & Boon Limited*

© Louisa Gray 1994

*Australian copyright 1994   Philippine copyright 1994*
*This edition 1994*

ISBN 0 263 78253 0

*Set in 10 on 12 pt Linotron Times*
*04-9406-80167*

*Typeset in Great Britain by Centracet, Cambridge*
*Printed in Great Britain by*
*BPC Paperbacks Ltd*
*A member of*
*The British Printing Company Ltd*

# CHAPTER ONE

OF ALL things—to be banished to Bath for her own good! As if it were *her* fault the Honourable Cuthbert Nettlesham had forgot himself so spectacularly at Carlton House, let alone that the Honourable Cuthbert's uncle had promptly ordered him from England until the scandal had been superseded by another. And here was she—the victim of his melodramatic importunities—rattling into the boring, *boring* provinces with beastly *Algie*, to stay with, of *all* people, Aunt Lydia. Allegra hugged herself into her sable-lined velvet travelling cloak and wished pointlessly that the Honourable Cuthbert had shown the only spark of intelligence he was likely to muster and fought that duel with Freddie Limmersham over someone *else's* 'Heavenly Azure Eyes'. It was the fact that Cuthbert had won and Freddie had still had the gall to approach Papa for her hand. . . Oh, well—Allegra tucked her freezing fingers closely round the silver flask of hot water hidden inside her muff—that was two people she could blame for her plight! Freddie, in fact, was particularly a wretch because he had been packed off to India, where he had secretly been longing to go for years.

It wasn't Algie's fault that he was protesting his own sudden exile out loud; nor even that his parrot would insist on noisily repeating every grievance after him. It was just that it was one vulgar squawk too many——

'Oh, *do* throw your coat over his cage, Algie! I never met a more idiotic bird——'

'Bird!' offered the parrot.

'*Algie!*'

Algernon Ashley, The Most Honourable the Marquess of Stonyhurst, made a far from honourable gesture with his tongue. Inarticulate with ten hours of gathering frustration, his much older sister—who really ought to have known better—made one back.

'That's rude—for a girl!' Algie reproved with ten-year-old majesty.

'Rude!' tried the parrot.

'If you don't throw something——'

Algie was out of his coat and smothering the elaborate golden cage before Allegra could utter another syllable. Ill-behaved he might be, and proud of it, but he had the liveliest sense of self-preservation and had long discovered it unwise fully to enrage his sister within the confines of a moving carriage. Out in the open—with several acres to lose himself in—then the horrid, cross-patch creature would see! Only there were no wide open acres in Bath, only old people, and improving lectures, and libraries, and *schoolgirls*.

'I can't see why you must always be snapping at my ears,' he objected, making a meal of the fact that he was cold without his coat by shivering loudly.

Allegra was not remotely sympathetic. 'You make me snap. In fact,' she added candidly, 'just about anything would make me snap just at the moment. I cannot believe Papa would do this to me——'

'*Us.*'

'Us, then. After all——'

'After all, you only encouraged that idiot Cuthbert to moon after you——'

'I did not!'

Algie grinned lewdly. 'And I suppose you didn't flirt with Freddie either!'

Allegra sat up—unwisely, given the careening motion of the carriage over these icy Wiltshire roads. 'Freddie! And besides the fact he is Mr Limmersham to you, you little toad, I did *not* flirt with Freddie! Freddie is a rake so one doesn't have to.' Then she remembered to whom she was speaking and amended hastily, 'I *never* flirt!'

Algie's roar of hysterical laughter was echoed, if somewhat muffled and subdued, by the enterprising parrot. The Marquess of Stonyhurst was laughing so much he all but fell off his seat, and would have done so were he not pinned heavily to the squabs by a long and monstrously overweight deerhound whose least attractive quality—of many—was to howl the moment anyone evinced amusement.

Brandenburg howled, Algie and the parrot crowed, and Allegra smarted.

It was *not* true, she had never flirted with anyone. . . she did not consider it the thing to do at all; unfortunately her Mama had died just too early to warn her that it was even less the thing to allow gentlemen to become so openly sentimental in the first place. Gentlemen, concluded Allegra with all the wisdom of her seventeen years, were simply and only a menace. After all, what else could one expect when they started out as specimens like Algie?

'Haw! Haw!' The parrot was well into his stride by now, so it was a great relief to Algie that the very moment Allegra leaned forward to murder his pet the coach offered the long-awaited signs of slowing its mad pace and at last the unremitting darkness of the open countryside gave way to a sky glowing softly with the reassuring lights of the city.

All Allegra could think to say was, 'Well, thank God for that, I suppose! At least in a few more minutes we shall be warm again.'

Everything would look better from the comfort of a roaring fire. Even boring old Bath.

Algie was the first to notice it. With a tremor in his voice that betrayed his very real exhaustion he tugged at his sister's velvet sleeve.

'Allegra, look; no one's home!'

'What? Oh, no, Algie, you must be looking at the wrong house. . .' Then her voice petered out. He wasn't.

It seemed that the whole honeyed façade of Great Pulteney Street was gilded with welcoming light; indeed one or two doors that very moment opened and an enticing candle-glow spilled across the frost-bright pavement — only one house was in darkness.

'Impossible!'

'What shall we do?'

There was only one thing to do. 'Aunt Lydia *must* be at home, Algie. Perhaps she is just having one of her fits of economising. You know how she can be.'

Even so, Allegra did not believe it. Somehow, as she descended from the carriage and approached the door . . .well, she could not explain it, but the house *felt* empty. More than that—her lively imagination was never very long subdued—it felt like a house deserted, and deserted suddenly, as if the people in it had, without any warning, and in real, urgent haste, gone away.

It was an impression compounded not one second later by the hush of still warm air as she knocked and the door swung wide on to a desolate hallway, its marble floor shining with chill hostility in the moonlight.

Allegra was more than relieved when the second carriage drew up—Herr Kraftstein; he would know what to do.

The most disquieting thing of all was that, as Allegra turned in a rush of relief to Algie's young Austrian tutor hurrying competently towards her, she saw that Herr Kraftstein was looking not just puzzled, as anyone might have done, but actually disturbed.

He was so disturbed, he ordered Allegra back to the carriage.

'I shall go in alone, your ladyship,' and there was no arguing with the quiet determination in his voice. 'Something is amiss and it is better that I attend to it alone.'

Of course he was right, especially as he had her father's largest groom and even larger footman to investigate with him. Allegra looked on as the men made their way inside, her eyes—she was not sure why—glancing almost nervously this way and that along Pulteney Street towards Laura Place and the junction with Henrietta Street. All deserted. Except. . .

Now that *was* strange. A man was leaning against a tree by the end house, as if waiting for a friend perhaps . . .only—only he seemed—Allegra felt it as a prickle of ice down her spine—to be watching her.

Even as she became sure of it the man disappeared.

One thing's for sure, Allegra thought, not really aware that she did so, I should know that man again. Anywhere.

Not that she would ever have to.

'Maybe someone has abducted Aunt Lydia.' It was Algie's half-excited, half-teeth-chattering tone that brought Allegra round to the real predicament.

'Nonsense!' She hoped to sound reassuring. The trouble was, where *was* their aunt, who had most certainly known they were on their way and exactly when they would arrive? Indeed, a note had been waiting for them at the inn where they had rested overnight just to reassure Allegra that she and her entourage were expected. Aunt Lydia was a great many things—and irredeemably irresponsible was one of them—but leave her young niece and nephew stranded in this way? No, that was not like Aunt Lydia at all.

Algie echoed her thoughts in his oddly grown-up way. 'Funny thing is, if we had been met by a dancing bear or a circus clown, or someone singing a Russian serenade, it would have been almost natural, wouldn't it? This isn't.'

'No. . .' And suddenly Allegra could stand it no longer. 'Come on, Algie, we're going in!'

They were met as they blundered their way towards the staircase by the young tutor hurrying the other way. From somewhere he had acquired a candelabrum and the means to light his candles. The sudden flooding of light threw into relief every last line of worry on his austerely handsome face.

'Not here, Herr Kraftstein?'

'No. No one. I cannot understand it, particularly in light of the letter Lady Limington sent your ladyship last evening.'

Allegra, though very far from a nervous dispostion, was nevertheless comforted by his matter-of-fact way of facing this perplexing development. So she confided, 'You have never met our aunt, sir; if you had you would be even more bewildered.'

'That's for sure, milady,' confirmed Lorcan, the tough young Irish footman, racing up the steps from the kitchen quarters at that moment, a carriage lamp in his massive fingers. 'I *do* know her ladyship. If I may make a suggestion, milady, you must not stay here. I'll send Williams for the Watch; you should go at once to the York——'

'Yes——' the tutor turned to the footman gratefully '—you are quite right. . .your ladyship and the Marquess must leave this instant. The hotel will be sure to accommodate you.'

Something strange happened to Allegra then. Perhaps it was the anxiety in the men's voices, and in their quick exchange of glances. . .but most likely it was the sudden eruption of long-fermenting resentment that yet again *men*, if you please, were deciding what she must do. She knew they had only her interests at heart, but. . .

So she said, 'I cannot understand this any more than you can, but I refuse to believe that anything so untoward has happened to my aunt that it would mean it were safer that we leave here. That is what you mean, isn't it — that this house is somehow *unsafe*?'

The tutor and the footman knew that tone and exchanged another eloquently anguished look. The tutor, the footman's straining eyebrow implied, was the only one who had a hope of overriding her wilful little ladyship now.

So Herr Kraftstein tried what he knew already to be hopeless. 'Yes, my lady — for a reason I cannot begin to give because I haven't a rational one, I *do* believe that something is very wrong here; it *isn't* safe.'

'But that is. . .well, it's absurd!' And suddenly it seemed so now the candlelight revealed the familiar comforts of this most elegant and unexceptional of houses. 'My aunt must have been called away ——'

'Taking all her servants with her?' For the first time her maid spoke up. 'No one is here, are they, Mr Kraftstein, sir? No one at all!'

And that was exactly the point. The reason why Allegra wasn't going to be sent off to some stuffy old hotel for anyone.

'Precisely, Sorcha, and I see that as all the more reason why we must remain. My aunt cannot have meant to leave the front door open for just anyone to walk in off the streets as they please. I should very much like to know where her servants have got to, and why, and I intend to be here to ask them when they come skulking home from wherever it is they have been carousing!'

It was not as if she did not know her aunt's servants after all—and what she knew most certainly explained *their* absence.

But not her aunt's

'No,' she added more firmly, 'I think—I *know* it is important that we stay here. Stay together. If something is wrong, if my aunt should be in trouble and need our help, where else would she look for us but here? We shall send for a constable in the morning.'

The tutor, because he had from the first considered the young Lady Allegra as much his duty to defend as his official pupil, tried one last time to dissuade her. The very tone of his attempt showed he knew only too well it was impossible.

'If *I* were to stay alone, my lady ——'

Even as she smiled at him—as she had never been able to help doing, for all she knew it would make Papa so angry—Allegra knew she was going to ignore his all-too-sensible advice. After all her word—without Aunt Lydia—was law.

'No—we stay.' And as if to make all further agument redundant she untied the ribbons of her fashionable little Polish hat and flung it carelessly on to a nearby ormolu table.

An hour later, the essentials of their luggage unpacked, Allegra was well in charge of what was turning out to be an intriguing, if not quite welcome adventure; now that she was warmed and had eaten an excellent supper—the very existence of which proved beyond doubt that her aunt had been expecting them, for all Algie's favourite cakes and pies were lined up on the vast kitchen table — Allegra found her initial alarm all but dissipated.

She had insisted that the whole company eat together, for it was necessary to arrange her plan of campaign for the morrow.

'We are, it seems, to be without a cook, or a housekeeper, or a butler, at least until the morning. . .'

She had known her maid's eyes would light up at the opportunity to display her housewifely talents to an appreciative and very handsome footman.

'Ah, but I can cook!'

'And I,' smiled the footman, 'shall just be a butler a little sooner in my career than anyone intended!'

It was a strangely comfortable moment, listening to their laughter here in the shadowy firelit cave of a kitchen, for Allegra always her favourite part of any house since the days when she had pleaded jam tarts from the chef as a little girl. And Algie all but lived in the kitchens, a fact which showed all too obviously in the distress of sundry seams and buttons. Brandenburg the deerhound snored in front of the flames, Herr Kraftstein's absurd little mongrel Schnapps curled between his great boxing-glove paws. Even the parrot was amiable in the general post-prandial languor.

So when Allegra smiled round at the expectant faces all about her — the only disapproval now evident being in the young tutor's clear grey eyes — she could not prevent herself from laughing.

To think that Papa had sent her to Bath to be overseen, ordered about and all but actually incarcerated!

'This is going to be quite an adventure,' she murmured to no one in particular.

'Venture,' sighed the parrot.

How long she had been sleeping Allegra could not say, for in the dwindling firelight she could not see the tiny enamelled clock at her bedside. All she knew was that it was not its gentle ticking that had woken her so abruptly. It was some other sound.

Allegra lay rigid for a full minute, holding her breath and straining her ears against the darkness, before she heard it again. The strangest scraping noise, gritty yet metallic, followed by an unmistakable click.

And yet. . .and yet there had been no response from Brandy or from Schnapps. Not even from the parrot who had been left downstairs where he could not disturb the human sleepers with his singing. The house was silent.

And yet. . .Allegra was not satisfied.

She should wake Herr Kraftstein, of course, or Lorcan. It was not the place of gently bred females to investigate suspicious noises. But then the most gently bred females were not a crack shot with a duelling pistol of their very own. Allegra leapt silently from her bed and, only just taking time to wrap herself in her sable travelling cloak, she picked up her Mama's pearl-handled pistol from her jewel case on her little Pembroke table and crept towards the door.

It was downstairs, whatever was making that sound. And still nobody else in the house had heard it. It was probably only a mouse. Or a rat.

No—the dogs would have been in baying pursuit of

anything so harmless. It was only burglars and assassins they would allow to go peaceably about their nefarious business. Smiling at the thought of little Schnapps even thinking to tackle a felon, Allegra pulled open the door and, using the moonlight alone for her guide, crept down the stairs.

There—in Aunt Lydia's study! Or more properly her late Uncle Barnaby's, the room Lydia never opened.

That was when Allegra's heart began its erratic beating, climbing inexorably into her throat until it seemed about to deafen and to choke her. Someone was in a locked room, a room to which nobody in this house but she knew where the key was hidden. So— somebody had come in from outside.

Allegra only hesitated for a second. Then she raced into the morning-room and rummaged blindly in her aunt's sewing table for the key. In her haste she dislodged a book which fell to the floor with such a clatter that she froze abruptly. Now she had made up her mind to confront the intruder it would not do to alert him to her presence too early—least of all because Pythagoras the parrot had been banished to this very room at bedtimes and could be all too predictably relied upon to make a rumpus.

Allegra pressed her ear to the door that linked the morning-room and the study and listened. There was a long silence. And then, at last, a footstep.

Taking a long, hard breath, Allegra silently turned the key and went in.

The man was bent over a desk that he appeared to have opened by means of a large and deadly-looking dagger. He was so intent on his search that for a moment he did not heed her entrance. Then, as abruptly as if she had spoken, he turned around.

'What the Deuce. . .?'

And suddenly all Allegra's fear fled away. Never had she seen a face more comical. So she said, quite calmly, 'I might ask the same, sir.'

'I —'

'And just in case you are thinking not to enlighten me I have to tell you that I have a pistol.'

From somewhere in the morning-room behind her came, quite clearly, the menacing echo —

'Pistol!'

'Be quiet, Pythagoras, and kindly leave this to me!' It was out even before she realised the absurdity.

The man was still staring in absolute astonishment, but he managed despite it to say, 'Pythagoras? You have a *servant* named *Pythagoras*?'

Allegra was too startled by his completely unembarrassed behaviour to do anything but reply, 'Well, of course I don't; I think you must be quite without your wits, sir! Pythagoras is my parrot.'

'Parrot,' confirmed Pythagoras.

And, to Allegra's final bewilderment, her burglar burst into the most unseemly laughter. And however hard he seemed to try he could not stop it.

# CHAPTER TWO

'I THINK you're very rude,' announced Allegra after a while when the man had still not ceased his laughing. 'Moreover I wish you would be quiet or someone will hear you!'

The man swallowed hard on his mirth then, with an all too evident struggle for self-control, enquired, 'Oughtn't you to want someone to come precipitately to your rescue?'

Allegra was affronted. 'Not at all! I can just as well shoot you myself if I have to.'

'Well, would you mind if I sat down for my — er — execution, ma'am? I've had a very tiring evening and —'

'I'm sure you have, if that was you — and I know it was, so don't pretend it wasn't! — lurking around the corner, spying on us —'

'*Lurking*! I never *lurk*! Anybody would suppose I were a common criminal! Furthermore I was not —'

'Spying? Now I suppose you are going to say you are just a law-abiding citizen who — in moments of aberration merely — breaks the windows of other people's houses and —'

'I did not break it! Good God, ma'am — well, do you *see* shards of glass all over the carpet? I am well aware that young ladies feed themselves on nothing but the most lurid melodramas these days but never would I

have imagined one would go so far as to accuse me
of——'

'Oh, really!' Allegra thought it was about time the
man actually saw Mama's pistol. Even in the moonlight
it was a menacing example of Manton's best workman-
ship, and it needed to be, for the stranger was unques-
tionably quite demented. 'And what, pray, would you
say to explain your. . .your intrusion?'

'I was looking,' explained the man, as if to the village
half-wit, 'for my brother.'

His brother? In a desk! Allegra really did think to
shout for assistance then. The poor fellow had most
certainly escaped from some asylum.

She tested out this theory. 'You are certain you are
not Bonaparte, sir?' Apparently it was quite the fashion
among lunatics to imagine themselves the Emperor of
France.

It was the man's turn to stare at her through the
distorting moonlight—a hard, unexpectedly assessing
stare that made her blood run instantly and inexplicably
to ice. Then, suddenly, he smiled.

'I know who you are. . .you're Allegra!'

Allegra all but dropped the pistol in her outrage.

'How *dare* you——?'

'Lydia has told me all about you—poor Freddie
Limmersham wasn't it?'

'Freddie. . . I don't. . .you *know* Freddie
Limmersham?'

'For my pains,' replied the man sardonically.

And at last Allegra began to register what she had
been too preoccupied with aiming her pistol accurately
to notice until that moment. He might be the most

dishevelled, the most disreputable-looking, the most mannerless person it had ever been her misfortune to encounter, but he was a gentleman. Everything about him shouted this unwanted information to her—his cool confidence of manner, his lazy, drawling, strangely authoritative voice—even the cut of his immaculately fitting coat. . .despite the tears in it, and the ominous-looking stains.

Gentlemen! Hadn't she been right all along? Men were bad enough, but the well-bred of the species! First Cuthbert, then Freddie—now this! And what was that he had said about Aunt Lydia?

'You know my aunt, sir?'

'Again, for my pains.' And, as if he had now reassured himself that he would not be summarily shot, the burglar sank gratefully on to the Holland covers that swathed a vast and lumpen sofa, with what could only be descried as a sigh of singularly misplaced relief. Allegra could only stare in incredulity at the impudence of the creature.

Not that she would really expect anything else of Aunt Lydia's notoriously eccentric acquaintance. Only . . .he seemed very young to be another of Lydia's—well, *amours*.

It was almost as if he could read her mind. Certainly he put his head on one side in the most offensive manner and laughed with open mockery. 'Am I Lydia's latest lover, you would ask if you were not so gently nurtured. No, my lady, I'm not.'

'I'm sure that doesn't interest me at all!' retorted Allegra pompously, then her reckless curiosity got the better of her. 'What are you, then?'

The odious creature leaned back on the sofa in a lazy, animal stretch of satisfaction. 'Damned,' he drawled absent-mindedly, 'if I have the least idea! Where's Lydia?'

He didn't know where her errant aunt had got to? Somehow Allegra had expected this strange incident to explain the other. The fact that it did not was more than unnerving.

Her companion saw the flash of anxiety shadow her face — he must have eyes like a cat to see so clearly in this gloom, she thought even as, disconcertingly, like that very cat, he was on his feet and crossing the room with quite extraordinarily threatening grace to her side. Too close — only she could not say why it so disturbed her.

Whatever the reason, Allegra drew back and deeper into the protection of her cloak, although cold was the last thing she felt as, without seeming to realise he should not, the burglar reached for her hand, as if he had quite forgotten the pistol in her other.

'Something's wrong. I knew it! And you're frozen!' His alarmingly strong fingers closed around hers as if to share the warmth of his body with her. Certainly Allegra felt as if he did. That was an even more disrupting sensation.

'Come.' He carefully removed the pistol from her now shaking fingers. 'I want you to tell me everything.'

She protested only once more. 'But you are a burglar. . .'

'No, I'm not, I'm just a reluctant intruder and you know it, silly creature!' And once again he gave that far too dizzying smile and added frankly, 'What I really am, my lady, is starving. Do you suppose. . .?'

And in an instant Allegra lost all wariness of him. He had sounded so like Algie, and was wearing so very much the expression of a small boy cruelly deprived of sustenance, that she found herself saying without a thought, 'We'll go to the kitchens, sir. It's warm there and there's plenty left over from our supper. . .'

She expected him to hurry then, lead the way, since he seemed to know the house a little too well for comfort. He did neither. The stranger stood stock-still and looked at her. Even in his shadow, his back to the moonlit window and towering over her, Allegra could see the intensity of his sudden scrutiny; certainly she felt it. It made her heart skip erratically with what was *like* fear only somehow she did not think it was.

Then he said, his voice almost unrecognisable, it was so serious, 'You're a brave child, Lady Allegra Ashley. You haven't even asked me who I am.'

'No. . .' It came out as little more than a whisper.

'I could be anyone. I could even be lying about knowing Lydia——'

And suddenly, as if he had at last proved beyond doubt his bona fides—Allegra smiled up at what she could see of him.

'Oh, no, you couldn't! You're just exactly the sort of person Aunt *would* have about the place. If you had come to the door, and left your card in all correctness, *then* I should have suspected you of some quite scandalous intention!'

'And so, because I prised the window open with my dagger, you trust me?' The laugh was not quite back in his warm and, she noticed at last, unusually attractive voice.

'No.' Allegra thought carefully through what she meant. 'Not *trust* exactly. I'm. . .um. . .reserving judgement.'

'And if I suddenly start to pack the silver into my pockets?'

'Then I shall prevent you, of course.'

He did laugh then, and Allegra felt a strangely pleasurable shiver run down her spine.

'But what with, you, you little goose, when I've just taken your pistol from you?'

Allegra just could not be perturbed by him any longer. 'Oh, *that*; for all I know it was not even loaded! You need not worry about me, sir; should the need arise I shall find something I can hit you with ——'

'Or spear me?'

'Well, that *would* be better.' Suddenly she became aware that her feet were bare and she had stepped from the carpet to the ice-cold oak block of the floor. 'Do you suppose we might got to the kitchen now, whoever you are?'

'The Honourable Luc Fleetwood, ma'am.' He effected a very sardonic bow.

It was Allegra's turn to laugh helplessly then — so helplessly that he was obliged to catch a hand to her mouth to stifle it.

'I can't imagine what amuses you so, my lady.' He said it rather stiffly.

Allegra enlightened him. 'It is you — and the fact that you could ever be an honourable anything at all!'

'You are the most impossible little——' the Honourable Luc Fleetwood began.

It was the parrot that finished for him. 'Brat!'

And Allegra—who had completely forgotten it was the bird's favourite utterance—promptly threw her aunt's discarded embroidery over his cage.

'I like that parrot,' remarked Mr Fleetwood with outrageous innocence.

'Good boy!' bragged Pythagoras, and Allegra, completely conspired against, fled the room.

The fire in the kitchen had fortunately not gone out. She only hoped she remembered what to do with the cooking pot she had so idly watched Sorcha manipulating on to the hook above the flames that evening.

She need not have worried. With a smile that was offensive in the extreme Mr Fleetwood relieved her of her burden and, hooking a chair towards her with one booted foot, said, 'Sit, ma'am, and let me do the rest. I refuse to have your incompetence in the kitchen deprive me of my supper.'

Allegra sat, mainly because her knees were suddenly shaking with what might have been shock in any other circumstances.

'You need not think to eat it all yourself,' she protested crossly.

'I wasn't. If we are to put our heads together to discover what's amiss you might as well be warm as well as I.'

'Oh, I'm so glad you think so!' retorted his victim acidly, then added even more astringently as she saw him tipping brandy into the soup pot, 'I suppose that is going to turn out the explanation of it. . .it often is with Aunt's friends.'

'Hardened drinkers, ma'am? That may be true of Lydia's female acquaintance, but not the gentlemen. Generally we are only gamblers, thieves and murderers.'

Allegra smarted. Just because he was older than she was, he need not think he could tease her as if. . .

And suddenly for the first time she looked at him properly. And had the most unwelcome surprise.

He wasn't that old at all. Probably not even thirty. He was tall and strong as the fittest athlete and had once been fashionably elegant. He was also the most handsome man she was ever going to set eyes on in her life.

Allegra hated him for it. She had no wish to like him and so he shouldn't look as if he was eminently likeable. The trouble was — she accepted her soup with very ill grace — he did.

He looked. . .well. . .friendly. None of Freddie's drowning melancholy which had proved so disastrously distracting in London; Mr Fleetwood's eyes were of the most languid dark sapphire-blue. None of Freddie's artfully disordered hair; Mr Fleetwood's was a strangely appealing mass of black dishevelled curls. In fact Mr Fleetwood was so like her friend Lord Byron as to be quite alarming. . . Byron looked like an heroic archangel too.

She knew she was right the moment Luc Fleetwood smiled. *That* was George Byron's smile too! It smote one instantly and devastatingly in the region of the heart — if not more intimately still — like a lightning bolt striking earth. Allegra knew better than to trust a man who smiled like that. Look at how George had turned out, after all, with all that deliciously indelicate poetry and. . .

'Don't you like me?' asked Mr Fleetwood, and Allegra became hotly aware of the unladylike nature of her scrutiny.

'No. You smile too nicely.'

'Well, of all the illogical——'

'It is not illogical at all. You might at least have looked *dangerous* or something, if you are to make a profession of——'

'Breaking and entering? Only I'm not. As for my profession. . .well, let us just say it is better that I do not look menacing. It is better, in fact, that I'm not very noticeable at all.'

And for the first time it occured to Allegra to wonder why a man as young as he was should not be at war. So she asked, curiously, 'Oh, you have a vocation, sir? As a highwayman, perhaps?'

'Only you would call Great Pulteney Street a highway!'

'So what *do* you do? I presume you to be a younger son; you look like one, and your clothes are a shocking mess and——'

'Meaning I have been cast out to make my poor way in this unfeeling world? How absurd you are! No, I'm perfectly comfortably placed, I assure you——'

'What a pity,' Allegra purred, and when she was sure it was real fury that hardened his beautifully sculpted mouth she added sweetly, 'So what are you?'

'That——' and here the Honourable Mr Fleetwood

turned on her with most quelling stare '— is none of your concern, my lady! Moreover, since we are being so impertinent——

'I was not!'

'You were! Let me tell you it is not I who looks too innocent to be true, my girl, it's you! Look at you, like some sweet, pretty little kitten; no wonder you've been causing so much uproar in the capital——'

'I. . .how *dare* you?' Allegra surged to her feet, loath to admit that being likened to a sweet and pretty anything was most gratifying.

'You're spilling your soup,' he added coldly, then finished with real disgust, 'I might have guessed you'd be another Lydia!'

Lydia! Allegra stared at him, her soup so far forgotten that Mr Fleetwood was obliged to remove her cup from her numbed fingers. He said she was like Lydia — the most exciting, maddening, ill-disciplined beauty of her generation!

Allegra should have been appalled. Instead she felt a little flame of near triumph ignite inside her. A *femme fatale*, Allegra Ashley! What fun it would be if she could be fatal to a man like this. . .

For the second time in their acquaintance he read her mind.

'And don't think any of it will work on *me* ma'am — because it won't!' He added this last word most emphatically.

Maybe it was the brandy in the soup, or the fact that she was only seventeen and had just been likened to the most heart-shattering female in living memory, but

Allegra did not believe him completely immune and her smile said so.

Mr Fleetwood saw it and raised a more than sardonic eyebrow.

'It won't, you know. I'm no Freddie Limmersham. Or Cuthbert Nettlesham. Or Felix Didsbury. Or——'

'*Felix*?'

'Yes. . .oh, well, I might have *known* you wouldn't have noticed; you spoilt little goddesses never do! I never met a more heartless female than Lydia — until now.'

It definitely was the brandy; Allegra felt as warm as toast inside; even her toes were curling with self-congratulation. She put her head on one side, puzzling over whose was the other name he had been about to mention.

Mr Fleetwood laughed out loud. 'No, I'm not going to tell you! My God, but they did us an ill service when they turned you loose from the schoolroom!'

And suddenly, because she understood that, just a little, he meant what he said, Allegra was hurt. Very hurt.

After all it never had been her fault. She had tried to stop Freddie being so asinine about her; she had done everything to prevent Cuthbert's foolishness. . .it wasn't her fault she looked as she did. So Ethereal, Cuthbert had sighed, like a Fairy Creature, so Fragile, so in danger from this Wicked, Wanton world. It was not her fault otherwise perfectly sane gentlemen took only one look at her and saw not down-to-earth, rather tomboyish Allegra Ashley but some frail Rapunzel trapped in her ivory tower. Just one look and even the most hardened roués were rushing for their snow-white chargers. It had got so out of hand that Papa had pretended there was smallpox in the house when he was last on leave from Spain; anything, the Duke of Alderley had roared, to spare him having every waking moment wasted by the pleadings of yet another witless suitor.

It wasn't her fault she looked exactly like her mother . . .or that Cleone, Dido and Lydia Gurning had been the most sought-after beauties of their age. If anything Allegra herself was even more lovely than her dazzling mother, but she would never know it. How could she know that the strength of character inherited from her father showed in her imperious little nose and haughtily abstracted smile? Or that, chestnut-dark where her mother, Aunt Dido and Aunt Lydia were fair, her lustrous curling hair set off a flawless ivory complexion that was even more luminous, more bitterly envied? How was she to know that her childlike inability to remain tidy however hard anybody tried. . .

Allegra scowled with real hostility at her companion. She might have overheard men say she was the Trojan Helen of her generation, but it was wickedly unfair of him to imply that she believed it. So she said stiffly, 'I am extremely tired, sir, and would very much like you to go away.'

'Not until——'

'Pray do *not* interrupt, sir! I was going to say that I need to hear what you have to tell me before I can permit you to leave——'

'Permit me! Oh, but. . .!' The Honourable Luc

Fleetwood's undoubtedly unseemly rejoinder dissolved into his all too ready laughter.

Allegra panicked. 'Don't make such a noise; do you want —— ?'

'Someone to come here and catch you entertaining a strange man in the kitchens. . .and you in your night attire ——'

'I am not!'

'Yes, you are.' And there was something in the warmth of his smile made Allegra pull the protecting cloak closer about her still.

'Well, it would do you more harm than it would me, sir, for I should tell them you had dragged me here against my will and ——'

'Gave you the best chair and heated up some soup, naturally. All quite usual behaviour for a vile brigand.'

'I think you're a beast!'

'Indisputably, ma'am. But you are now going to answer all my questions.' He held up a hand as she began to speak and something in his extraordinary eyes silenced her completely. 'Good. You will start by telling me where your aunt is.'

Afterwards Allegra told herself that the brandy was again responsible for her dramatic pronouncement of, 'Gone, sir! Vanished! Into thinnest air!'

Only his deep and lasting viciousness of character could have been responsible for his vulgar laughter. Allegra all but hit him. 'Hush up!' It was the most lamentable lapse, and something she had culled from the far from couth young Algie.

'Ah, yes,' drawled her tormentor, 'you have a brother, don't you?'

Allegra subsided into steaming silence.

'So — ' the Honourable Mr Fleetwood stirred the logs on the fire with his once immaculate top-boot ' — Lydia is now missing too?'

'Too?'

'My brother.'

'Oh!' She had forgotten all about his brother. 'Has he vanished as well? How very singular.'

Mr Fleetwood was seen — all too plainly and he would pay for it! — to stifle yet another burst of laughter. Even so, it flared all too treacherously in his eyes.

'Isn't it just! Faron — he's the Earl of Hawkhurst, by the by — disappeared into — er — thinnest air on Friday last.'

'But. . .it is Thursday, sir!'

'As you so accurately say, ma'am, Thursday. And on Tuesday he was meant to join me at Fleetwood.'

'But maybe — '

'No, he *would* have come if he could. It is. . .we have a tradition — Tuesday was my birthday, you see.'

Strangely Allegra did see. Even the tone in which he spoke of his brother suggested a great affection for each other; she understood that. Algie was the most reprehensible little thug but she adored him. So she asked, 'You thought he might be here? I don't quite understand. . .' And then she did.

'Exactly, ma'am. It is Faron, not I, who is your Aunt Lydia's — ' And suddenly, as if he for the first time recognised Allegra's extreme youth, he broke off.

Allegra saw it and felt a happy glow of revenge at his awkwardness.

'No need to mince words for me, I assure you, sir.'

She smiled kindly. 'You mean your brother is my aunt's latest lover.' Then she finished somewhat naïvely, 'She does have rather a lot of them.'

His smile held quite another quality then, and Allegra found she could not look at it. All he said, very gently, was, 'Yes, she does, doesn't she? What a life your family has led you, Lady Allegra.'

And Allegra felt the sting of tears in her eyes because it was true. Poor Papa, doing his best for King and Country in the Peninsula and now France, and no one left to entrust his children to except flighty, unashamedly selfish Lydia. And because Papa had had no choice Allegra had never complained, just shielded Algie as best she could from the worst of it and closed her eyes to it for herself. Sometimes she thought her very childishness, her need to be so indisputably young and so untouchable, came from the cynicism that had been born in her as young as fourteen years old, the first time she had had to barricade herself in her rooms against the attentions of one of Lydia's drunken house guests.

And yet it would be disloyal to let a stranger see how she felt. So she swallowed her tears and replied steadily, 'Oh, no, not at all.' She was looking away, so she never saw that he did not for a moment believe her.

Carefully Mr Fleetwood changed the subject. 'And now I come here and find not only no brother but Lydia away. It makes no sense. . .'

'My aunt knew we were coming, sir; she wrote me a letter.'

He said the strangest thing then. 'Are you sure that Lydia wrote it?'

'But of course. . .!' And then Allegra stopped short. Was she sure? Moreover, how could she be sure? Lydia had barely written a letter in her life, and certainly never once to her niece or nephew.

He saw her hesitation. 'So you're not certain?'

'I. . .well. . . I don't know that I can be, and yet. . . yet who else would the letter be from, sir?'

'A fact that whoever wrote it could rely upon——'

'You mean that because it would never occur to me it was anyone but Aunt Lydia I wouldn't look to see if it really was?'

'Incoherent——' he smiled gently, taking the sting out of his mockery '—but more or less what I was thinking. You don't happen to have the letter, I suppose?'

'No. . .I never thought to keep it. . .'

'No, of course you didn't; why should you?' And suddenly his voice was grim.

Allegra was really frightened. 'I don't know what you're saying, sir. How. . .? I mean why. . .? This makes no sense at all; I——'

'Must leave here at once with your brother.'

'I can't!' She meant it literally, and realised she had to explain it. 'Our London house is closed, sir, my father away. Where else could we go?'

For a long while Mr Fleetwood stood silently looking down into the fire, then he smiled. It was a strange smile, thought Allegra, watching more appreciatively than she meant to; amused, affectionate. It was the smile of a man she could like. . . Only she wasn't going to—if it killed her!

Then he said, without thought of contradiction, 'You

will go, Lady Allegra, to my grandmother. . .brother, servants, dogs, parrot and all.'

The most startling thing Allegra did that whole strange night was say, with absolute meekness, 'Yes, I shall.'

'Might I ask,' put in Allegra after a few moments' bemused silence — she astonished at her meek and compliant tone, Mr Fleetwood all but startled to death by it — 'who is your grandmother, sir?'

'The Dowager Lady Hawkhurst, ma'am.' Mr Fleetwood was so far thrown by her docility that he forgot himself completely and was within an inch of being courteous. Then he pulled himself together. 'My father's mother; you will like her, she is just like you, not the least clue how to behave on any occasion you'd care to mention, nor any inclination to act upon it if she had. She's French,' he finished, as if that went a long way to explaining everything.

Plainly it did. 'So was Mama, at least *half* of her was.' Allegra's not unexpected revelation was met with a sardonic smile so coolly amused that she all but snapped at him, 'And *now* what amuses you, sir?'

The trouble was Mr Fleetwood could not answer that. It was not that he did not have the answer, just that she would not like to hear it. If she even understood. How was a child like this to comprehend just how like the affectedly cosmopolitan Lydia she was, she who had no affectations at all, when he who had met the world head-on with half-bored cynicism that had been hardening ever since he was Allegra's age didn't understand either? Carefully he side-stepped disaster.

'What was her other half?'

Allegra was distrustful. That was far too normal, if encroaching, a question for Mr Fleetwood, and asked in far too civil a tone to be anything but suspect.

'Why do you ask?' she demanded suspiciously.

She got what she deserved. Luc Fleetwood laughed out loud at her. 'Vulgar curiosity, my lady!'

Allegra pounced. 'Yes, it was tasteless. I suppose no one ever troubled to teach you that such very personal questions are all that is offensive!'

Mr Fleetwood suddenly found something of overwhelming interest to stare at in the fire. Whatever it was so fascinated him there, it was visibly causing his shoulders to shake in a most peculiar fashion. But his voice was steady enough.

'You mistake the matter, ma'am. . .my family are all that is *bon ton* and were tireless in drilling me in all matters of masculine grace and etiquette. I just wasn't listening.' Then he turned back to her, eyes hot with what was unmistakably laughter. 'And you, you little hypocrite, you weren't listening either! If anyone ever succeeded in instilling so much as the first lesson of ladylike deportment into you then I'm the Pope! So answer my vulgar question; your answer may be as indelicate as you choose.'

And Allegra, for all she knew she was being laughed at, could not fight him. It was only, she told herself, that he was so like her adored George Byron that made her like his odious smile, that was all — if George were here she would not notice Mr Fleetwood at all. . .of course she wouldn't! Something had to explain her smiling almost shyly back.

'Mama's other antecedents are Irish and Italian, sir.'

She was not remotely surprised at the response. Far too many people had blamed her own wilfulness — and the Honourable Cuthbert had blamed her Fatal Charm — on these exotic facts alone.

'Dear God, but what a cocktail! And I thought my family the recipe for chaos!'

Allegra was piqued; she had never been able to see that Italian volatility — and somewhat eccentric morality. . .stirred in with French arrogance and wide-eyed Irish trickiness was anything to be ashamed of; it was not as if her English half were not staid enough. . .Papa even had relations who were bishops.

'I think you are being ruder than ever ——'

'Probably, if there is such a word as ruder. . .'

'More rude, then! But then ——'

'But then I was not meaning to insult you, and you know it, silly child! How could I? My own great-grandmother was Venetian, my father all but French, so you see, ma'am, we are neither of us remotely respectable. . .'

Suddenly, and without even realising why it happened, Allegra was quite serious. 'I know. Since the war with Bonaparte it has not been so very amusing, has it, being different. . .*foreign*? Mama used to tell me that when she was a girl it was quite the most romantic thing in the world to be a Frenchman; her Papa was an *émigré* — he had actually escaped from one of Monsieur Robespierre's prisons all by himself. I dare say your grandmama's family ——'

'Were on the run from the Terror, everything lost but their pride and *savoir-faire*?' Suddenly it became imperative to Mr Fleetwood that he lighten her strangely shadowed mood. 'Oh, yes.' Then without warning his own mood darkened. 'In fact I believe it is still very glamorous of me to be what I am. Possibly because now it is just a little dangerous.'

There was such bitterness staining the edges of his casually light tone that Allegra stared and found herself asking almost nervously, 'Dangerous?'

'Yes.' Mr Fleetwood's eyes were back on the fading fire, almost as if he regretted something he had said and could not look at her in that moment. 'Dangerous.' Then he turned back and dark mockery was all that was to be seen in those vivid, puzzling eyes. 'After all, ma'am, just which side are we on, we mongrels; to whom does our loyalty belong?'

And she remembered in that moment that his brother—the all but French Earl of Hawkhurst—had mysteriously vanished. Along with her aunt, who had always been so flauntingly proud of her Continental blood. Remembered too the comments she had over-heard as a child as the country slipped into war with Napoleon; snide, wantonly cruel remarks about her mother and about the steadfastness of her father's loyalty to his King, so besotted as the Duke of Alderley was with his *foreign* wife. For too long now Bonaparte had been synonymous with France and all French people with Bonapartists, whatever the truth of their politics. People looked at the Alderleys and doubted in whispers behind their hands—wicked, unjust doubts that had roused her strong, gentle father to fury, and her mother to a rage of impotent tears. All of them comments Allegra should not have heard. Allegra thought then of how she had lived since, knowing that

only the fact that she was heiress to a great part of the
Alderley fortune, the richest in England, protected her
from the same prejudices, so politely chilling, and the
subtle exclusion of all those who did not completely
belong. That was the kind of thing Mr Fleetwood was
talking about.

'We mongrels,' he had said. . .and she wondered at
last what had made her so exciting to her suitors. Was
it that she was — were it not for her fortune — forbidden
fruit? If she were not Lady Allegra Ashley she would
be unacceptable?

It hurt, the more so because she was young enough
to have trusted the things men told her, to have
believed just a little that it was herself they wanted,
and only herself, but the main sensation that swept
through Allegra in that moment of revelation was a
healthy anger.

'How absurd they are; what side could you be on,
sir?'

The trouble was — Allegra glanced at the enigmatic
Mr Fleetwood — it was a question she could all too
easily ask about him herself.

Did she know she looked so — what was that look?
So alone, so sad, almost frightened. The shock of what
he saw puzzled Luc Fleetwood. Until he understood.

He should not really have been surprised. She too
was wondering. . .what he was and where he really
belonged.

It would be all right so long as she never found out.

He regretted in that moment the need to take
Allegra to his grandmother; she was better off out of

this business altogether. But someone had to look after her.

There was the strangest look in his eyes, thought Allegra, so distant, hard, she could not look at it; it scared her. *He* frightened her suddenly. There was something secret about him that his gentle, all too infectious humour so effectively disguised. Something tense and remote, something that walked alone. Something that led in quite the opposite direction from the security she had felt with him till now. Allegra noticed that the fire was dying and shuddered.

Mr Fleetwood saw the pallor of half-understood fear bleach her face. If his voice was a little harsh when he spoke, Allegra was too preoccupied to notice it.

'You must go to bed now, Lady Allegra; you're exhausted.'

And suddenly she realised that she was. So much so that she could only nod at him.

Mr Fleetwood moved then, almost as if he would come towards her, but if the hand that reached out to her had meant to take her own he changed his mind. Something in her eyes told him they were no longer friends.

He smiled suddenly at the thought, because that was exactly how it felt. They had been friends. They were meant to be. But not now. He had no place for friends at the moment. Least of all pretty little children who did not even begin to understand how disturbingly vulnerable they were.

'I'll come for you tomorrow; we cannot go to Grandmother very early, for she rarely rises before noon.'

'No. . .' Allegra was so tired suddenly, she could not

even recognise its cause; she was only vaguely aware of a new and uneasy heaviness inside her, a dragging feeling that made her want to cry, she who never cried at all.

Luc Fleetwood saw and thought he understood. 'I'll stay in the house until the servants wake, just to make sure I'm the only visitor you have tonight.'

What did he mean? Then Allegra saw. She stared at him, eyes wide with shock. 'That is what you think, sir, that someone else. . .?'

Damn him for a fool! Mr Fleetwood cursed himself. It was something else that had been worrying Lady Allegra than the thought of other intruders and now he had added to her troubles! He could not help himself. One hand reached out and touched her cheek — only briefly — and Allegra's exhausted body stung back to life at the shock of it.

They looked at each other silently for a very long moment. Then he said, with a calmness he no longer felt though he could not say why, 'No one will come tonight. Not while I'm here, I promise you that.' Then he forced the careless laughter he had become so used to affecting. 'I shall have to leave at dawn, of course.'

'Of course. . .' came a dazed whisper.

'I don't want to be observed clambering back out of the window!' And the absurdity of the picture brought real laughter back to his eyes at last.

Allegra found she too was laughing again, reassured. 'You might always try the door just for once, Mr Fleetwood.'

'So I might, Lady Allegra!' It was a long time since he had seen such courage. It was a new courage in her;

one that saw the danger and no longer cared. It would not do to let her see he understood, though; she was reckless enough without any encouragement from him. So he smiled — all too devastatingly like George Byron had he only known it — and said, 'Now, off to bed if you please, ma'am.'

Allegra found herself halfway through the door before she realised she had obeyed him again; before she realised she was not even annoyed at herself for doing so. Almost, it amused her to do it. After all, obedience was such a very novel experience.

'What a strange night it's been,' she mused out loud.

'Very strange,' came the carefully expressionless rejoinder. 'Perhaps I should make a habit of this felony business!'

Allegra really did laugh then.

'Why do I suspect, Mr Fleetwood, that you already do?'

'*Touché*!' The reply seemed to come from the gathering shadows. And before Allegra could speak again the all but French Mr Fleetwood was gone.

Allegra turned and ran towards the stairs. Silently. Like a cat — just as he had vanished into the depths of the shadows, with all the subtlety of a night creature. Strange, disconcerting Luc Fleetwood. Somewhere in the house still. Comforting. Or dangerous?

Allegra was so caught up with her thoughts of him that she did not hear, somewhere above her, a door very carefully closing.

# CHAPTER THREE

THERE was one thing wrong with the Honourable Mr Fleetwood's plan, one singularly awkward fact which leapt out of half-consiousness and struck Allegra most unwelcomely as she sipped in dreamy fashion at her morning chocolate. How was she going to explain this sudden invitation to stay with Lady Hawkhurst—who did not even know that she had issued it—when as far as Algie and Herr Kraftstein were concerned neither she nor they had ever heard of the lady? Moreover, how had the Dowager come to learn of their plight when as far as everyone knew Allegra had spoken to no one but themselves since arriving last evening? Algie would ask troublesome questions—Allegra idly bit off a corner of dry toast—Algie always did; but he could be fobbed off with any old story, the more outlandish the better. Algie was not really the problem. Herr Kraftstein was going to prove the fly in Luc Fleetwood's otherwise ingenious ointment. Allegra faced it squarely; Herr Kraftstein was almost certain to insist they return to London and arrange for Allegra to stay with friends there. And Herr Kraftstein, in lieu of other authority, was almost certain—after a struggle—to get his way.

But not if Allegra could help it. Bath, which had seemed so deadly dull only yesterday, had suddenly become so very, very interesting. Allegra was not going home for anything.

So thinking, she dressed carefully in her most fragile and innocent of muslins; Herr Kraftstein's romantic soul was an open book to Allegra and if she was to save the day she must appeal to it. Making certain she looked tired and wan enough to be convincing, Allegra made her way down to the breakfast parlour resolved to faint to the carpet with fatigue if she had to, anything to convince Herr Kraftstein that to expend one breath more energy than it took to walk to Lady Hawkhurst in Laura Place would see the early demise of the Duke of Alderley's only daughter. Then all she had to do was fend off Herr Kraftstein's fussing questions until Mr Fleetwood could arrive with a plausible explanation. She had not the least doubt that he would. The problem was when.

For the first time she was grateful for Algie's rudeness. From behind a muffling mouthful of kidneys he announced, 'You look *terrible*, just like someone who's drowned or died or something.'

Allegra did her best to look still worse, sinking into the chair the tutor held for her, wearily sighing out her pedantic retort, 'People who are drowned *are* dead.'

'Not always! Not if someone rescues them at the very last minute!' Algie made rescuing gestures towards a crumb floating in his tea, then bit into his toast so loudly that Allegra quite genuinely winced in pain.

Herr Kraftstein was horrified.

'My Lord Marquess, if you *please*!'

Algie didn't please; it was the strangest thing but without Aunt Lydia to stare him into silence he was having a wonderful time. Odd that, he mused, excavating another kidney from beneath a wedge of beef, how Aunt Lydia could be so stupendously scatter-brained but still one did as one was told. . . Herr Kraftstein need not think Algie was wasting this unexpected freedom on doing as his tutor bid him.

Until Allegra murmured fraily, 'Yes, Algie, *please* be quiet, I am. . .I feel. . .' And Algie, who had not been remotely convinced by her act a moment ago, believed her.

It was all Allegra could do to keep her face straight as she watched Algie begin to chew *silently*. Pulling herself together, she shivered as consumptively as possible and glanced feebly at Herr Kraftstein; one long, soulful look and he believed too. He usually did.

'Please not to worry yourself a moment longer,' he began in his shy and charming way. 'You must leave everything to me, my lady, not disturb yourself with even the smallest problem; I shall manage it all!'

Allegra knew she could never overdo it with Herr Kraftstein. 'Oh, I know that, and I am *so* grateful! I am so completely fatigued I declare I could not move an inch even if the house were to burn to the ground!'

Algie could not be asked to control himself for long, least of all when offered such dramatic prospects as these. 'I would, and I'd fling you over my shoulder the way they do in stories and save your life and be blinded and crippled myself, of course, and be enormously famous for——

'*Algernon!*'

'*Algie!*'

Simultaneous outrage from both his victims. Algie

subsided into silence again, his mind finally made up that only aunts and parrots were any fun at all.

'I do apologise, my lady!' Herr Kraftstein's tone was martyred. 'As I was saying I shall take everything upon myself. Indeed the very first thing I shall do after breakfast is send Lorcan to arrange your removal to the York ——'

'*No!*' Then Allegra realised she would give herself away if she were not careful. She lifted an enfeebled hand to her brow and repeated faintly, 'Oh, no. No, not yet; *surely* there is no need. . .'

She then sustained her greatest shock so far. Herr Kraftstein was adamant.

'Forgive me that I must dissent, my lady, I mean no disrespect, but no, my mind is made up; it is not correct in any way that you remain here.'

'In my aunt's house?'

'An aunt who is not here, nor any other lady to act your chaperon.'

Never had she seen her brother's tutor so stern. If he had been anyone else Allegra would have said that he was obstinate. Almost as if he had a reason for it — a reason she did not know.

Allegra panicked. Had he seen Luc Fleetwood last night? Had he heard him? And imagined some low and sordid intrigue? Was that his reason for being so determined to take her away? Allegra studied the tutor carefully from beneath her lowered lashes; no doubt about it — every line of that handsomely Teutonic face was resolute that she would leave here.

Herr Kraftstein confirmed this. 'It is imperative you repair to an hotel, my lady, for these extraordinary circumstances when they are known can only cause the most unwelcome comment. Until you are recovered sufficiently to return to London. . .'

London! She had been right to fear it. He meant it. Allegra took a deep breath and thought fast. Could she defy his authority? What would Papa have to say about it if she did? Did Papa and his inevitable and volcanic wrath matter just at this moment? Not at all. . .time enough to worry about that when it happened! But that did not help her. Even if she did try to argue with the tutor, what could she say? Where *was* Mr Fleetwood? Allegra seethed inside. It was all Mr Fleetwood's fault, she decided unjustly; what was the point of mysterious adventurers if they were not to help her when she needed them?

This injustice was borne in upon her even before she had time to cheer herself with planning just what she would say to the wretch when he did appear, because Lorcan entered, plainly relishing his unexpected promotion in the household, and announced in very convincing butlerish fashion, 'Mr Fleetwood, my lady, apologising for the inappropriateness of the hour but he feels it is most urgent he should speak with you. I understand he has a message from your aunt, my Lady Limington.'

Allegra was so astonished at the Honourable Mr Fleetwood's audacity that she almost let her guard down and showed it. She remembered herself just in time. 'Oh, yes, I believe my aunt *did* mention such a gentleman; perhaps——' here she rose to her feet to hurry from the room before her inexplicable blushing could be noted by the observant Herr Kraftstein '—he can explain our mystery. . .'

The man was. . .well, he was outrageous! Even as she reached the door Luc Fleetwood was coming through it as if he owned the place, a most convincing look of benevolent concern on his impeccably noble features.

'My dear Lady Allegra!' How was it that he even seemed to add ten years to his age, he sounded so exactly like a worried uncle? 'Forgive my intrusion but, well, I should have come at once last evening but I had not realised you had arrived. . .' And he took the hand she held so helplessly towards him and bowed over it. Only Allegra was aware of the firm pressure of his thumb against her palm as he warned her not to show her astonishment. The only thing he did not do was wink!

Allegra was furious, horrified—and all because just the touch of his immaculately gloved fingers and she was blushing as furiously as the most timid débutante. Furious too because he seemed to think that it was funny. She already knew him well enough to see the tell-tale gleam of laughter in his far too innocent blue eyes.

She wanted to kick him. But she had no choice but to play the role he had assigned her. Poor, nervous little Allegra Ashley relieved to have a *man* she could rely on.

It almost choked her to say it. 'Oh, but I am so glad you have come, sir! Perhaps you can tell us. . .?' It was as far as she got—the glow in his eyes became a positive flame and she knew that in one more second she would strangle him.

Not a trace of that laughter escaped into his strangely altered voice; now he even sounded older too. Not like Mr Fleetwood at all. Not dangerous, not undermining. Just ordinary, ineffectual, more than a little bit distracted.

'Indeed I can, ma'am, and if you have suffered any alarms it is all my fault! I have no excuse at all, ma'am, none, for I mistook your aunt's instructions. . .'

So that was to be the tale—Lydia had told him what she was doing; plainly the fact that Aunt Lydia might turn up any moment and tell quite another story bothered Mr Fleetwood not the least.

Allegra played up to it. 'Oh, so then you know where she has gone, sir?' Had she overdone the relief? Allegra was acutely conscious of Herr Kraftstein's eyes upon them, shrewd, assessing. It worried her and she must have shown it. At least something in Luc Fleetwood's expression quickly reassured her she was doing what was wanted, though his features altered not at all. He was, she found herself thinking helplessly, the most extraordinary person. Even she was beginning to believe him.

'Indeed I do, Lady Allegra, and I shall never be able to apologise enough! You see, your aunt, Lady Limington. . .' he dithered out the words so convincingly '. . .was called away urgently; I cannot say I am at all sure of the reason, although she certainly told me . . .not that it signifies. . .thing is——' and here he smiled so hopefully that Allegra almost gave the game away; he was so like that idiot Cuthbert Nettlesham, she was laughing almost before she realised it '—thing is, can't always follow what Lydia is sayin'.'

Allegra turned her choke of laughter into a cry of relief. 'Oh, but I am so. . .well, I cannot say how *pleased* I am, sir! For we have been worried to our wits' end that something had befallen my aunt. . .' She could go no further. Mr Fleetwood's quelling stare saw to that.

And Allegra was furious again. It was his fault she had laughed! He had deliberately mimicked Cuthbert, she knew it now, just to tease her; she knew because he was doing it again.

'And I am abject, Lady Allegra, *abject*! But when I think what anxieties you must have *suffered*!' The only thing he was not doing was speaking in Cuthbert's habitual capital letters. 'But rest assured I have come to make amends. My grandmother. . .Lady Hawkhurst . . .thing is, your aunt and my grandmother had it all arranged that you must remove at once to Laura Place.'

Allegra dug her nails into her palms to calm herself— both of her desperate urge to laugh at this Cuthbert-like incoherence and so as not to kill its perpetrator.

'Laura Place?' It took all her strength to follow his lead by asking a bewildered question.

'Indeed, Laura Place. My grandmother is even now expecting you. . .'

Ought she to look unsure? Defer to Herr Kraftstein? No—Mr Fleetwood had at least had the sense to say these were Lydia's orders. There was nothing Herr Kraftstein could do. And he knew it. Allegra would have been shocked by the tight anger on the tutor's face had she not been so busy trying not to like Mr

Fleetwood again, and answering, in her best fluttering
heroine tones, 'Oh, but how kind of her, sir, and what
a relief! I cannot tell you, sir, how. . .well, it is not
very *nice* to have a mystery. And I had not quite liked
being here without Aunt Lydia. . .'

'Indeed no!' Then Mr Fleetwood went too far. 'Not
the done thing at all!'

Allegra fled the room in choking incoherence. 'Oh
dear. . .I. . .please excuse me, I heard. . .I think. . .
the parrot. . .!'

Behind her Algie dropped his loaded fork and
stared. First at Herr Kraftstein, then at the agitated Mr
Fleetwood. Algie groaned. Another Cuthbert
Nettlesham! Why was it gentlemen went so instantly
peculiar when faced with Allegra. . .and was he himself
doomed one day to be so utterly sickening about girls?
Algie drowned the horrifying thought in a gulp of tea
that brought a blistering reproof from an unusually
short-tempered Herr Kraftstein.

The oddest thing was, Algie thought, as he listened
with one ear — the only one he ever used in such
circumstances — to the ensuing homily, but he could
have sworn just as he looked away that Mr Fleetwood
was laughing.

Allegra, safe in the morning-room with the innocent
and still dozing parrot, knew it. Knew and seethed.
Seethed and boiled and all but bubbled over with rage.
I *hate* him — she luxuriated in fury — hate, hate, *hate*
him! Luc Fleetwood was. . .well, she could not think
of a word bad enough to describe him; even Algie
hadn't taught her any. Mr Fleetwood had done that
quite deliberately to undermine her, quite ruthelessly

deliberately, and she was never, ever going to forgive him. Never, ever. . .stop laughing! That was the horrible truth. Allegra thought again of the way he had so perfectly employed Cuthbert's favourite word 'abject' and hugged herself in an agony of laughter.

'Oh, how much I hate that man and he'll pay for this!' she wept hysterically.

'Hate?' enquired the parrot.

The Dowager Lady Hawkhurst resided, and always had done, just along the street on the corner of Laura Place. Having long since expressed the opinion that the countryside was unhealthy and any other parts of Bath were, by nature of their steep hills and lurking farmyard fauna, even more likely to prove fatal to one with the glitter of Paris in her veins, she had taken virtual root in her favourite spot, a heavy, somewhat masculine library chair of attractively crumpled leather placed for her convenience in the morning-room window. It was thus she was accorded an excellent view through her opera glasses of the approach of a quite preposterous retinue. A girl, a small boy, a handsome Germanic youth, a maid, two more than ill-assorted canines and . . .a parrot, this last in the unlikeliest hands of all — her favourite grandson's. The Dowager Lady Hawkhurst was so delighted at the prospect, she quite forgot her standing in the town and rapped with ear-splitting abandon on the window.

In return the Honourable Mr Fleetwood raised a lazy hand — the one that was not holding the parrot — to shield his eyes against the dazzling April sun, then lifted the other in a wave of indulgent greeting. Since this hand did contain Pythagoras he was most roundly sworn at.

'Damned!' squawked his victim, clinging to his rocking perch with every available claw.

'Oh, *no!*' Allegra, still in flames of temper at Mr Fleetwood's evil behaviour, was even now, half an hour after the crime, struggling to compose herself and losing; consequently her pet's antics took on even grosser aspects of the embarrassing than ever. 'I wish you would control yourself, Pythagoras; I cannot begin to think——'

'I can,' put in Algie, scuffing and hopping along behind, quite delighted by the latest turn of events now things were beginning to happen at last. 'Papa taught him.'

'Algie, what a corker. . .um, I mean a shocking untruth! Papa would never do any such thing!'

'Yes, he *did!*' The Marquess Stonyhurst was adamant. 'I caught him once, teaching Pythagoras vulgar things. . .to say in front of all your silly suitors——'

'*Algie!*'

Allegra prided herself on never once, at least since her Come Out, having been put to the blush—not by anything or anybody. After all, blushing was not the mark of a budding *femme fatale*. Today was proving one long, red-faced nightmare. One choke of laughter from the odious Mr Fleetwood and her ears were burning so hotly that only the concealment of a particularly fetching bonnet of bluebell taffeta prevented the shameful discovery.

She might have known Luc Fleetwood would torment her anyway.

'*All* your suitors, Lady Allegra?' His eyes rested with insufferable innocence on her now flaming cheeks, and his smile was infamous.

Allegra, long since cemented in her determination to kill him, lifted the haughtiest possible nose at him and retorted stiffly, 'Algie only ever talks nonsense, sir, as you must be able to tell just by looking at him.' Here she turned a look of her own on her brother that would have incinerated a less hard-boiled personality to cinders. 'Algie is being impertinent and I for one am taking not the slightest notice of him!'

Algie stood stock-still in the middle of the road and stared. Never had he seen his sister behave so oddly before. He felt betrayed.

'Well, of all the — *ow!*'

He was hauled by the ear out of the path of a fast descending carriage. Herr Kraftstein liked to think himself a fair man and as indulgent as any with his charge's youthfulness and high spirits, but enough, Herr Kraftstein had decided — painfully — was enough.

'You will forgive my charge, sir,' he said in the tone of one who would take some persuading to forgive the miscreant himself, at least in this lifetime. 'I fear that all this excitement has gone to his head and got the better of his manners.'

'Think nothing of it,' murmured Mr Fleetwood politely.

It was Allegra who stood still then, bringing the procession to a stumbling halt. And not — although that was startling enough! — because of Mr Fleetwood's very first evincing of civilised behaviour. Never had she seen anything quite so. . .well, so puzzling as the stiff, rather distant smiles the tutor and Mr Fleetwood were now exchanging. If she did not know better she would say they had taken an instant dislike to one another and that that dislike was growing by the minute, and yet nothing could be more impossible. Herr Kraftstein was everything that was charming and, for all the tutor could possibly know about it, so was Mr Fleetwood. And yet she had not seen such quiet, almost cold assessment in anyone's eyes as the two now turned so courteously on each other. . .not since the time Aunt Lydia's ousted favourite had chanced upon that lady smiling all too bewitchingly at his successor anyway.

But then — Allegra knew to blame Luc Fleetwood — anything would be odd in the company of such a person. Never had she felt quite so puzzlingly on edge herself and she did not like it. Consequently she treated him to an exhibition of her most dishonestly sweet and ladylike demeanour.

'I do hope Lady Hawkhurst will not be too put out by you forcing her to take us in like this at so short notice.' She was careful to keep her voice down so that only her victim would hear it.

'Grandmama? Not in the least. Even when I put aside the thumbscrews she was quite amenable to what I was suggesting.'

His tone was so matter-of-fact that for a moment Allegra did not hear what he had said. Then she did and was infuriated — most of all at herself for not being able to cope with his insufferable teasing.

'I wonder that she let you in the house at all, sir, when you must always be so flippant and annoying!'

'Perhaps she thought to get into practice for meeting

you, Lady Allegra.' And, for the first time, there was
a note of real exasperation behind the blandness of his
set-down—enough to overheat Allegra's ears again,
for being so snappy and letting him see how easily he
could goad her; enough to see her resolved to be civil—
if only in front of his grandmother. After all, it was not
Lady Hawkhurst's fault that one of her offspring had
so carelessly produced a son such as this and let it loose
on the unsuspecting community. Lady Hawkhurst
probably spent twenty-three hours out of twenty-four
wanting to wring his neck too. Regretfully biting back
a rather clever retort, Allegra tried again for uncontentious conversation.

'Does your grandmother always live here?'

'Yes.'

Allegra flashed a puzzled glance in the direction of
that grudging monosyllable. He was angry about something—very—and she could not like the feeling that it
might be something to do with her; after all, obnoxious
he might be but he was also their knight in—somewhat
tarnished—armour. It was galling to admit it but she
was not too certain what she would have done without
Mr Fleetwood's high-handed intervention. She had but
the vaguest idea as to how to go about finding Aunt
Lydia; did one set the Bow Street Runners after errant
Society widows? And how did one call in the Runners
anyway? Allegra had the not unfounded conviction
that the local constabulary would make an even bigger
mull of things than she would. Algie had once been
brought home by a constable, having eluded both his
nursemaid and his two bodyguard footmen in the
Sydney Gardens maze. It had been Algie who had told

the constable how to get him home, not the other way about; Algie had at the time been only four years of age. . .and home not two hundred yards from the entrance to the Gardens. No, constables were a waste of time and the Runners were in London. That left the Honourable Mr Fleetwood and the unwelcome obligation to behave with grateful decorum. And to, somehow, coax Mr Fleetwood out of his current sour temper.

Allegra tried again. 'I only asked because I have never met Lady Hawkhurst and it seems very strange since I have stayed her with my aunt so often before.'

Mr Fleetwood's voice was even more wooden than his face then. 'My grandmother is not of your aunt's circle, my lady.'

He said it very quietly but to Allegra it was like a stinging blow to the face. It was not the first snub she had received just for being related to the cheerfully amoral Lady Limington, but it was the most chilling. The most hurtful. Perhaps, she realised, because it was the most inexplicable. . .she had thought Mr Fleetwood liked her. And the most outrageously hyprocritical. Who was he, of all men, to judge Lydia?

Allegra's own tone was a thousand times more icy. 'Ah, I had forgot; your grandmother is so much more elderly than my aunt — perhaps it is that she does not go out in Society as much as she was used to.'

There was no doubting the heat that flashed briefly in Mr Fleetwood's eyes then — mainly because it was so bewildering and upsetting that Allegra looked hastily away. But all he said was, 'That is so, Lady Allegra.'

And Allegra was left to silence and the cold, vengeful

vow that she would pay him out for this. For the insult to Aunt Lydia, of course, not to herself. . .as if she cared anything for Luc Fleetwood's opinion; he was not even worth despising! Luc Fleetwood was. . .

It was not a hundred yards to Lady Hawkhurst's door but it seemed to take a hundred years, the atmosphere between the two was so chilling.

It was not improved by the expression on the face of the Dowager's butler who, it seemed against his better judgement, compelled himself to open the door to let them in. The look on the old man's face was the last straw to Mr Fleetwood's blackening humour.

'Yes, Cardew, I *am* holding a parrot, which you will now be so obliging as to take from me.' Unceremoniously he dumped the protesting Pythagoras on the goggling butler, adding, 'You will also speak nicely to it, Cardew, because it has the most disconcerting habit of reporting back everything it overhears.'

'Ya!' Pythagoras bellowed agreement into the butler's horrified features.

Algie, never one to be sensitive to atmosphere, jumped in with both boots to make matters worse. 'He picks up curses best of all, Mr Cardew, so if you feed him any raisins — he *likes* raisins — try not to let him bite your fingers, and if he does make sure you don't — '

That was as far as the Marquess Stonyhurst got. It would be hard to say which adult reached out to cuff him to silence first.

'*Algie!*' Allegra was humiliated.

'Algie!' Pythagoras was having the greatest time.

'Dear God!' Mr Fleetwood's eyes had taken on an

aspect of pure murder. For the first time in their short
acquaintance Allegra realised something not very comforting about her rescuer. He was the proud possessor
of a ferocious temper. That and Algie's uniquely
undisciplined tongue were going to prove utterly disastrous if she did not step in quickly to calm things; Mr
Fleetwood would so regret his impulse to rescue them,
it would be next stop her seventy-year-old godmother
at Budleigh Salterton till Papa came home; Allegra
could see it all. Unless she managed to patch things up
with Mr Fleetwood there was no way in the world they
could remain with Lady Hawkhurst, not without the
spilling of gallons of blood. And Allegra wanted to
stay. If only to get even with Luc Fleetwood.

Consequently the Most Honourable the Marquess of
Stonyhurst could in all honesty say his sister had never
sent him a look the equal of it, nor sounded a fraction
so ruthless.

'Algie, you will remain silent until you are spoken
to, is that understood? I will not have her ladyship
judge us all by your appalling manners. Moreover you
will be good enough to take charge of your parrot, if
you please; I cannot think what Mr Fleetwood was
about letting you foist it upon him in the first place.'
Here she turned to Luc Fleetwood, hoping against all
hope that he was not still angry with her.

She need not have worried; he was coolly, sardonically, unforgivably amused. It was Allegra who fought
for the last scrap of self-control just to be able to smile
charmingly up at him, 'I really must apologise again,
sir. . .'

It was not working. She could see it in his eyes. Their

expression softened, she was sure of that, but only for a second before, if anything, they became even more shuttered and aloof than ever. And she understood. He knew perfectly well what she was doing, hoping to pour oil on to troubled waters, and had he not said last night that it would never work on him? Only, she was not flirting him into better humour, she never did things like that. . .not knowingly. . .she really did want to make whatever had so strained the atmosphere between them go away. Instead, almost as if she had mistaken the origin of his displeasure, she had only made it worse.

His voice was calmer now than when he had thrown the parrot at the butler—calm and chillingly, courteously remote.

'Think nothing of it, ma'am.'

Allegra was left feeling snubbed again and knowing that this time it was for herself. Not Aunt Lydia and her tattered reputation. It was something about Allegra that Mr Fleetwood found distasteful. What disturbed her most was not the newness of such an experience when gentlemen had always been so kind and approving before; it was the fact that it was Mr Fleetwood and that she minded that *he* did not like her.

She must be very tired; after all she had had no more than an hour or so of sleep. Something had to explain what felt very like tears threatening at the back of her eyes. Allegra looked away—she could never know how coldly—and it was on to this scene of unresolved tension that the Dowager Lady Hawkhurst broke like an incoming wave, enraged with her grandson and with

not the least care how far up Pulteney Street they knew
it.

'Well, really, Luc, what can you mean by keeping
poor Lady Allegra standing about in the cold in this
fashion? I cannot think what it is with you, you are
behaving so strangely this morning!' And before
Allegra could take in what was happening she was
clasped firmly by the cuff and spun dizzily up the stairs
behind this whirlwind personage, unable to utter so
much as half a startled syllable. Not that she would
have been able to prise one in edgeways even if she
had been in any state to try it.

'The man is—oh, well, that is men for you!' Lady
Hawkhurst pursued her topic with absent-minded
vigour. 'As I don't doubt you have discovered for
yourself, *mignonne*, you are quite disastrously pretty,
quite enough to have seen the very worst of the idiot
creatures. I suffered greatly in my day—oh, but the
*irritation*!—so I know of what I speak. And now Luc!
Never did I think Luc—no, never! I always thought
Luc had broke the mould—*comprenez*?—had been
born with at least the *stirrings* of common sense, and
yet now what must he do but *insist* on my getting out
my bed so early it is actually *daylight*? Before *noon*
may the good God preserve us! Not a word of explanation, you understand, nothing! *Rien*! *Luc*! It should
not be possible that *he*. . .but what would you. . .? *Et
voilà*!' And still on the same operatic breath she swept
Allegra into the most charmingly dishevelled of morn-
ing-rooms, packed to every last inch of the skirting
with spindly, exotic and very moth-bedraggled furniture dating from one or other of the extravagantly

tasteless King Louis, and whirled her down on to an inviting tumble of cat-mangled tapestry cushions littering an otherwise rock-hard Elizabethan settle by the fire.

'*Bien*! Now. . .*Gorringe*!'

Allegra could only stare in silent fascination as a young woman came all but steeplechasing the clutter to obey this ringing command, as if nobody ever did anything quietly in this household or at anything but at the double or faster either.

'Ah, Gorringe, a glass of hottest chocolate for Lady Allegra. You may warm some brandy for me!'

Without even knowing it Allegra turned mutinous. Always it must be soup or sweet, sickly chocolate when never in her life could her spinning nerves more have done with something a great deal stronger!

To her horror the Dowager Lady Hawkhurst choked with laughter. 'Oh, *mais là*! But what a face, madam! but then I have heard all about the pistol; Luc, he has told me *everything*. What a petulant little thing you are! Even so, no brandy for you. Chocolate with plenty of sugar and cinnamon, and perhaps even a little pepper. It is about time, I think, that you followed a more ordered existence.'

A blunt if uncensorious reference to Aunt Lydia's eccentricities again and Allegra was stunned. But not to anger as she had been with Mr Fleetwood. She burst into the most unseemly laughter; how could she ever have been able to help it?

'Ordered! *Here*!' Then she realised the enormity of her *faux pas*. 'Oh, but. . .I'm sorry!' But it was no use; she could not help herself. '*Ordered*!' It was shocking, unforgivable; Allegra knew it even as she knew that she would never be able to take a word of it back. What must Lady Hawkhurst think of her?

She might have known that uniquely forthright lady would tell her, with that infectiously ribald Gallic laughter of hers.

'Ah, but it is good to see you speak your mind, *petite*. I get so tired of all this simpering and soothing and being civil to me if it chokes them just because I am somebody's grandmama. It is the most irksome thing to be the Dowager Lady anything; it makes one feel so *old*! Or do I mean that it makes me see other people think I'm old when I don't feel a day above seventeen. . .?'

She was irrisistible. Even so, Allegra knew her only chance to speak for the next six hours was to hurry in while Lady Hawkhurst drew theatrically mournful breath.

'I was not meaning to be rude.'

Lady Hawkhurst waved away this protest in the same imperial gesture as dusting aside a gargantuan and malevolent-looking ginger cat so that she might sit on the other end of the settle.

'Think nothing of it!' The cat, plainly blaming Allegra for his banishment to the lesser comforts of the Louis Quinze, sent her a hot green look that said exactly the opposite. The Dowager saw it and added mildly, 'Oh, dear, I had forgot. He is quite the nastiest cat in England; you must tell me if he holds anything against you for he is inclined to bear grudges for weeks on end and then pounce with ruthless abandon just when one imagines one is safely forgiven.'

Even before she had finished speaking she had rounded up the seething animal and sat it on the already mutilated muslin of her skirts. The most evil cat in England promptly rolled over on his massive back and purred. It was the blissful sound of one contemplating a large helping of revenge, taken cold; Allegra shifted several inches in the opposite direction.

She was just struggling for something to say that was appropriate to the extraordinary circumstances of her morning when she heard a sound that chilled her to the bone.

'Aw! *Aw*! Leave orf, guv'na!' Pythagoras.

Surely even Algie could not so far forget himself as to bring his benighted parrot into the Dowager's presence.

Allegra was just practising her most venomous 'Algernon!' when Mr Fleetwood, with an insouciance that was breathtaking in its recklessness, strolled into the room announcing, 'This should shake up that mangy villain you like to call a cat, Tiffy!'

Tiffy?

None of this was really happening! Mr Fleetwood — no, not even he could possibly have just addressed his grandmother as Tiffy!

But it seemed that he had; certainly the Dowager was beaming up at him in unmistakable adoration. Even the old villain in her lap sat up and all but gurgled with pleasure. . .until he saw the parrot.

The Dowager did not share her pet's opinion. 'Ah, but what a beautiful creature! I'm sure that he and Napoleon will get along famously!' exclaimed Lady Hawkhurst, fatally unaware of what this betrayal might mean to the unmarred whiteness of her beautifully kept hands as the cat began to flex his tiger's claws.

Napoleon—and Allegra was no longer surprised by anything that was happening now; why not name a cat after the arch-enemy of the realm after all!—dug those claws ruthlessly into her Dowager Ladyship's knees and exited the room, pausing only to spit his contempt at a delighted parrot.

Every nerve in Allegra's body froze then. She knew her Pythagoras, and not even the eccentric Lady Hawkhurst would stand for what was all too inevitably coming next. In the final second before Pythagoras ruined forever her chances of remaining a member of decent society Allegra thought, I wonder if I shall like it with Godmother Arbuthnot-Ridley at Budleigh Salterton. . .?

'Well, I'll be bu——' began the parrot.

Then the miracle happened. Mr Fleetwood, in a voice that brooked no rebellion, least of all from parrots, looked the giggling bird right in the eye and announced baldly, 'What you will be is dressed and spitted and dished up for dinner if you don't learn to mind your manners, you misbegotten heathen!'

The only thing the parrot did not say was sorry—it being a word he had disdained to acquire. Feathers fluffed and apologetic, he glanced warily sideways at Mr Fleetwood, and suddenly Allegra understood the exact nature of the miracle. Whatever Mr Fleetwood's mood not ten minutes before, however angry he had been with her, however hostile, Pythagoras and his stevedore's vocabulary had chased all the shadows away. Mr Fleetwood was laughing as if he had never known ill-humour in his life and she found that she was laughing with him — and that his laughter at last reached his teasing blue eyes — and that his gaze for a long moment seemed as if soldered to hers.

It was a moment Allegra was never really able to explain later, or even remember in detail. It was something she was only ever able to feel, not analyse. She did not understand it. Except that suddenly from bewildered and tired she felt alive, excited, hopeful. And safe. Looking about the battered, homely room, she thought, everything is going to be all right. What she refused to hear was a small, buried voice adding, because Luc Fleetwood is here.

It was the Dowager who put paid to these comfortably unnerving musings.

'Well, now, Luc, dispose the parrot where you will. . . I note you have already disposed of our little Marquess somewhere——'

Luc plainly had the knack of interrupting his grandmother. 'He is flattering marmalade fig cake out of Auguste in the kitchens and his tutor has snatched the opportunity to take the two dogs for a very long walk, because they are apt to howl in unison like some infernal choir if he forgets them. So we are quite alone.'

Allegra looked sharply at Mr Fleetwood then. He meant something by this last that she could not begin to understand. But it seemed his grandparent followed it.

'Excellent! Because you know, Luc, Allegra — I shall call you Allegra, I think, it is such a pretty name — we really must get down to business, and, it being our

relatives who have elected to behave in so rum a
fashion, it is nobody's affair but ours. And it had better
to remain so, or I cannot answer for what I shall have
to say about the matter! I think, Luc, that it is better
even that you remove that so charming parrot, after all
. . .well, parrots *will* repeat things, *non*?'

Never had Allegra heard anyone sound half so
conspiratorial. The Dowager Lady Hawkhurst, one eye
on the doors as if she expected that at any moment
some unwanted party must burst through and entrap
them with their family scandals showing, lowered her
voice to such a pitch that both Allegra and Mr
Fleetwood felt obliged to lean almost intimately close
to hear her. Pythagoras, dumped still in disgrace upon
a convenient music stand, crane his neck though he
might, had not the smallest hope of catching even the
most innocuous syllable and cawed his disapproval in
such a shouting voice that, in Lady Hawkhurst's sibilant
opinion, even such a hardened listener at doors as
Cardew the butler had not a hope of discovering what
was going on.

Allegra found that she was holding her breath. This
melodramatic atmosphere was catching. And. . .well,
somehow Mr Fleetwood seemed suddenly too near. . .

His grandmother, however, was quite oblivious to
her new charge's suddenly glowing complexion. She
had the battle in her sights.

'Well, now, Lydia Limington and that half-wit
Hawkhurst are vanished and we are going to have to
find them — before every malicious tabby with a tongue
to gossip with all but advertises in *The Gazette* that
they know the reason why!'

## CHAPTER FOUR

THE glass of foaming chocolate spiced with cinnamon,
honey and the barest pinch of pepper was delivered to
Allegra at the centre of a theatrically silent tableau,
held mute by the Dowager's warning eye while anything so alien as a maid remained in the room. It
proved unexpectedly delicious. But that was possibly
because not five minutes later the Honourable Mr
Fleetwood took the opportunity of one of his grandmother's wilder flights of alarm — eyes shut, arms
thrown out in hectic appeal — to lean on the back of
the settle and tip a dash of brandy into Allegra's cup
from his own glass. It was a gesture as unexpected as it
was welcome and made Allegra, who had always
thought herself so very sophisticated, feel suddenly
much more grown-up, although she found at the same
time that she did not dare smile even so much as shyly
at Mr Fleetwood for if she did she knew that she would
blush again. Instead she just smiled to herself with
intense satisfaction and was not too offended when she
heard from behind her his indulgent, if faintly mocking
laughter.

Quite how long Lady Hawkhurst had been holding
forth did not seem to be the issue of the household.
Either Mr Fleetwood was the very model of manly
patience — which Allegra knew from bitter experience
that he was not — or he loved the old lady very much

indeed. Allegra glanced surreptitiously at him while he recaptured Pythagoras, who had taken a desultory flap about the room to cast a critical eye over his new surroundings, and made the bird comfortable on the edge of a dangerously valuable Chinese vase, and she thought, He really *is* a nice man.

And yet only half an hour before she had hated him. She was sure she had not forgiven him, because his contempt for Aunt Lydia was unforgivable. It was just that there was something about being in his warm, intoxicating presence that made such things as honest revenge in defence of family honour superfluous. It was as if, Allegra thought, she could not choose her feelings when he was near to her, nor her reactions either.

Allegra, disturbed even as she felt so comforted and secure, wondered idly just how much brandy he had added to her chocolate then pulled herself hastily together because the Dowager was saying, 'Well, I must say you two are quite the most useless children; we seem to have got precisely nowhere!'

'We?' There was such gentle teasing in Mr Fleetwood's voice as to remove all sting from a very real reproof.

His grandmother looked as near to chastened as such a grand and headlong lady could ever come.

'Oh, Luc, I know I do run on, but. . .but, *vraiment*, *you* had nothing of the least use to contribute——'

'I? Good God, ma'am, but——!'

'No, it is true, Luc! You gentlemen always think you are so clever but what have you said that is of the least help to anybody at all?'

'With you talking at such a —'

'You might always interrupt me like a sensible person! Really, Luc, I cannot think what has got into you since you took up that new appointment with —'

'*Tiffy!*'

Allegra sat up with a start, realising she had all but dozed off as she watched the pantomine unfold before her. There had been real warning in that one urgent word. And never would she have expected to see the Dowager half so contrite.

'Oh, but I forgot, Luc —'

'Well, continue to forget, Tiffy! Jupiter, I must have been out of my mind to tell you in the first place!'

Secrets, Allegra divined through her fog of brandy — really it was a wonderful substance and she could not think why Papa had always banned it from her. Luc Fleetwood had a secret he was very anxious that no one should know. . .

Allegra smiled. He was a gentleman after all. . .a man, anyway. She would have the secret from him by sundown if it killed her.

She might have smiled a little less complacently had she understood the nature of Luc Fleetwood's sudden uninhibited laughter as he looked at her. However, she certainly understood the firmness of the hand beneath her elbow and his outrageous whisper not ten minutes of ever more fruitless speculation later.

'Don't hold your drink like your father, do you, my lady?'

It was rage that brought Allegra to her feet then. How dared he? And how dared he be so familiar in front of his grandmother — especially a grandmother who was gazing at them with the most Gallic of benign curiosity?

Then Allegra remembered where she was. Lady Hawkhurst had made it perfectly plain that this was a most unusual household so Allegra behaved unusually — at least, it was unusual for her. . .in public.

'Let go my arm, you barbarian! As if I cannot stand without your assistance!'

'You can't!' he retorted bluntly, and to her horror Allegra's buckling knees agreed with him.

'Drunk,' opined the parrot.

Lady Hawkhurst, inevitably, reacted as if intoxicated débutantes were an everyday occurrence in her morning-room.

'A walk, Luc, that's the thing for it! A good brisk walk. Do you not think so? To go out and find this tutor of the little Marquess who has the dogs. That is the best thing. A good *long* walk!' And she shuddered in horror at the very thought of such unwarranted excess.

Since a walk was exactly what Mr Fleetwood had been planning — or, at least, cornering Lady Allegra on her own for the purposes of grilling her about Lydia — he already had the far from steady victim through the door and down the stairs, where he solicitously reinstated her gloves and parasol, never for one second wiping that condescending smile from his loathsome features. Allegra stood meekly — it was too much to fight him and stay upright at one and the same time — and thought, Half an hour ago I hated him, ten minutes ago I didn't. Now? Now. . .well, I am going to do my best to murder him as painfully as good taste allows!

'Luc!' called his grandmother over the balustrade as if this were perfectly usual behaviour for ladies of her station. 'Do not you be going anywhere without her ladyship's maid! The child has her reputation to think of!' And through what could only be described as her grandson's most vulgar laughter she added imperatively, 'And do you not even *think* to be late for luncheon!'

The cool mid-morning air struck Allegra like a second slug of brandy. The sun smiled beneficently down on the classical gold elegance of Laura Place and she had the horrible sensation that she might sing out loud if she were not too careful.

Drunk, he'd said. No, that was Pythagoras — who had seen his last beakful of plum from her for a very long time. Was she? How utterly humiliating! Allegra smiled lazily to herself and, tossing her head at her maid's dawning comprehension, found she had skipped several yards along the pavement before she realised what she was about.

When she did realise she turned, all ready to do battle, on Mr Fleetwood, who was strolling innocuously behind, only to find that he was smiling again in that unfairly disabling fashion.

Patronised — for she had frequently smiled at Algie like that when he was a very little boy — she put her head on one side and demanded crossly, 'What is so amusing, sir, that you must smirk in that ridiculous fashion?'

It was the social equivalent of putting one's head above the parapet mid-battle. Mr Fleetwood's grin shot her down in flames of embarrassment.

'You, of course. But thank the Lord you look young enough to be my baby sister or ——'

'I do *not*!' raged the toast of fashionable London.

Mr Fleetwood even more infuriatingly dismissed this outburst with a smile still more unsettling. 'What are you doing, by the way?'

Allegra was baffled. 'Doing?'

'Yes. . .every time you step on a crack in the paving you go back and start again.'

The next blush all but cremated Allegra where she stood. Dear God, but she would never touch brandy again! She simply could not have been doing such a childish thing and not know it. . .

'You mean. . .?'

'Is stepping on the cracks bad luck or something?'

Not brandy, not champagne, not anything stronger than milk *ever*! she vowed. And yet, appalled as she was, her very first response was a peal of laughter.

'Oh, lord! Was I really? It was Algie's favourite game—when he was little, I mean; he's much too big for it now. Now he only cares for catching things in jars so he may—er—oh, dear. . .'

'Scientifically observe them,' supplied her enemy helpfully.

'He always lets them go afterwards, of course. Only he doesn't always remember to put them back where he found them so one finds the oddest things in one's sewing box and walking boots. . .'

By now Mr Fleetwood was quite literally shaking with amusement and Sorcha the maid seemed to find it necessary to turn away and pick some foreign object out of her shoe. She appeared to be shaking too.

'How odd precisely?' enquired Mr Fleetwood.

'Barn owls,' explained Allegra, no longer caring whether she was foxed or not since it felt so wonderful. 'Poor Pythagoras was most put out. He found one sitting on his favourite perch one morning. Not that the owl wasn't even more astonished. Algie said it fainted but Papa said it died of shock.'

Of course it was not really possible that she was standing in the middle of Pulteney Bridge, above the soothing rustle of the weir, gazing down towards the buttresses of the great grey abbey, discussing extinguished barn owls with what amounted to a complete stranger. It became necessary to enquire, '*Am* I really drunk?'

'As a good score of wheelbarrows, I'd say!' Just for a moment that strange shadowed look she had seen before stole into Mr Fleetwood's hypnotic eyes before it was burned away in another flame of laughter, 'I wish I could say that I am sorry for spiking your chocolate!'

And even as he came towards her, as reassuring and as friendly as he had seemed last night when she should have been so frightened, Allegra felt a sudden chill twist and stab in threat at the base of her spine.

Had he known that the brandy would do this to her? Had he meant it to? Why?

So when he held out his arm to her Allegra, suddenly as sober as a bench of judges, edged away, wary and distrustful. Unsure of him again. The sun seemed to have gone in.

*    *    *

She had been right to suspect that Luc Fleetwood was intent upon some dubious scheme of his own and that she played the greater part in it; but what that part might be she did not know. All she knew at this moment was that the smiling and not in the least to be trusted Mr Fleetwood was tugging her quite ruthlessly by the elbow to the very last place in Bath any sane young person would wish to go on such a bright and hopeful morning.

As the great abbey entrance yawned univitingly before them she demanded, a great deal more plaintively than she realised, 'Why are we going in *there*?'

Her captor was implacable. 'You'll see!'

Allegra, like a small child thwarted of an outing she had long been looking forward to, dug in her heels, hanging back just literally enough to cause a severely starched-up-looking matron to raise pained eyebrow plus vulgarly bejewelled quizzing-glass in Mr Fleetwood's direction. Allegra knew that look; and the one he cast so haughtily back. The 'Heavens can he not control the monstrous child?' expression, returned by the 'Believe me, ma'am, she's living on borrowed time; just wait till I get her home!' tight-lipped smile. How often had she been forced into such winces of humiliation by the antics of her beloved Algie?

Very well, then, if Luc Fleetwood must make a fool of her, well. . .he did not know the meaning of embarrassment! But he was going to find out! Allegra wondered venegfully if she remembered how to throw a real crowd-pulling tantrum.

'I'm not going in there!' would do to be going on with.

To her final and everlasting fury Mr Fleetwood, not having been apprised of the script, smiled so good-naturedly at her that had he been anyone else she would have been well and truly disarmed.

'No?' was all he said. . .towing her ever closer towards their chilly destination.

What to do with a man who would not argue in a proper fashion? Allegra, seething and utterly bewildered by the wretched creature, tried a far too belated appeal to reason.

'But it's cold; besides, I've seen it before and it's boring. And it smells all musty. Why cannot we go somewhere else?'

It was useless.

'Because we can't, that's why!'

And Allegra, all but gaping in astonishment now, found herself trotting meekly in his immaculately coated wake, the iron grip he had on her aching fingers allowing for no more protest than an outraged gasp of sheer pain. This was not right; this simply was *not* the way gentlemen behaved towards her! Freddie would never have been so unsporting—and Cuthbert. . .well, Cuthbert had long since declared himself Willing to Die if Need Be, it being his Destiny to do Whatever his Divine Allegra's Adorable Little Heart Desired.

There was no getting away from it. The Honourable Luc Fleetwood was no Cuthbert Nettlesham. Nor Freddie, nor Felix, nor any one of the poetic and passionately adoring young men who had fallen like autumn leaves in a hurricane at her richly shod and 'Exquisite Little' feet from the very first day she was launched into adult Society. Mr Fleetwood was like no

one she had ever met in her life and, a great deal less
experienced in the arts of mortally wounding her
masculine quarry than she had thought, Allegra had
not the least idea how she should deal with him.

Only that she would. And he was not going to enjoy
one second of it!

It was silent in the grandly austere darkness of the
abbey and empty, she noticed, of all but what appeared
to be warily watchful couples anxious neither to be
seen nor overheard. The deeply-slanting shadows hid
their faces and the vaulting ceilings disguised the echo
of their nervous voices. The place was full of whispers.

Mr Fleetwood's blunt question was not one of them.

'Very well, Lady Allegra, now we are safely where
there is not the least risk we shall be overheard, tell
me, other than my poor brother just how many other
men has Lydia trapped writhing helplessly in her talons
at this——?'

He got no further. Allegra might have been keeping
her voice down but her tone was volcanic with fury as
she hissed, with a singularly unfortunate disregard for
her surroundings, 'Be damned your impertinence, sir!
But how dare you ask me such a thing?' And she got
to her feet to stalk from their secluded corner. She got
not further than the length of his arm which snaked so
efficiently and intractably about her waist to hold her
fast that her very first thought was, I was right,
abominable rake! Most certainly this was not the first
time he had behaved in so depraved and dishonourable
a fashion.

If ever she had doubted it Mr Fleetwood's unforgivable murmur of laughter, much too close to her burning

ears, assured her, 'Don't think I'm letting you flee, Lady Allegra! Not until you have told me everything I want to know. And don't——' he patiently unfurled the clenched and seething fingers that were flexing even now to do him lasting damage '—hit me, scratch me or inflict any other of the abuses to my person which you are planning, you little hoyden!'

'I shall scream!'

She knew how foolish she sounded long before her voice echoed derisively back at her off the nearest funerary plaque. Who here would come to her assistance when they were none of them meant to be here in the first place?

Luc Fleetwood confirmed her opinion of their fellow 'worshippers'. 'Morning service is long since over, ma'am. These people are not here for anything so innocent as God!' There was such cold, contemptuous cynicism in his voice that Allegra stared at him, deeply shocked. In the arm still locked ruthlessly about her waist she felt a tension building that she could not begin to understand. But even as she sensed it he shook his head in a gesture of icy dismissal. 'But then where else could they come, in a society such as this that will not allow people to love whom they please and acknowledge whom they will in public?'

What an extraordinary, confusing man he was. Allegra, feeling in her acutest awareness of his hold about her that his rage, his tension must become hers any moment, as if it were possible to transfer emotion, body to body, through the barest touch, was almost frightened by him at last. By that touch. . .

Touch? He should not be holding her!

This time as she pulled away he let her go. He had
made his point, after all. To anyone who heard them
quarrelling now they were just another thwarted couple
breaking intolerable rules. Or so Allegra misunderstood it. And there was nothing in his suddenly shuttered face to say otherwise.

It should have occurred to her then to hope that
nobody who knew her had seen her enter the abbey
with Mr Fleetwood, accompanied by her maid or not.
Sorcha's presence would count for little when the abbey
plainly had a universal reputation as a trysting place.
She should have demanded that they leave. That they
take a turn about the abbey churchyard like the most
respectable of tourists, stroll innocently to the Pump
Rooms and sip the unappetising waters, or down the
road into the safe, crowded anonymity of the Stall
Street emporia. But suddenly she knew this was not
the time for petty concerns. Suddenly she understood
why he had questioned her so clumsily.

'It is your brother, is it not? Are you *so* worried
about Lord Hawkhurst, sir?'

She could never have expected such a reaction.

'*Worried*! By God!' He all but shouted it, flinging his
head into his hands in a gesture of frustration so un-
English that Allegra suddenly remembered their talk
of last night. Remembered why he had reason for
concern; that some families, only grudgingly accepted
already, had a lot more to lose and sooner than most
once scandal struck with the full force of Society's
unflinching hypocrisy. And that was the least of the
things that might have befallen his missing brother.

Tentatively, not really aware that she did so, Allegra

put out a hand to his shoulder. 'But. . .forgive me if I seem stupid, sir, but I can't know unless you properly explain. Why should it be so strange that his lordship has vanished? I know you said that he would never miss your birthday but. . .perhaps if he was called away——'

'He would let me know.' He was so calmly certain that Allegra without hesitation believed him.

'But. . .well, what if he could not, sir? Perhaps he did not expect to be away so long as for there to be need to tell you, but for some reason he has been detained. Perhaps there has simply been no time to get a message to you.' Then she realised what she was saying. She knew as well as he did that where his brother was, so her aunt must be. The likelihood of the two of them vanishing simultaneously but for different reasons was outside intelligent consideration.

There was a new, hard chill settling around her heart now as she asked, at last beginning to understand, 'That is why you ask about my aunt having other admirers, isn't it? You want her to be with one of them? So it wouldn't be true that she has. . .bolted. . . with your brother?' That cold rigidity inside her was setting fast into humiliated anger, an anger echoed in the bleak remoteness of her voice. 'Would it be so terrible a thing that they had run away together, sir? That is what you think, is it not — that they have eloped?'

What Mr Fleetwood said then took her breath away. Never had she heard such intensity in his voice, nor seen it blaze so wildly in his mesmerising eyes.

'Terrible? Dear God, no! Lady Allegra, don't you

understand yet? That I *hope* it is as simple as that. Because the alternative. . .God, but it *has* to be that!'

'*What*?'

Mr Fleetwood's next action was as instantaneous as it was unforgivable. Even as Allegra drew breath to speak again his hand covered her mouth so painfully that she was all but choking beneath the force of it. Instinctively, frantic for breath, Allegra bit him hard.

Patently the better quality the glove, the more repulsive the taste.

'Ughh! Mmnn!'

Mr Fleetwood correctly interpreted this as, Let me go, you vile snake, or I swear to every god there has ever been that I shall kill you!

'Not if you're going to do that again! For pity's sake, you wretched child, I brought you here particularly so we might not draw attention to ourselves, not to have you bring the roof down with your screeching!'

'Grrr!'

'And don't even think of biting me again, my lady! I have a particular fondness for these gloves. *Ow*!'

Allegra was discovering a particular fondness for the delicate little kid-skin half-boots she was wearing, soft as silk. . .all except the tiny but imperative heel now sunk into the arch of Mr Fleetwood's agonised foot.

His grip tightened. Even in the gloom of their discreetly shadowed corner Allegra's eyes spat flames of fury. Mr Fleetwood's iced over in unforgiving rage.

'Very well, ma'am, war it is! And believe you me, you have no hope in the world to win it! Now, are you going to be silent and listen to what I have to say or are you not? I am quite content to smother you all day if need be, keeping one hand free for when I can no longer control the urge to throttle you!'

Since Allegra's most urgent concern was to breathe again she nodded her head vigorously. She might even mean it, she thought. After all, he had a very great deal of explaining to do. She could floor him afterwards.

'Good!' He withdrew his hand and scowlingly inspected what he could see in this darkness of the damage to his glove.

He had just made a very elementary mistake and Allegra inwardly crowed at it. He believed her! He actually believed all he had to do was bully and misuse her and she would be as good as gold! Meekly she dipped her head to hide the triumph of her smile. It was all she could do to keep the laughter out of her whisper.

'Very well, sir, explain! For you must own. . .well, how could you expect me to do other than exclaim——'

'Bellow.'

'I did nothing of the. . .!' Then she remembered she was being civil so she changed course hastily. 'You must admit, sir, it was quite the most shocking thing you said!'

'Shocking?'

Mr Fleetwood was plainly astonished by her choice of word—and Allegra understood for once. Her humiliation was absolute, burning into her face until her ears throbbed with the pain of it. Of course he would not think it strange of Aunt Lydia to do something so vulgar as to elope. He had already made his opinion of that lady's morals hurtfully plain.

Subdued by the truth of his implied criticism, aching with hurt, Allegra whispered, with a quiet dignity that was shocking in itself, 'Well, to *me* it is a shock, sir.' To her horror there was almost a break in her voice.

Mr Fleetwood mistook it for tears. Before she knew it he had taken her chin so gently in his hand, needing not so much as a fraction of the strength she felt so sternly held back to turn her reluctant face towards him. However hard she tried to look away, Allegra knew she never could. Mr Fleetwood, with that simmering gaze of his, was becoming more and more disturbing by the second.

And yet she had never heard him so reassuring. 'Come now, what would be so wrong in it, kitten, that your aunt and my idiot brother have run away together? A trifle unorthodox perhaps——' he smiled even as he said it, knowing how implacably respectable society would disagree '—but if they care for each other, and I believe they do as well as either ever can, and both are free. . .'

'But. . .' Allegra did not know how to say it. How did one say, But your brother would be ruined by it, sir, for my aunt is considered little better than a well-bred harlot? How did one admit that just the barest family connection with one's own relation could annihilate forever Mr Fleetwood's own prospects of a comfortable future too? Surely he must know it?

Allegra, dazed as she was by his closeness, and the soft caress of his fingers against her cheek, tried to see it in his face; that he knew and she would never have to say it. Admit her family could ruin his.

He knew. And as Allegra watched the grim twist to his expressive mouth she thought, I don't believe he cares.

He didn't. Almost urgently now, and leaning closer to her than perhaps he realised, he whispered quickly, 'I believe my brother loves her, child. Whatever I think of that, all I want is for him to be happy. My brother is . . .he has always *needed* to be happy, *needed* pleasure, for life to be only a harmless game. Our mother called him "the golden one", her child of the gods; he is very bad at being unhappy.'

'Is not everyone?' It was her own voice, Allegra knew it, and yet it sounded different. Strained. As if it belonged to someone new, someone much more grown-up. Much more sad.

He shook his head, even more urgent to make her see. 'No, child not as he is. You, I, we can be hurt, we rage at it, we fight it; sometimes it seems to destroy us but it never can. It always ends; it fades away. It is not like that for him.'

Allegra understood now, so much so that she wondered how she had never really seen before, so she spared him the need to say it. His brother and Aunt Lydia belonged together; they were both of them gilt, not gold—easy to love, easy to live with and laugh with, but *only* laugh; both weak. It was not true joy of living that drove them, it was a child's fear of the dark should ever that joy be snatched away. When they were happy it was for them, and everyone around them, as if the sun shone only in their orbit and the

world around them warmed and brightened for it, but
it did not last and they could not stand alone; they
could not live without finding something new to fuel it.
It had become their drug and without it they were
nothing.

She knew it to be true of Aunt Lydia, so much so
that she knew she would never see her aunt in the same
way again. She had always adored her and she always
would. She would be charmed and delighted by her
presence, miss her a little when she was not there. But
she knew, quite undramatically now, that she would
never be dazzled again.

She did not want to *be* Lydia any more.

What a terrible thing — Allegra shuddered as if she
were cold right through to the bone — to be like Aunt
Lydia and need so desperately something so few people
ever truly found. To breathe only for a wild, sen-
sation-seeking happiness that could never be found in
one place for long, nor in one person. Not where there
was no contentment, not without the capacity for real
love. She found that she was shivering quite violently,
for she had never seen anyone in such a light before,
nor life either. She had never really pitied anyone
before. Or been afraid of what her own future might
hold.

Lost in a daze of newborn understanding, Allegra
was half expecting to feel Mr Fleetwood's arm slip
about her waist once more. Not the iron grip of anger
now, but meant to comfort her. She was not surprised
that it did. Nor that she felt its immeasurable reassurance. And yet never in her life had she been more out

of her depth, and sinking deeper every second. She
was shaking in her efforts to fight it.

There was something so strange about his voice now,
as if he found it difficult even to whisper, a harsh, torn
sound that was soft and exciting all at the same time.

'Don't be afraid for them, sweetheart. It is how they
want to be. It is all they have ever known. They are
too beautiful, the two of them, too spoiled. One can
be indulged so long that one never understands there
can be an end to it. It is safer they never find out. Let
them be as they are. Wild, the pair of them, greedy
and selfish as babies but just as innocent. They *are* just
children, Allegra, and I for one hope they neither of
them ever need to be any other way. Now they have
each other—yes, I know what you're thinking, that
they will be shunned by our precious Society, be
damned to its smug hypocrisy! But do you think they
will care? Not if they are safely together. Would you?'

'Would I. . .?'

'Yes, you. If *you* loved someone whom it would be
ruin to love. . .'

Allegra's whole being reeled; she would never know
how they had come to this point. Talking of such things
as she knew, had she never met him, she would never
have thought about at all. This was not part of the
world as she knew it. Such fierce, dangerous words
were not part of what she had ever seen. They were
not what Freddie Limmersham had meant by love;
they were not what Cuthbert Nettlesham professed.
Two men who had walked out one morning and tried
to kill each other for her—risked killing, anyway—and
she had thought it just a game! And the most terrifying

thing was, it had been. They had neither of them even a fragment enough of imagination to begin to understand words like these. They could play games to the death without ever knowing there was nothing in them but a hollowness of spirit. No heart. Nothing like this. They would never understand.

What Allegra now knew was that she did. She understood with a wrench to the heart that all but stopped her breathing, in a tide of blood scalding through her veins as if she were alive for the very first time, and really feeling it. Nobody in her old world talked like this. What had she to do with a world as desolate as that?

'Would you throw the world away for him? *Would* you?'

The answer was out long before the thought itself seemed real to her.

'Yes. . . I think.' Then, leaving all she had ever known of herself behind for good, she said, with a passion that would never again surprise her, 'Yes— yes, I know that I would!'

He said the strangest thing then. So quietly, she barely heard it.

'Then let us hope, my lady, that whoever he is you love so bravely loves you so completely that he would die before ever he would allow it!'

That was the moment when Allegra had to get out of the abbey, out of his explosive presence. She was on her feet and flying like a wild thing for the door before she knew it. The midday sun struck a stinging blow to her already shaken body. She felt like that. Shattered, torn up by her very roots, wrung out. Half understanding what was happening to her; half wanting to stop it. To turn time back and be the Allegra she had been before. The one it was so much easier to be. Safe, shallow little Allegra who reigned over every susceptible heart in London and did not feel a thing.

Allegra leaned against the ice-cold stone of the abbey wall, dragging breaths of gentle spring air into her aching body as if she had any hope of calming it. Oddly the only thing she was aware of was her maid's pale, bewildered features.

I've grown into a world I don't understand, thought Allegra. I am growing into a person I did not know I would ever be.

And all of it was because she had met Luc Fleetwood.

# CHAPTER FIVE

ALLEGRA was more than subdued as they made their way back towards the security of Great Pulteney Street and safe, normal things such as Algie rebelling loudly against his tutor and Pythagoras eyeing the choicest morsels of their luncheon and plotting how to snatch them. Subdued enough to listen with as near to calm as she felt she could ever come again to what Mr Fleetwood was explaining to her.

He too seemed unnaturally quiet. Almost, Allegra felt, as if that moment of urgency—no, real passion and self-revelation—in the abbey had never been. He did not want it to have been. This was more than just the awkwardness that even good friends might feel after exchanging their most private secrets. Withdrawn, almost as if he had reined in that so powerful magnetism of his so that it might not reach out and encroach, touch her; that she might not encroach upon it. Withdrawn completely. He walked as far apart from her as he could and not cause a nuisance to other users of the pavement. Not once during the whole ten minutes did he smile at her, or even really look at her at all.

'It is the best we can hope for, my lady—that Faron and Lydia are in some hare-brained scrape together. The alternative is that we have two mysteries on our hands and not just one that has a simple if all too infuriating explanation. I know it seems the worst thing in the world to you at the moment and yet, however disastrous such a marriage may at first appear to both our families, we shall ride out the storm. After all, we have faced out worse; do not think I don't know the evil gossip from which your parents suffered at the beginning of this savage war with Bonaparte, yet no lasting harm has come of it. Your father is Duke of Alderley, after all, and a man respected as much for his character as his courage in the field. He is well-liked, my lady, and so—God knows!—are you. So am I, come to that; there is no one bears any of us real malice. Faron and Lydia—well, in their way I think they are very much needed. Society would be a much drabber place without them, and everybody knows it. They might be snubbed for a time, child, but I sincerely doubt lasting damage, to any of us.'

Not to me, Allegra thought, for as you have just reminded me I am far too rich; but it could bring unconscionable harm to you. Young as she was, she was far less forgiving of the shallowness of Society than he seemed to be, now that she had seen it at last for what it was; she was far less optimistic. What she actually said was, 'But, Mr Fleetwood, how can you be complacent about such a match, for my aunt must be so many years your brother's senior?'

Now he laughed at last and Allegra realised that it felt a very long time indeed since she had last heard its intoxicating sound, and she had missed it. Even so, this was a joyless sound, soaked through with that cynicism in him that always so effectively pushed her away, left her a little in awe of him. It was so far from his habitual good humour, jarred so with the capacity for easygoing contentment, that she felt instinctively to be his true nature. She felt again a stab of regret that he had something private, something he would never let free, that made him so jaded, so angry and unhappy.

And yet even as she puzzled at it and wished she could make it go away she found that he was smiling at her at last, really smiling, and she wondered if she would ever be able to keep up with his volatile reverses of mood.

'It is you who are young, Allegra, that is all! Silly child! Your aunt is but five and thirty and my brother not a year her junior!'

Allegra was so astonished not to have thought of it for herself that she did not even resent the inadequately veiled reference to her own muddled immaturity.

'Oh, but then——!'

'Then there is no reason in the world why they might not marry, and all the time in the world for there to be a coven of little Lydias born to frighten my poor brother into the need for a proper sense of responsibility!'

Children. An heir! For a moment Allegra, separated from her aunt by a gulf in generation that felt so much greater than its mere eighteen years, could barely take in what Mr Fleetwood was saying, let alone the quite astonishing calmness with which he seemed to be saying it — almost as if he could not see what it must mean to him. If Lord Hawkhurst and Aunt Lydia were to wed and produce an heir to the titles it would make Mr Fleetwood's own position in Society all but impossible, thought Allegra, and fatally damage any chance he might have of marrying himself in time, least of all respectably. While he remained his brother's heir he had probably some hope of riding out the in-breaking scandal; after all, a man one day to be Earl of Hawkhurst and possessor of a far from negligible fortune would not so swiftly be turned away by the more intelligent of matchmaking mamas. But if Aunt Lydia and his brother were to have a son, let alone in the wake of such a public flouting of all the intractable *ton* held dear, Mr Fleetwood's position would be untenable. A younger son, comfortably situated though he seemed to be, was still a younger son, and, tainted with a family from planets far beyond the social pale, what kind of future had he in that?

And it really could happen. Allegra had never thought of it before since there had never been any suggestion that Aunt Lydia might marry again. Aunt Lydia had always been Aunt Lydia, and aunts were always, if not exactly old, *too* old. Too old for children. . .

Dear lord, Allegra closed her eyes against yet another kick of humiliation. What a child I am! How naïve! What a fool I must seem to him!

Risking a glance at Mr Fleetwood, she received an even sharper pain. Quite deliberately he turned away. She knew it. He would not even look at her with that indulgent, tormenting smile. He was not even thinking about her at all. She was so much a baby to him that he could never. . .

That thought was broken off then and there. There were feelings taking root inside her that she would only ever want to stifle. Feelings about him, of course, and she wanted with all her heart that they would only be anger. . .because he had walked into her life and turned it upside-down, and inside out, and every way but how she wanted it, and he did not even care that he had done so. He probably did not even know.

Maybe he was not so very different from his brother after all? For how could anyone of feeling not know—what he had done?

Only Allegra did not know either.

It was as if she had woken this morning in a different world, as someone else, but someone who remembered her old world, her old self and wanted to go back. So close, only yesterday, and yet so far away, she could never return.

He had done all that and all he could do now was turn away from her as if the only thing of interest in the whole of the universe was the bizarrely undignified antics of a duck who appeared to be in the throes of making unexpected advances to a swan of quite the wrong gender, right in the middle of the spring-swollen river.

Allegra watched him as he gazed down at the swan's heroic defence of its virtue and the duck's consequent life-threatening embarrassment, watched the harsh, almost hostile set to his powerful face, knowing he was shutting her out. Not for the first time. And not for the first time she did not know why.

She knew only one way to deal with it.

'Come, Sorcha, I do not know about Mr Fleetwood but I declare I am about to expire if I do not have my luncheon!'

It was with no little satisfaction that, as she turned

coldly away, she saw Mr Fleetwood swing round to her, and as she walked — it felt stiffly, even clumsily, as if suspended in a dream — towards the corner of the Grand Parade to turn right towards Pulteney Bridge and Laura Place beyond she felt his eyes follow her, felt them as physical contact, as if they — he — had the power to reach out even across the growing distance and hold her back. Even as she felt his gaze searing to the very core of her spine Allegra knew that she was shaking with cold as if she had a coming fever.

He did not hurry to catch her up of course, so it was Allegra who saw it first. Saw her. She *knew* she saw her!

Yet even as she called out, 'Aunt Lydia! Aunt *Lydia*!' without a thought for the twitters and gasps of middle-aged outrage all about at such grossly unseemly behaviour, even as she turned and cried out, 'Oh, Luc! Hurry! Quickly, it is Aunt Lydia!' the vision was gone.

It was almost, for a moment, as if she had never been there. But she was. Far away at the very end of Pulteney Street, just a butterfly-flash of Lydia's favourite malachite walking cloak, hovering near the entrance to Sydney Gardens, flitting towards a dark, unmarked carriage. Aunt Lydia who never did anything discreetly, who had never been known to hurry in her life. . .

'*Where*?'

Allegra came round to the fact that Mr Fleetwood was beside her, and suddenly she knew nothing at all in the whole world but the tension pulsing through him, feeling it, hearing nothing but his harsh, quickened breath as he measured the distance with his eyes and judged that he had the speed to cover it in time, even though the carriage door was already closing. . .

He almost did. Allegra watched with an awe that was truly breathless, clutching without thought at her maid's sleeve as both she and Sorcha forgot themselves completely and urged him on.

'Oh, *run*, Luc! I know it is she!'

'That it was, my lady, as sure as these are my eyes in my own head! Oh, *look* — '

'He's going to do it, see!'

'If I hadn't seen I'd never have believed. . .no man ever ran so. . .it is impossible!' Sorcha was almost jumping on the spot in her excitement.

But Allegra believed. Luc Fleetwood ran as if there were no obstacle between him and his target, let alone Bath's languid cohorts of elderly visitors making their leisurely way along his route, all of them impeded every step of the way by crossing sweepers, itinerant knife-grinders and the quite demented traffic that nobody in authority seemed to have the least inclination to do anything about until someone inevitably was killed.

Luc cut through it all as if he were alone in the world, and all the time he ran Allegra gazed after him, mesmerised. It was as if her whole body was aching to follow him, yet knowing no one on this earth could ever catch him. Effortless, it was as if he had been born to run like the hero of Marathon. He never faltered and he only failed because, just as he made to sprint the last few yards across one of the busiest junctions in England, a stately barouche of hazardous antiquity, and dragged by a team of bays even more decayed, stumbled its way round the corner into Pulteney Street pursued first by a flurry of ferocious barking, then bodily by the plainly rabid dogs themselves, leaping and hurling abuse and all too painfully familiar to Allegra who watched numb with horror as the whole lethal entourage missed Luc Fleetwood by the barest inches. By the time it had lumbered out of the way, Luc quite unmistakably cursing the driver to perdition and beyond, the mysterious carriage and Aunt Lydia were gone.

Gone!

Allegra swayed in a shock of disbelief and rage. Luc had made it, run like a god and all for nothing! Aunt Lydia had escaped him. And she knew the word to be the right one. Because now she was sure that her aunt must have heard her call her name.

Allegra had no illusions at all about the noise she could make when she had to. Unladylike it might be but when one owned a younger brother of the stamp of Algie one needed the lungs of a fleet commander and the uninhibited audacity to use them. Algie could hear her coming across a good ten acres when he had to. Aunt Lydia had been no more than three hundred yards away.

It had to have been Lydia.

If Sorcha had not at that moment said the same, emphatically, Allegra would have begun to doubt herself. Doubted that she would know that cloak anywhere; that she had judged the distance correctly and that the lady had come from Lydia's house.

'I. . .I don't understand! She *must* have heard you!' The little Irish maid was staring in equal disbelief.

'They'll be using you to sound the Last Trump! She *must*. . .but she would never. . .'

'Never ignore me?'

No. Or so Allegra had always believed. Now she did not know what to think. Except that she must reach Mr Fleetwood and she was quite ready to run to do it.

It was Sorcha who held her back.

'No need, my lady; look you there, that was our dogs, no mistaking them when there is a riot on. . . Herr Kraftstein has just caught Brandy, see. And just where the carriage was. He cannot fail to have seen my lady Limington!'

'No, you are right—oh! Oh, but Sorcha, he does not know her! He has never met her! Come, oh, do come *on*, Sorcha, and *quickly*!'

Sorcha, however, was made of sterner stuff than most who ever encountered Allegra's headlong personality.

'Not an I end up letting you disgrace yourself again for at least the fifth time today and I'm any kind of witness to anything, my lady! Not that you haven't been ripping about the place like some painted heathen quite enough, I suppose, and calling out——'

'You shouted too!' Allegra was not going to stand for injustice however much she knew her maid to be in the right of it. One glance at the halted promenaders all about her told her that it would be a very long time indeed before she could hold up her head in this town with any degree of equanimity.

Consequently she held it even higher than usual, all but tossing it—in fact it was a very real struggle not to dip an impertinent curtsy to her avid audience—and

delivering a deliciously quelling stare at a young gentleman who had so far forgot himself as to grin in her
direction with helpless admiration as she marched
away. But, she was almost sorry for that glare when
she saw the one the boy was consequently awarded by
his mama.

It was acutest agony to walk, even at such a pace as
it was a matter of the most exquisitely debated seman-
tics as to whether or not it could be called a canter,
and it seemed forever before they at last reached Mr
Fleetwood and the tutor at the entrance to Sydney
Gardens.

And walked straight into what appeared to be a war.
Not of words: Mr Fleetwood would no more stand for
the tutor forgetting his place than Herr Kraftstein
would dream of so far offending his personal dignity as
to argue with his superior. Even so, Allegra felt she
could have moulded the air between them in her
fingers, and then only with difficulty, so thick was it
with hostility and, on Luc's part, burning, frustrated,
uninhibited rage.

'You *have* to have seen her!'

Plainly he had trod this ground several times already
but the tutor was adamant.

'I saw a carriage, sir, as I have told you, but I did
not see the lady. Besides,' he added with what was
almost asperity, for all its Viennese suavity, 'I should
not know the particular lady if I were to see her.'

'But *we* saw her!' Allegra had caught her breath by
now.

And so had the maid. 'Aye, 'twas her ladyship, no
doubting, sir, no doubting at all!'

Still the tutor repeated, 'I saw no lady!'

It was impossible. Allegra cast her eyes about. The street was not empty, but nor was it so busy that he could have missed Aunt Lydia, let alone dressed in such a vividly obtrusive green, climb into a carriage not ten yards from where Mr Fleetwood had caught up with him.

Unless. . .

'That *damned* barouche!' Luc exploded completely now. 'Those infernal dogs! By God, Allegra, but do you own not even *one* animal that can comport itself sensibly in public places? Must you adopt only the very lowest forms of life?'

'*Ja, ja, das*! *Das*! That was it!' Herr Kraftstein traitorously sold the dogs to Luc's damnation in return for peace. 'It was the dogs, of course! There was a spaniel in the barouche, a most unpleasing creature.' Here the tutor looked sternly at their own unrepentant canines and Allegra understood what had happened. Planted firmly—and for their own safety—on Herr Kraftstein's perfectly polished boots were an exhausted Brandy and Schnapps proudly lapping up all this unexpected attention. 'It would have taken an army to capture them any more quickly, my lady. . .' Here he gave his hardest stare—the one that frightened even Algie—at the deerhound who was after all not his own dog and therefore entirely to blame. The little mongrel he picked up under his arm the better they might hear themselves think once it ceased its yapping. 'I was so concerned they might cause a serious accident. . .'

Allegra had always liked Herr Kraftstein, indeed had never met one person who was not taken with his charm and grace and air of impeccable breeding. She hurried at once to reassure him.

'Of course, that will be it—it was not your fault you saw nothing!'

'Well, I still can't see how he can have missed seeing Lady Limington!' Plainly Luc Fleetwood had no such tender feeling for the tutor.

Allegra, startled at the harshness of his tone, looked at him then, and excused him even such shocking rudeness. If the only reason he was out of breath was healthy fury, he had still just run like a Derby winner and it showed in the softened dampness of his hair where it clung to his sun-gilt brow.

Allegra was puzzled as she tried to speak and nothing came out. Her throat seemed suddenly as dry and raw as smoke. She tried again, and managed a husky whisper. 'You did your best, sir!'

His reply astonished her. Especially since he was not even looking at her but right at the carefully disinterested Herr Kraftstein with eyes that would have burned the poise of any lesser man to a crisp.

'So it's *sir* again, now, is it, my lady, when it was "Luc" bellowed halfway across Bath for all the world and his wife to hear it not five minutes past?'

Never had she heard him half so savage. Nor seen him look it. His face was tight with rage and she could not believe she understood even the half of it.

'But I. . .'

'Might as well stay with using Luc now you have forgot yourself so completely——'

'I——'

'*Well*, Allegra?'

Allegra felt her flush of pleasure bewilderingly combining with a fury so elemental that it felt as if it would choke her. But she just managed, 'Yes. . .very well. If you wish——'

'*Luc*!'

'Luc.'

And before she knew what was happening to her she had been taken firmly, almost proprietorially, by the arm, and—was he ever going to stop hauling her about the city as if she were some parcel of potatoes?—all but frog-marched back the way that they had come. He was walking but Allegra was panting to keep up with him. However, it did not stop her delivering herself of the very heartfelt opinion, 'If I have ever seen rudeness the equal of it! Poor Herr Kraftstein——'

'The man's a fool!' Or so, at least, Allegra interpreted the snarl that was all she got in reply.

'It was not his fault——'

'He says not.' Implacable. More than that. Sardonic.

'Oh, really! *No*!' Allegra stopped, boiling over with rage and her reputation so long since in shreds that another public scene was of little consequence. In fact she was going to enjoy it! 'You really are the most intolerable man I ever met in my life, and you're behaving. . .you're behaving. . .'

'*Well*?'

'Well, just like *Algie*, that's what! Like a spoilt schoolboy! And I will not be dragged about the pavements by you as if—*ouch*! Where are we going——?'

She could have forgiven him anything even then but what he did next.

With absolutely no warning whatsoever Luc

Fleetwood burst into the most electrifying laughter and without thought for anyone else in the world pulled her ruthlessly towards him till she was balanced helplessly on her toes, and kissed the tip of her by now scarlet nose. And before Allegra could be sure she had not just died from the shock of it he said, with all his old tormenting mockery, 'I promised Tiffy I would not make you late for luncheon.'

Allegra was left with just one thought. . . Well, that is just about what one would expect of a man who calls his grandmama Tiffy! I just do not understand why I have fallen in love.

So, absurdly, she demanded, 'And why do you call Lady Hawkhurst Tiffy? I think it is——'

'Her name!'

Love!

The thought was so outlandish that Allegra was halfway through luncheon before she really recognised she had thought it. Algie and Lady Hawkhurst were engaged in a mild dispute about the nesting habits of bats in belfries and the Honourable Mr Fleetwood was minding his unusually innocent business investigating the remains of a slice of cold chicken as if he already knew one always had to be on one's guard with Algie on the premises. He found the undesirable object he was looking for and passed the marble calmly back to its grateful owner.

'Yours, I believe.'

And Allegra knew it was all true. Just the faintest laugh in that uniquely unsettling voice and she was quite helpless with love for him. Just one surreptitious glance at the way his beautiful, strong fingers reached for his glass of wine; and an even more furtive glance at the way—as he turned towards his grandmother to point out that bats could hardly be expected to want to reside in Algie's bedchamber however fond that youth had become of the one he had found hanging up in the rafters that morning—every muscle of that powerful athlete's body tautened so distractingly beneath the dark blue superfine of a coat that reflected its colour so dramatically in his eyes.

He had washed and changed his clothes since his exertions of the morning and Allegra was left with the delightful task of trying to decide if he looked his best like this, immaculate without the least effort, or how she had seen him not an hour ago, racing with all the God-given grace of a thoroughbred, when she could see as she came closer to him where his collar caught against his burnished skin as he barely broke sweat. . .

Allegra stared into her plate, her cheeks blushing so hotly that she all but reheated the contents; she simply could not make herself eat. There did not seem room for food. Not with a heart flooded to twice its size with excitement. Not with the spiralling rapture flooding through her veins, her nerves, catching at her breath so urgently that she simply could not have joined the conversation had she wanted to.

Allegra looked once more at Mr Fleetwood while he was safely occupied with the future of Algie's bat.

She did not trust him. He shouted at her, he patronised her. He kissed her on the nose in the middle of Pulteney Street. She was in absolutely no doubt at all that she hated every inch of that arrogantly perfect body. And even less doubt that she wanted it. Him.

Allegra was sure love was not meant to be like this. Nobody else's seemed to be. Her friends giggled and blushed, to be sure, but all they ever talked about was the sum of their beloved's fortune and their own capacity for spending it. They talked about how comfortably placed they would be, of how good it would be to have a home of their own with no Mama breathing down their necks, of how amenable their fiancés seemed, how personable. Her friends, though far from ecstatic, really seemed to *like* the gentlemen they had chosen to love.

Allegra was sure she didn't. Like Mr Fleetwood, that was. She liked a great many things about him. He made her laugh as no one ever had before. He had not one manner fit for presenting to decent Society, let alone a whole set of manners like everyone else. And he did not care in the slightest! He seemed, too, to have the measure of young Algie already, if Algie's clatter of incoherent chatter and eyes of glittering admiration were anything to go by. The odious man plainly adored his grandmother. . .who was quite the most interesting person Allegra had ever come across. Pythagoras patently thought he was wonderful, and Pythagoras was most particular. . .

But he had hurt her. There was contempt in him, and anger, and once too often he had levelled both at her. He made no secret of the fact that he despised Aunt Lydia. Worse, he had made Allegra understand at last that Lydia could be despised. He had insulted Allegra herself, ordered her about, ignored her, told her off to do as *he* pleased and not a word for what *she* wanted. He treated her like a child. He saw her as a child.

It was never meant to happen to her. Not to the Allegra Ashley she had been planning to be. The Allegra who had already set London ablaze and was destined to break the hearts of princes before finally she was married, to wails of loud despair and the attendant seclusion in sundry monasteries of all her thwarted suitors.

Suddenly all that was a very long way away. And this really had happened—to her. When it couldn't, just *couldn't*!

Allegra faced it as the bitterness rose into her throat in a stinging tide of pain. I have fallen in love; this is what love is like. But he will never love me.

Fighting back what felt dangerously like tears, Allegra looked at him again. I must face it. Just as he said. . .people like us can be hurt but it will not last. It *will* be over.

He saw the tears caught against her lashes and misunderstood. Without a thought for their company Luc reached out a hand across the table and covered her own where it lay helpless against the gloss of Sheraton mahogany.

'Don't fret, Allegra. Please, you mustn't be unhappy. We shall sort this out, I promise you. We shall find Lydia safe and sound, I swear it!'

And Allegra knew. It would never be over. He had reached to her out of kindness, because he was a kind man; right to the very core of him he was kind and generous. She knew it even though he had so badly hurt her with a coldness she would never understand. She had fallen in love with him and she could only fall deeper. Time had nothing to do with it now. Certainly it would never heal her.

She just managed to control herself as she rose unsteadily to her feet and excused herself. Let them think me stupid, weak and silly, frightened for my aunt and not grown-up enough to cope with it! she thought. Let them think me ill! Let him think anything but the truth!

She could never let him know it. Because of that other truth. That he would never want to know it; because he would never want her.

Allegra only just reached her bedchamber before the tears came. Curling up on her bed, a worried deerhound snuffling comfortingly into her neck, she thought, That mustn't be true. I mustn't let it be true. He *has* to care!

But Luc was not like any man she had ever met before and she did not know how to make him.

What she did know, an hour's fruitless misery later, was that she was going to try. After all, she *had* nothing, so she had nothing to lose.

So resolved, Allegra poured herself some water from the jug on the wash-stand and repaired herself as best she might for facing the rest of the afternoon.

She was not given long. She was just putting the last touches to her sadly dog-disordered hair when the door cracked back on its hinges and Algie burst in.

'Come *on*, Allegra. . .hurry *up*!'

'I. . .what — ?' Algie already had her so violently by the sleeve, he was but one tug away from separating it from her person.

'Stop making such a fuss,' cut in Algie, pre-empting the one he could envisage coming if he did not leave go her sleeve in the next few seconds. 'We're going hunting!'

'Hunting? Oh, Algie, not more of your revolting bats!'

'Of course not; besides, they are not revolting, they are very pretty if you look at them closely; I've got one on my bedpost——'

'Algie!'

'Well, I was telling you, wasn't I? It was you would insist on mentioning bats! Luc says we have to look for every last clue as to what might have become of Aunt Lydia——like letters, you know, inviting her some-where, that she forgot all about, or forgot us. . .just like she *does* forget things. . .'

'Luc?'

If only he had not laughed then at the sound of his name uttered in such puzzlement as Algie dragged her bodily down the stairs towards him.

'Didn't Algie tell you? I want all hands on deck.'

They might have all been living together for years, it seemed so natural. Allegra's heart turned over and she smiled at him.

For the second time he quite deliberately looked away.

# CHAPTER SIX

It was Algie who ultimately wrested the all-important key to Aunt Lydia's domain from the more than reluctant Herr Kraftstein, whose wise inclination, born of long, wearying experience, to disbelieve every last word his Most Honourable young lordship uttered was on this occasion rooted in the quite breathtaking implausibility of the tale Algie had concocted for him.

'I told him that I had left behind my Latin grammar and a book of Greek verse that I most *particularly* wanted.' Algie waved the key triumphantly at his sister and Mr Fleetwood as they descended the steps of the Hawkhurst residence into the early afternoon tranquillity of Laura Place. It was the fact that Allegra did not laugh at the outrageousness of his monstrous story that alerted Algie to her new predicament. Mr Fleetwood, Allegra would have seen had she been willing to look at him even once, which she was not, appeared to have noticed nothing wrong in her at all.

At least, he *behaved* as if he had seen nothing, mused Algie, deeply puzzled. Grown-ups were the most peculiar animals, Allegra with her nose in the air *because* she liked Luc and didn't want him to know it, Luc pretending he had not seen for a reason undoubtedly far too adult and thus idiotic for Algie to have any patience with it at all . . .

All in all Algie thought he preferred the company of bats.

It was strange to enter the Limington house to the cold mustiness of a place seeming months deserted and not just a few short days; Allegra shuddered, unaware that Mr Fleetwood was now watching her intently through the masking shadows of the hallway, all expression fiercely reined in, as if it was a look he could not prevent yet he was determined she should never feel it.

She looked altered — he had seen it at once as she descended the stairs to come out — changed even from the incipient tears of luncheon; she walked as if she would avoid all contact with even the air around her, bruised, frightened that something was waiting in the darkness of her mind to hurt her, eyes shuttered, lashes lowered against cheeks one moment pallid as ice, the next flushed as if in the throes of a fever.

Even if he had not seen it he would have sensed it, because he had been watching her almost every moment they had been together since the very first second they met; watching against his will, fighting, failing. . .

Even if he had not been watching he would have known the change in her, as if he too began to feel the inner chill that caused her to huddle so closely into her bright Venetian shawl as if she did not know the cold was inside her, hard and fast as granite, and could not be warmed away.

Just as he knew he must not look at her a second longer, because he would want to help her — because he would have to hold her and soothe that fear away

. . .because that was the last thing he ever wanted to
happen — Allegra turned and saw his eyes, unveiled,
raking her with unleashed emotions she could never
hope to read. She felt the heat of them as if she had
just passed through the sun. It felt to her in her
vulnerability that he was angry; what else could burn
such torment into his eyes? She turned away.

He was angry. But not for the reason she thought.
Now it was he who turned away, raging at something
he had never expected in his life to feel. He had meant
to shut her out; he *had* to; instead, just as he should
want her to do, it had been Allegra who had closed
herself to him and he was the one left totally disorien-
tated. His anger at it was palpable. Even Algie felt it
and was glad to flee the unsettling scene the moment
he was given his orders. They were curt, as if Mr
Fleetwood's mind were a million miles away.

'Algie, we are to search this house from top to
bottom. You go up to the servants' quarters and work
your way down to meet us in the morning-room. I want
to know anything that seems unusual to you, anything
out of place; I want you to look particularly for letters
to your aunt, or for notes from your aunt to her
servants, anything that might explain why she has gone
away and to where. Bring anything you find with you
and do it as quickly as you can. I think we have no
more than fifteen, perhaps twenty minutes before your
tutor pursues us to know the reason we are keeping
you so long from your studies.'

Suddenly Algie began to realise this was not quite an
adventure; adventures should not feel quite so. . .well,
*important*. But he did not know why he felt this. There

was a quaver in his usually ebullient horn of a voice when he asked, 'But could not Herr Kraftstein have helped, sir? I mean, surely the more people we have to search——'

'No!' It was so abrupt a refusal, it brought Allegra out of her stupor of personal unhappiness into a confusion even less reassuring. Because when Luc Fleetwood said, 'No, Algie, I shall explain it better to you later but this *must* be kept a family affair, your family and mine,' she did not quite believe him.

And now she was alone with him! Only ten minutes ago she had promised herself that she would make him notice her, make him see that she was no longer just the silly schoolgirl he so plainly thought her. He *must* see it! Now she was here with him, the house so quiet, she could hear his calm, steady breathing, feel it murmuring through her blood as if each long, comforting breath were her own, and she was helpless. He would not even look at her; when he did, just the sight of her seemed to all but enrage him. And she could not think why, or begin to guess at what she had done. It was as if—sometimes—he were another person and not the Luc Fleetwood who had called her brave, and silly, as he fed her soup in a firelit kitchen. . .only yesterday!

And yet his voice when he spoke was gentle enough, brisk, cool but—she felt it now—so painfully impersonal. It was only now he had withdrawn from her so completely that she realised what a friend she might have had. Instantly, instinctively they had liked each other, she was certain of it. . .

So what was happening now?

'Come, Allegra, I was not in jest that we must hurry. And not just for the reason I have given Algie.' He was making his purposeful way for the ever-locked door of her late uncle's study. And he had the key!

Allegra's eyes opened in near awe when she saw this — she had never seen him take it! *Felt* him take it. From the pocket of her cloak where she had slipped it automatically after she had opened the door last night to discover Luc breaking into the desk.

He saw her open her mouth and find herself quite unable to say a word and to Allegra it was as if a miracle happened; briefly, but unmistakably, she saw the ironic quirk of his uniquely fascinating smile. Then he murmured, 'Well, you said it yourself that I was a villain born, my lady!'

And she found that somehow, despite the fact that she was shaking like a fool just to have him be kind to her again, she was laughing too.

'But even I did not think. . .!' But her words were lost in a sudden, aching flush as she realised how close he must have come to her to take the key; as she realised she had not noticed because it had not been the only time he had been too near her. Realised that all through that strange encounter in the kitchen she had kept close to him, and he to her, as if drawn quite naturally to the warmth of each other's body. Instead she swallowed hard and finished, 'But surely we are wasting time in here, sir, when you have searched the room already?'

It was Luc's voice that was inexplicably strained now, nothing more than the huskiest breath. 'Not the desk, remember, kitten — I would be a riddled corpse else, the way you could not wait to shoot me!'

And suddenly Allegra felt she did not need her shawl any more, nor her feet either; suddenly there was only air to walk on because he had called her 'kitten' again. Even though it was only said to tease her. . .

He saw the lift to her spirits reflected in her glowing eyes, and smiled again. Such a child, after all, and this was only a harmless adventure to her. He meant to keep it that way. Play it through without her ever really knowing what was happening, end it — and never see her again. He was almost sure now that it must come to that.

Forcing a smile to lips that suddenly felt as cold as ice, he added, 'Hurry up, Allegra, or Algie will discover everything before us and then we shall never hear the end of it!'

He was wrong. Someone had got here first, but it was not Algie so innocently turning out every last drawer in the attics. It was whoever had opened the desk since last they had entered this room. Someone, moreover, who had not needed a dagger to open it with. . .

Someone who had had the key.

'Oh, dear God, Luc!' Allegra started forward, then she sank helplessly on to a sofa, shaking her head in bewilderment as she tried to keep pace with yet another impossible twist of events.

They both said it at once.

'Lydia!'

Luc Fleetwood searched the desk anyway, as if it were something he did every day, in his sleep if necessary when some dangerous mission called. And in the back of Allegra's brain something stirred, the beginning of an answer to one question at least. She was going to make him answer it.

Carefully taking on to her lap an elaborate Florentine writing box and going minutely through the contents, she asked, as if only vaguely interested in any possible reply although it took all her strength to keep her voice steady, 'Mr Fleetwood——'

'Luc!' He did not even raise his eyes from his perusal of a long and frantic missive from one of Lydia's discarded conquests.

'Luc, it is something your grandmother said. . .about what you do. About your taking up a new appointment . . .and I was wondering, you know. . .well, so many young men are still with the army. . .?'

He had been waiting for it, and since long before Tiffy's idiotic mistake. Allegra was far too quick-witted not to have reached this point eventually. He knew exactly how to deflect her. After all, lying through his immaculate white teeth was the better part of his qualification for his present occupation. . .

So he sat down in the dust of the holland-draped sofa beside her and said very carefully, with the air of one about to draw her into his confidence, 'How much do you know about this war, Allegra—this war that has so abruptly turned to peace?'

With luck she would be like every other débutante it had ever been his ill fortune to encounter and the sum total of her knowledge would be which handsome young military marquess looked better than which dashing duke in his best dress regimentals. But he knew even as he thought it that Allegra was not like them. She never could be. Her father had been in the thick of this titanic struggle with Bonaparte from the beginning to its all too raw and recent end; she would know every last move of the armies down to the smallest detail.

She did. 'I know that Paris was taken three weeks since on the last day of March, but that Wellington was not warned in time that the Emperor was defeated and so made his move against Soult at Toulouse, that seven thousand died needlessly——'

She broke off then; it had been four days since she had learned that her father was not among them, in a message sent express with Wellington's couriers to England. It was only two days since she had read Papa's safety confirmed in the London newspapers. She gave nothing of her feelings away in her expression now because she had for years held every frightening one of them at bay, afraid that if she let them touch her even for a moment they would overwhelm her; she had simply waited, waited for peace, until the moment when she truly believed that peace would last, then she would think, then she would feel. Then she could let the years of fear flood in and engulf her until they were finally washed away. Allegra had not cried for her father once throughout the past fifteen years. She was waiting for the moment he finally came home.

Luc guessed it, and it defeated him. Even as he fought to stop himself he reached for her hand.

'Your father is more than safe, Allegra. . .indeed he is in terrifying good form if his dispatches to the Foreign Office are anything to judge by! What he has omitted to call those bungling idiots are words yet to be invented, and what he *has* said I can't repeat to you; I would not even teach them to your parrot!'

And Allegra, her secret struggle with years of terror seen so simply for what it was, clung to his fingers as if he were all that was saving her from drowning, grateful not just that he had understood but that he had had the unique grace to make a jest of it.

She did not even notice that Luc had all but answered all her questions about himself. But he did; so he explained, fingers lacing through hers without even really noticing any longer, it seemed so natural, 'As you know your father is perhaps the man closest to Wellington, they have fought side by side for so long now; he is the only man I know to whom Wellington will pay even the smallest heed, for you must know Old Nosey has the Devil's own temper and the arrogance to make even Boney seem diffident, and only your papa has anything like the obstinacy it needs to challenge him. Without Wellington we could never have won our part in this war — and without your papa to curb him we would most certainly have lost. You must know what friends they are become, for all they are so very different?'

'Yes.' Arthur Wellesley, so ambitious, with so much to prove, so single-minded; Papa so restful, so far-sighted, so stubborn, so wise. All of them great — dangerous — qualities in a soldier, and both were dangerous men.

Luc was saying so, and with a passion that saw Allegra looking at him as she had never felt she would again, seeing yet another Luc when she had thought she had seen all that there was. Seeing even more that she could respect and admire.

'It has made them both so powerful now because they have the people behind them. Not because they are this war's greatest heroes — we haven't won alone, we needed our allies — it was they who took Paris after all. No, the people, and most important of all the army, are behind your father and Wellington in anything they do now because they *ended* the war. God knows, but it has bled this country close to death! We could not have stood another summer of it. Ending it has made Wellington our greatest force at the peace negotiations in Paris.'

Allegra knew more than Luc could ever have expected. 'And yet they have begun without him! The Treaty of Chaumont was signed the day the Allies took the city! Luc, what are you trying to say?'

'I am saying that there is a much more dangerous battle beginning now, for much greater stakes than the world has ever seen, and someone is trying to keep Wellington and your father from bringing their influence to bear in it. Someone is working to weaken their position. . .'

'The Allies. . .the Prussians? The Prince of Orange is too inexperienced. No ——'

'No! That is exactly how we — I — worked it out!' Here Luc turned to her and took her other hand between his, urgent to make her see, because he knew now that as far as he could he would tell her the whole truth, as far as it was safe for her to hear. 'Allegra, listen to me, because I think this could well be my last chance to tell you and, because your father is so closely involved, I know that I may trust you with it.'

She snatched her hands away, stinging with hurt. 'You could trust me anyway!'

God, but what a fool he was! The pain lashing from her eyes ripped through him like an exploding shell, leaving him sick with rage at himself — most of all for the weakness that now made him reach out and take her shoulders, one hand, against all sense and will, stroking the tumbling curls away from her trembling throat.

'Dear God, child, do you think I don't know that I can?' Then, because he could feel all control slipping through fingers now intent only on the silk-softness of her hair as he ran it so sensuously between them, he went on, each word forced out so carefully in the only hope he had to stop what he swore must never happen. 'Listen to me, Allegra, and fight me later! Even in public if you will, for all you will care, having all but beaten me to a pulp in the street on at least two occasions I could care to mention!' Thank God for it that she laughed! Though nothing altered that dazed, dangerous drugging of her darkening eyes. 'Allegra, it is not the Allies would thwart Wellington and our English ambitions, although God knows it might as well be with the whole of Europe to be carved between us; and it will be; can you see any of us setting one single nation free? For certain the Austrians will want the greater say in Europe's future, while the power of the Prussians grows dangerous, and to take what they want they must weaken our position at the bargaining table; I know all that and yet I'm still certain it isn't

they who mean Wellington and your father harm. It is
the French for certain.'

'The French! But it is all ended; they are finished!'

His tone then was unreadable. 'The Emperor will
never be finished until he is dead, Allegra, believe me.
In exile people will forget all the havoc he has wreaked
and have only their memories of his undoubted great-
ness to salvage the tatters of their pride; he will be a
martyr, a messiah, he will be a thousand times more
dangerous than he has ever been because he will
believe it of himself! And so does someone else! I
know enough of the plot already—it *is* the French.
There are so many who stand to lose all they gained by
revolution if the Bourbon King returns. It is the
French—and someone here.'

'*Here*! In league with the Bonapartists? Impossible!
To do what, and *how*? I do not understand this!'

'No. And that is why I'm here. That is what it is my
job to discover.'

'Here? *Bath*? But. . .no, you cannot mean. . .! Aunt
*Lydia*?' Allegra could not take it in, because none of
this was real, of course. Nothing was real anyway while
he held her like this, touched her so gently that one
would have thought she were the very kitten he called
her. She would have moved away, shaking her head in
disbelief if but one muscle of her body were left in her
control. Stiff, mute, dizzy, disintegrating beneath those
hypnotising fingers, she could only gaze her question
at him, longing for him not to have meant what he
seemed to be saying.

But he did.

'Allegra, try to understand. I have been investigating

this plot from the very first moment Wellington was warned of some danger by his brother Richard. You may not know much about Richard; few people are really certain what he does, only that his influence reaches into every office in the government. And that is the thing. Let me explain if I can. Until six months ago I was on Wellington's staff at St Jean de Luz in France, not just a soldier any more, not exactly a civilian. A trusted courier, if you like. . .'

Allegra knew what he meant now. He meant a spy.

'I worked only between Wellington and his brothers here in England, the only people he believed he could trust. . .then. Now — well, now rumours are circulating here of a rivalry building between the brothers. Richard wants to be our man at the Paris peace talks, and he has support here from those who think Wellington too powerful already. Yet I would swear Richard loyal to his brother; so would Wellington; he is certain there is a deliberate move to divide them. So he sent me home with a spurious injury. I was manoeuvred on to the staff of Lord FitzCarlin, another government manipulator ranking just below Foreign Minister Castlereagh himself, and well-known to have ambitions that require the removal of both Richard Wellesley and his war-hero of a brother. FitzCarlin must move against them soon for Wellington is to be rewarded for his service and it can be nothing less than a dukedom; the country would stand for nothing less. FitzCarlin must move now.'

He had known Allegra would see the connection at once. FitzCarlin. Until supplanted by Luc's own brother, Gerald, Lord FitzCarlin had been the most favoured of Aunt Lydia's lovers. Certainly the closest of her cronies.

'Oh, dear lord!' It none of it made any sense, except that she could see how Luc had been led to Lydia.

'Lydia——' dear God, but he almost hated the woman in that moment for putting such a child through this '——was also once close to——'

Allegra was so used to it, she finished the sentence for him. 'Arthur, Viscount Wellington. She met him through Papa many years ago. But——'

'How can I connect FitzCarlin to the French? I can't. But I have got to! Because if I cannot discredit him. . . think, Allegra; with Castlereagh tied up for months ahead by the coming peace talks FitzCarlin is all but master at the Foreign Office.'

'So you must work for him to work against him?'

'I must! Because only your father and Wellington can add the strength of the people to balance our cause at Paris. Castlereagh needs them.'

'And Richard Wellesley was the one who warned his brother that FitzCarlin might be a traitor?'

It sounded so absurd to her ears! Like something that might happen in a book, not here. Not to her. Not really.

'Yes—because he wants as prime a place at Paris as his brother; Richard wants the embassy. If he can unmask FitzCarlin and protect his brother, Castlereagh might just be moved to give it to him.'

Allegra still felt as if she had stepped off the world and was spinning helplessly in space. Never had the politics of peace seemed so confusing, when she had thought in her youth that they must be so simple.

'But the Bonapartists, Luc? How can you connect FitzCarlin to them? Surely you cannot *invent*. . .?'

His hands fell from her shoulders so abruptly then that she knew she had perhaps committed the worst offence she ever could against him. She had questioned his honour, his integrity, and he would never forgive her for it. Yet all she could think was, I shall die if he does not hold me again; I shall waste away in the cold!

His eyes were slabs of ice. He plainly had such contempt for her that he disdained even to address her question. 'FitzCarlin and Wellington have both been Lydia's lovers, and FitzCarlin is an overweening fool. A careless fool — so convinced of his own omnipotence, he thinks himself invulnerable. Quite careless enough to trust a woman with the secrets of his ambition. He would even try to impress her with them! And Lydia — God knows, the whole world could see he would do anything to keep her! If I could find just one letter, the smallest indiscretion ——'

But Allegra's brain, shocked back to life by the contempt she had seen in his eyes, was as clear as glass now and one step ahead.

'And Aunt Lydia is all but French; that is what you are trying not to say!' Suddenly Allegra saw it all. Saw that he thought he had found his connection to France. Saw that he meant Lydia might be his traitor!

She was on her feet in a rage so frozen she could barely feel it was rage, soothing, numbing; never would she forgive him for this. Because her quick mind had taken another leap towards the answer to this terrifying puzzle. She knew what it was he was really afraid of. . .

'You seem to have omitted one thing, sir.' Was it

even her voice? It sounded so distant, so steady in its ice-hard anger, she could barely believe someone as young as she had uttered it. But then she did not feel young any more. 'You seem to have forgotten that FitzCarlin is ousted from my aunt's affections by your brother. And your brother too is French!'

He caught her before she had moved even so much as a yard towards the door and she knew the instant his arms came about her in a grip of steel that she could not fight him; that he was infinitely dangerous; and what she had just said was the most dangerous thing of all. Because he loved his brother; she had always seen it. He was loyal, maybe to family alone. Yes, she was sure of that. His brother would come before everything for him. And Luc too was all but French!

It was impossible even to breathe, she was held so violently against him, his grip hardening as if he meant to force the life from her. She had never felt such anger before. Nor endured such pain. Not physical. A heart that was crumbling into nothing left no place for the feeling of physical hurt.

It was as if the whole world were suddenly disintegrating beneath her feet, taking her with it, and time too; she never was to know how long he held her like that, silent but for the ragged fury of his breathing.

Luc the soldier. The spy. She had seen everything all along really; she knew it. From the very first moment she had found him breaking into the desk. From the moment she had seen him run after Lydia as if he would pass through a battlefield unscathed, and unseen. As if he so often had. Luc the 'courier'? Luc the Foreign Office man.

Luc the traitor?

'No!' She could not bear it. Not even the thought; if she could tear it from her mind she would, with her bare hands. It could not be. He could not be lying to her! But then, he could not really believe her aunt a traitor. . . 'No!'

'No! Exactly, madam! My brother is no traitor!' She felt his breath as it scorched against her cheek in an eruption of fury she could never have anticipated even in him. 'My brother who fought in the Peninsula beside me although he was never fit for it. My brother who all but coughed his lungs out into the black Spanish snows! My brother who took a blow to his head at Coruña so wicked he still remembers nothing of it; my brother who for a whole two *years* could not even remember *me*! Who has only just now come to speak again like other people, who, though it went against his whole spoilt, self-centred nature, would not let me go to Spain alone. He came to *protect* me, the little brother who has always been so much stronger than he will ever be! My God, but if you ever speak of him like that again——'

And in her horror—her shame, though she could not have known about any of this; how could she?—Allegra flashed back, '*You* accuse *my* aunt, *my* family!'

'It is your family I am trying to save, you little fool!'

'Save us? When you would drag my aunt through——'

There was no other way to silence her. Burnt out by a rage of injustice, Luc had to make her see. See what

she had said and why he would never forgive her for it.
Already he knew she was not really at fault, but it
made no difference. She would have believed treachery
of him. . . Now she had to hear it all. And there was
only one way. . .

He kissed her so hard then that Allegra had nothing
left to fight with. No warning. . .and all strength swept
away in an eruption of heat that scalded the axis of her
being away. Took the whole world with it but Luc and
what he was doing now—as she had longed for him to
do from the very first second she saw him. As she
would kill him for doing now, so violent was her hatred
for him. . .

It had to be hate. It *must* be! It was too frightening
that love could be so helpless, so absolute as this.

The whole world went black as she closed her eyes
and without ever knowing that she did so she began to
kiss him back.

'Oh—um. . .I    say. . .dashed. . .um. . .awkward,
what? Well——' cough '—I say, you fellows, haven't
found a thing!'

And, neither really conscious of why, Allegra and
Luc fell apart at the interruption—yards apart, Allegra
moving back so clumsily towards the settle that she
knocked over the writing-box she had almost finished
searching. Luc had his back pressed against the wall as
if he needed it to restrain him.

Only—from doing what? He still did not know why
he had done this; or, at least, he did not know how he
had let it happen. He who was a legend among his
fellow officers for his ruthless self-control, most of all
with women who might get in his notoriously indepen-

dent way. Luc too had stepped off the edge of the world. Where he never wanted to be.

It was Algie, glowing with childish horror at what he had just witnessed, who broke the stifling silence.

'I say, Allegra, what a funny colour of paper. . .'

'I. . .what?' At this moment Allegra did not even know what paper was. Against the throbbing ache of her lips she felt the bitter taste of blood and marvelled at it. Luc had done that! And he had not wanted to, she knew it! But he had!

'Paper.' Algie progressed hastily towards collective sanity. 'You have your foot on it.'

Allegra had just one second in which to see it, glancing down as if from some far remote height at something of no interest whatsoever except that it seemed to be important to Algie. . .

It was Luc who moved so fast then, catching her aside by the waist, his eyes blazing in triumph. She knew why. She had seen it too: a pale, almost lavender-coloured paper, not English. And writing whose words were French but whose style of hand was not. She saw the initial that stood alone because it was all that he would ever need. 'N'.

Luc was gone from the room, the letter safely out of her reach before she could even stop him. On legs that barely agreed to move Allegra followed with Algie to see Luc standing with the front door already half ajar, staring at the paper as if it had struck him. So much so that he had forgotten all about her, and about all that had passed so savagely between them. All he said was, 'This was not there when I searched before.'

'No. . .?'

'No. That writing-box was the first place I looked last night. Now why? No. There is something I have missed. . .'

And Allegra could only stare at him in horror, thinking, He has a letter from Bonaparte in his pocket. A letter found in Aunt Lydia's possession!

Impossible though it was, he had found his French connection, and her whole world would be destroyed by what he chose to do with it.

'*Why*?' He might just as well have been alone as he ran his hand through his hair in a way that stopped the breath in Allegra's throat, turning every last nerve to water.

Algie, concentrating passionately on the puzzle so that he might pretend that all the unsettling things he had just seen had never happened, and with not the least idea why the foreign-looking letter should have affected his new friend so powerfully, pitched in then, 'That's easy. It's been put there.'

Luc managed a smile, as he always did for Algie, and nodded, still preoccupied. 'I know. Now what I want to know is *who by!*'

It was as if it came from another world, so wrapped up were they all in their own tangling thoughts; the door was rapped upon with such gusto that it flew back against the wall, all but taking Luc Fleetwood with it.

Allegra would believe anything now. Even what she saw beaming at her from the doorstep, like a hopeful, irredeemably dim and clueless puppy, adorned in the tightest of sickly green coats and the most lurid salmon-pink waistcoat. Cuthbert Nettlesham!

'But. . .but I thought you were. . .you had been. . . banished from the country!'

Cuthbert doffed his ludicrously tall and overbrushed hat in the most breathless, the most pleased with himself of bows.

'Oh, but not at all; you are plainly most sadly misinformed, my Dearest Lady Allegra! *To* the country, not *out* of it, you follow, not the same thing at all! Besides——' And Cuthbert pulled himself up to his full negligible height, looking even more like a strangulated pheasant than ever. 'Besides, Wouldn't Go, don't you know! No, not the King himself could see me go Willingly from *your* Divine Presence; should—er—Kill myself First, you see!'

'And be deprived of her Divine Presence for All Eternity instead!' put in Luc Fleetwood in such a caustic tone that Allegra was left gaping at him in astonishment as Cuthbert steered his constricted person forwards and scooped up her hand the better to kiss it in his most affectedly besotted fashion.

Algie took one look at Cuthbert, one look at Luc and thought, Aha! Then, Aha, I *think*! Certainly Luc looked unreservedly furious.

But even as Algie made his enterprising deductions Luc's expression altered completely. Just the briefest smile, one that Algie would have found most unnerving had he been speared upon the end of it, then the most coolly timed of interruptions.

'Ah, hello, Nettlesham, my dear fellow. Wondered what had become of you since popping a hole through poor Freddie. . .'

Allegra was so stunned she could no longer stand

up. She slumped to the nearest stair in final amazement. Luc did not speak like that! Ever! Not *Luc*! Sounding—and she remembered at last that it was not for the first time—just exactly like Cuthbert and his dandyfied young cronies.

Cuthbert, forced by both her collapse and his own unmistakable surprise into dropping her hand and wondering awkwardly what now to do with his own, turned from her, looking—as Algie later expressed it so aptly—as if you could have prodded him off his perch with a feather.

'Oh, I say. . .that you, Fleetwood? Wondered where you'd slid off to; someone said you was ill—your foot and that, what? Come to Bath to dip toe in the remedial pond, eh?'

'Thought it might do the thing; been dashed painful, let me tell you. . .' replied Luc, doing the impossible and sounding more half-witted even than Cuthbert, and he returned the Honourable Mr Nettlesham's bow with a sardonic quirk of one all too expressive eyebrow that thankfully only Allegra could see.

Cuthbert—whose habit was to bow until his head usefully polished the parquet—thus held preoccupied, Luc looked straight at Allegra across the anguished seams of her suitor's far too close-cut coat. There was no smile in that look, nothing but the briefest, the most contemptuous twist to that wonderful mouth, but there was real warning in it, and hate him though she did Allegra knew to take it.

She had just remembered what she knew Luc to have been thinking all the time.

Cuthbert Nettlesham was Lord FitzCarlin's only nephew and his heir.

And now Cuthbert too was unexpectedly in Bath.

Allegra got to her feet as if Luc had actually spoken. Carefully adjusting both her expression and her shawl, she said brightly, although she had felt not a moment before that she would never speak again, 'Well, I am so very glad to see that you are not really in disgrace, Mr Nettlesham, because it *was* all Freddie's fault after all. . .'

Cuthbert made a lunge for her arm even before she thought to offer it, patently to put paid to her offering it to Luc instead. Allegra almost laughed then, though from where she dredged up amusement she would never know in the midst of this fast growing out-of-hand dilemma.

Luc, seeing the tell-tale signs of laughter threatening to sneak into her far too betraying eyes, glared at her sternly and she read his unspoken words again: Get us out of here! And I do not care how you do it! Just make certain that to Nettlesham it seems as natural as may be.

And suddenly Allegra could not help herself. Because Luc had hurt her, and did not want her. Because he had kissed her as if he did. . .when he never would. . .and besides she loathed him. . .

Cuthbert had never been cast such a captivating smile as now was all his. Nor heard her voice cooing so sweetly, 'Oh, but I'm so pleased to see you, Cuthbert; do say you will join us, for Algie has been tormenting us for hours that we must go to Sally Lunn's for one of their famous buns——'

'I. . .we only just ate luncheon!' Algie got no further, simply because Mr Fleetwood kicked him ruthlessly on the ankle.

Cuthbert had not even heard him. Allegra had called
him by his given name at last, just as she did Freddie
Limmersham. . . Cuthbert was orbiting the moon.

Allegra steered him from the house, leaving Luc
Fleetwood to close and lock the door behind them, still
acting a part, she could feel it, still the Luc Fleetwood
Cuthbert and his coterie knew in London. Not her
Luc. . . .

For she saw the wince of pain as he moved. Heard
his carping tone. 'Since we came for your Latin grammar, young Algernon, I take it you have now found
the book and will strive not ever to be so careless
again!'

Algie, who was brighter than he looked even to
himself, hauled a book out of one cluttered pocket,
earning a smile of real amusement from Luc. Latin it
was not — and if he had the right of the quite stunningly
licentious contents Algie was never going to lay his
hands on it again! — but it would do.

'Good fellow,' returned Luc, so insufferably that
Allegra almost choked again. How could anybody help
it? 'Now run along and enjoy yourselves while I deliver
this safely to your tutor.'

He was not coming with them!

Only Cuthbert — thinking the day every dog was
graced to have had come and this was his! — all to
herself with only the hefting bulk of Algie to protect
her from the inevitable proposal!

Even as she hated Luc, even as she wanted him out

of her sight because every second he was within it she felt herself physically shaking, so drained was she of all strength by her efforts to control the maelstrom of feelings he had unleashed inside her, he could not do this to her, he must not go!

But he had. Even as she opened her mouth to speak he was bowing punctiliously to them all and leaving. Limping.

Not once in all the time she saw him afterwards, with anyone outside the family present, was he ever to forget that he was reputed to be severely injured.

So convincing. Every change of mood and manner — how to believe any of it? How to believe anything about him or one word he said?

How could she still care?

Tossing her head to dismiss him from her thoughts, she turned the dazzled and ecstatic Cuthbert firmly in the direction of the abbey, Sally Lunn's and the pot of tea she knew was all but going to choke her. She could never concentrate.

She didn't.

Disastrously, she did not.

Cuthbert had managed somehow to catch her for one second to himself, while Algie inspected an insect jar in a shop he knew just around the corner. It was all it took.

'And you *will*, won't you, *won't* you, my *Divine* Allegra?'

'I. . .what? Oh, yes, of course, Cuthbert, just as you say. Now, will you not have another cup of tea?'

It was only Algie's agonised groan as he returned that moment with a pickled grass-snake and a shrimping net, compounded by the sharp pain of Cuthbert's frantically clasping her hand to his palpitating chest, that alerted her.

Allegra had just assented to become Mr Nettlesham's bride.

# CHAPTER SEVEN

'Luc! Oh, Luc!'

He was the only one who would know what to do and Allegra flew up the stairs and into the morning-room at Laura Place as if she had the hounds of hell behind her. She certainly had Algie, making at least as much commotion.

'I mean, *Cuthbert*!' he was yodelling for the hundredth time since they had managed to shed a joyous Mr Nettlesham somewhere in the precincts of Pulteney Bridge.

'*Luc*!'

Allegra barely knew what drove her to call out for him and no one else. She only knew that the most terrible thing in the world had happened and that she wanted him to make it go away again. She wanted him, just to be there. Only Luc. . .

She was met by a Dowager Lady Hawkhurst wide-eyed with startlement for the very first time in their acquaintance, as well she might be.

'But oh, my dear child, what is it?' It was plainly something serious, not to be joked about. 'Did you not know, but Luc has gone to London?'

Gone?

'*Gone*!'

Allegra did then what she had never thought to do in front of another person in her life; at least, she never

133

had. She sat with a dull thump on the edge of the Elizabethan settle and cried as if her heart would break. . .

As it could not, of course. It had shattered long ago. And now Luc was gone, taking—she hiccoughed dramatically—the pitiful remains of what was left of it with him. She wanted to keep silent, wanted no one ever to know her misery, her shame. But she could not stop them, the sobs of rage and anguish.

'Oh, I hate him! I *hate* him!'

The Dowager understood at once. But then she had understood the very first moment she had seen them together.

'Of course you do, my dear, because you have fallen into love with him. It is only natural.' By which she meant, among other things, that she would deem it most unnatural in any young girl to fail to be felled by her grandson.

It was Algie who executed the *coup de grâce*.

'Yes, and now the great, utter *bird-witted*, imbecile, *shatter-brained*, butter-headed *booby* has gone and got herself betrothed to *Cuthbert!*'

For the very first time in the whole of her seventy years of existence the Dowager Lady Hawkhurst felt she really *had* to sit down.

Allegra had never spent a night the like of it. Neither able to stay in bed nor to bear that feeling of raw, cold vulnerability when she was out of it, she hovered between the two, tossed disastrously between tides of anguished—misspelt—outpourings to her absent parent—who had no business to be missing in such a crisis—and her rage at Luc, who had. . .though she could not quite explain to herself why she thought so . . .even less right to so desert her when he was needed most. His second in command in Laura Place simply had not been up to the task; nothing the Dowager Lady Hawkhurst had said had comforted the by the second more outraged and self-recriminating Allegra. If anything, it had only made matters worse.

Before he had departed for London Luc had accepted, with a sigh of misgiving born of a deep understanding of his grandparent that the Dowager Lady Hawkhurst must be told as much as he dared to tell her of what had been found at Lydia Limington's. Thus she was briskly apprised of the fact that he had made a discovery that could have the gravest repercussions within the family, and which necessitated his reporting at once to whomever it was he was really working for. . .

Who was that? Allegra *had* to know. The Wellesley clan and therefore the incumbent government? Or FitzCarlin, a man who saw advantage in bringing the government down, or at least in weakening it until it was little more than an impotent tool in his hands? Allegra had met FitzCarlin often and had never liked the languid, supercilious, if undeniably handsome creature. Too young to understand his lecher's interest in her own maturing person, she had understood only that his motives for attaching to Aunt Lydia were not all that they appeared. And yet he had seemed to be quite besotted. . .

Seemed? Suddenly everything in the world and everyone in it only *seemed*, and she could not be sure of anything any more. Except—Allegra flung herself down on to her counterpane and demolished her pillow in rage and horror—she was going to have to marry Cuthbert!

She had no choice at all. Unless—unless he got himself involved in another embarrassing scandal— which he wouldn't, because Cuthbert was that tiresome sort of individual who *would* learn his lesson the first time he was shown it. No hope, unless Papa refused to countenance such a hasty, let alone unpalatable arrangement.

Unless—oh, there was no unless! She should know; she had been trying to think of one all night.

Facing up to one's own heroic stupidity in the chill loneliness of the dead hours was not something to which Allegra took easily. Therefore—well, it *was* all Luc's fault for so upsetting her! If he had not left her so angry, so distracted, she might have attended to the wretched Cuthbert and. . .

No, that was not fair. She had never attended to Cuthbert in her life! And now she must spend the rest of that wretched existence in harmonious tandem with him!

Even before she had met Mr Fleetwood the very notion of an alliance with Cuthbert would have appalled her, but it would have made her laugh. Now it coiled through her blood as real, stinging nausea. . .

Now there could never be anyone but Luc. Luc who had gone to London to betray her family! All of them. If Aunt Lydia was involved with the French the whole of the Alderley clan would pay for it. Nothing, not even Papa's great friendship with Wellington, could help them now. Indeed that friendship would bring Wellington and all stability crashing down beside it.

And Luc would do that to them. To Papa. To Algie. To her!

Why?

He could not possibly believe that Aunt Lydia would be involved. Aunt Lydia never got herself involved in anything; she had long upheld that opinions fatally wrinkled one's complexion.

But Allegra had seen the letter too. Unmistakably the hand of Bonaparte; she probably knew this better than did Luc. She must have been one of the few people in England ever to have seen it before, when her other aunt, married long ago to a French *vicomte*, had sent the Emperor's signature to her niece as a souvenir, along with that of the great Prince de Talleyrand too. Allegra still had it somewhere.

An innocuous letter, just a personal note to the *vicomte* regarding some trivial family matter, the betrothal of a cousin of one to the third cousin five times removed of the other, some such nonsense as that. But written on the same paper, and in the same unmistakable hand.

No doubt at all but they had found a letter from Napoleon himself in Aunt Lydia's writing-box. And now, bearing all its damning evidence, it was halfway to London and disaster.

Allegra all but tore up her sheets with rage.

I will kill him for this! I would stop him if I could! she cried silently.

But it all came to the same thing: betrayal. In being loyal to his country Luc was betraying her. She felt it

like that. As if it were personal, and it were she alone
he meant to harm.

And yet, lying here, staring into the moonlight till it
hurt her eyes as if it had been the sun, she wanted Luc
to come home. Because only Luc could help her. . .

Then suddenly she sobered. Maybe, unwittingly, he
already had. Her nausea sat inside her as painfully as
lead. After all, from the moment it was broadcast
about Aunt Lydia the Honourable Cuthbert
Nettlesham would be free from all his obligations.

It was the strangest thing to find oneself doing in the
middle of a night as terrible as this, but Allegra started
laughing, laughing as if she would never be able to
stop.

The Dowager Lady Hawkhurst, just as restless,
paused outside her guest's door and debated. What to
say, what to do to help the child? She had nothing that
she was *sure* of that she could say, so she could only *do*
. . .what the Fleetwood family seemed to hold in hand
for every emergency known to man. . .

Allegra was burst in upon with a very brisk, '*Et
voilà*! *Et maintenant*. . .!' and found herself on the
receiving end of a very large brandy indeed.

It was to a world that felt it would split her head to
pieces that Allegra woke the next day; a world so full
of agonising noises that she took to her bed gratefully,
the better to nurse her by now pulsating temples.
Besides, it was the only way she could think of of
avoiding Cuthbert.

Algie reported progress from the morning-room
when he brought her the only food she could bear to

have look her in the eye. . .for indeed the cherry cake
seemed to her to be glowering balefully back.

'You really are going to have to stop swilling brandy.'
Algie plumped himself heavily on her feet and looked
critically at her. 'Tell you what; go down and let the
Honourable Cuthbert see you like that and he'll run
away and then we'll all be shot of——'

'Algie!'

'Hmm?' This through the largest possible mouthful
of cake.

'Be silent, and do not you even think to mention
Cuthbert!'

'It's all over town; I overheard Cardew saying so
to——' This he drowned in a vulgar slurp of her tea.

'That's mine, you despicable little glutton!' Allegra
sat up, relieved to find that she could mind such
ordinary things as her brother demolishing her breakfast. . .or tea, or supper or whatever it was.

'What time of day is it?'

'Sunday.'

'Sunday! But oh, but I *can't* have done——'

'Snored like a dragon for a whole day. . .this is the
most wonderful cake, Allegra; you really ought to
try——'

'Well, leave some on the plate, then!'

Algie grudgingly obliged, while polishing off the tea,
which was the part she really wanted.

'Is Cuthbert really downstairs?'

'Been there all morning since coming back from the
abbey; the Dowager's going——'

'Lady Hawkhurst is becoming a trifle irritated, Algie!
Can you not at least try to amend your language?'

'No.' Algie wiped his mouth on what he took to be his clean handkerchief but was in fact a somewhat older specimen containing remnants of his own luncheon for the parrot. Allegra threw them at him and herself out of bed. Then she climbed back in again.

'I cannot go down with Cuthbert there. . .oh, Algie, whatever am I to do?'

'Whatever's Papa going to say, don't you mean? *AND* he'll be home soon——'

'Home?' Papa home! Forever and ever, at last. She had missed him so long she had never let herself believe this moment would arrive. Let alone that her very first sensation would be dread.

'Sent a letter,' explained Algie, nibbling into one of Pythagoras's scraps which he had decided was too good for the bird. 'Herr Kraftstein found it at Aunt Lydia's this morning.'

'Herr Kraftstein? What on earth was he doing at——?'

'Looking for our letters, of course, silly! Anyway, Papa says he will be home maybe as soon as June. And even you can hold Cuthbert at——'

'Algie, if I hear one more of your insufferable crudities——'

'Well, you ain't all that good at keeping 'em at bay, are you? Ain't seen you seein' off anyone to speak of, in fact——'

'And just what is that supposed to mean?'

And inexplicably Algie blushed. 'Well, Mr Fleetwood. . .Luc, I mean. . .'

Oh, dear God! Allegra felt herself burning a million times more fierily than Algie as the memory rushed back at her—if it had ever really gone away. 'Algie, it wasn't what you think! Mr Fleetwood only. . .only wanted me to be quiet!'

'Oh, and I was born in a bucket!' scoffed Algie, making the phrase up on the spot and very much liking the sound of it.

'It's true!'

And to her puzzlement Algie's eyes dipped away, and he sounded almost childish when he said, 'You mean you *don't* like him?'

'No! I utterly and entirely loathe him!'

Algie got up then, dusting crumbs all over her counterpane for Brandy to clean up later. Never had she seen him look so lonely.

'Does that mean. . .well, does that mean he can't be *my* friend?'

And Allegra almost burst into yet another flood of tears. But she knew better than to follow her desperate urge to hug him as she was used to do ever since their mother had died and she was all he had to turn to with Papa away. So taken up had she been with her own misery that she had only barely understood that to Algie Luc Fleetwood was someone very special indeed. Someone unpredictable and mysterious, exciting, who talked to him as if he were a grown-up, someone who understood that, in his own way, the Most Honourable the Marquess of Stonyhurst had a good brain and could, on occasion, surprise everyone, including himself, by using it. Someone who simply knew what it was like to be a boy.

'No, of course not, you owl!' she returned with carefully judged scorn. 'Just because I never want to

see him again as long as I live, it does not mean that
you may not; just do not let him near me, that is all I
ask, unless it is to bring me what is left of the monster
in chains!'

It made her feel almost better to see Algie's bursting
smile.

'I won't! Only. . .why won't I? Can't you like him
just a little bit?'

'No! And why you won't is because I am going to
kill him!'

None of which stopped her leaping up from her
theatrically rumpled sickbed every time she heard a
horse or a carriage so much as slow half a step beneath
her windows. None of which stopped her longing every
time for it to be Luc.

Her room was by now all but filled with the numbing
fumes of the thousand exotic blooms Cuthbert had so
valiantly struggled to find for her in Bath in April, and
her dressing-chest awash with his it seemed endless
stream of alarmingly fervent messages. Odes most of
them. Concerning the fragile charms of young females
dying of the consumption and leaving their lovers,
bereft, to pine feebly away on their gravestones. Not
entirely encouraging in their tenor had she been anything but faking her indisposition. Allegra squinted at
another epic in real distaste; Cuthbert was still going
strong — this time clambering about icy mountain
passes, battling evil barons uphill and down implausibly
bluebelled dales, distractedly in search of his Long Lost
Love — a whole week after their disastrous betrothal.
She did not even look up when the door opened so
softly, lest she be sleeping and woken by the intrusion,

and Luc Fleetwood came in, taking care not to close the door completely behind him.

He had come to make his peace — somehow. And not just because he still needed her co-operation. Apprised by his grandmother of the true nature of Allegra's sickness — a life-threatening allergy to Cuthbert — he had been expecting to see her perched here, merely hiding in her room playing some idle game with her brother or reading the latest blood-curdling novel, until Cuthbert could be forced, if only by chimes of midnight and the Dowager's exhausted collapse, into seeing himself off the premises. . .never this. She was pale as ice and had visibly lost a great deal of weight. And she had been as fragile as a bird to start with.

He had come to coax her, to tease her out of her doldrums, and promise her that her father would make everything all right. To tell her most of what he had done in London, and to ask for forgiveness for what had passed between them before he left. But he could not do it.

Whatever was eating away at her it was serious; it was as if she was in the acutest physical pain from it. Dropping the violets he had brought her unheeded on the counterpane, he went straight to her, towering over her as she gazed up at him, eyes wide with shock and unrelieved misery, and taking her chin in his hand looked into their swamped indigo depths as if he would burn the truth from her. Much more was wrong here than simply Cuthbert Nettlesham.

Even as she tried to wrest her chin from him he sat beside her and his grip tightened.

'Oh, kitten!' was all he said and to her horror Allegra fell into his arms in such a flood of tears she could never have believed it could happen. Except that she had longed for it as if her life depended on it, and now he was here. Here and stroking her hair so softly, murmuring to her that it was not like her to cry and that everything would be well. Whispering that she was the most unmitigated little fool, and to have a care for it not to ruin his coat, which was brand-new, in her violent hysterics. . .saying anything, it seemed, just so that she could hear his voice and be calm.

Allegra felt his arms tighten about her as her angry sobbing abated. . .tighten as her shaken tears gave way to a trembling she had never known before, which was not born of cold, nor distress. . .nor anything but that he was holding her so closely and she had lived for every moment of this too.

'Silly kitten!' She had never heard him sound like this before. He was laughing and yet it was almost as if he could not believe that he was. Almost that he had suddenly found out something he did not know. . .

Then she knew. Of course he had. She had clung to him as if he was the very centre of her existence. Luc was not a fool, nor was he a man who had ever been ignorant of women, nor ever could be. He must have faced this a hundred times before. Of course he knew she loved him.

What was he going to do about it?

Allegra was too afraid of him rejecting her to find out. She shook herself from his embrace, the urgent desperation of a cornered bird.

Luc stared at her hard, and she stared at him, he not

beginning to guess why she had pushed him away, Allegra hoping with every breath that he would pull her back again.

He almost did. At least he reached out to smooth away the hair that was clinging to the tears latticing her cheeks. He sounded almost too normal when he said, 'Well, what an idiot! Cannot I leave you for a second but you must become betrothed to the likes of Cuthbert Nettlesham?'

And groping pointlessly for her handkerchief — pointless for Algie had long since gone off with it for fell purposes of his own — Allegra found that she was laughing. Really laughing. And that — impossibly — that laughter was echoed back at her in the bemusing glitter of his eyes.

'You would prefer it had been Freddie Limmersham, Mr Fleetwood?' she managed huskily.

'I should prefer it that it was no one at all!' There was something so harsh in his tone for a moment that Allegra flinched away — and was stopped by his hand catching into her shoulder in a grip that made her heart race in awe. Until he said, 'But, as it has turned out, it might prove very useful that you have poor Cuthbert in thrall!'

She was meant to laugh at it, she knew. But she could not. Because she wanted him to rage at it, at her; she wanted him to be angry with her, jealous, not tease her as if he didn't care. He was only ever going to be indifferent. But Allegra laughed anyway, because she had to. She had shown all she would ever show of her true feelings. She closed her eyes against the revealing sting of pain — and felt his hand against her shoulder as if it could break her in a thousand pieces. She had to look up, into those eyes now so black it was impossible to tell they had ever been blue. . . Eyes that made her feel she must dissolve completely into nothing, into him. . . She saw his jaw tighten, and the pulse beating faster than it ought to just where it joined his ear. . .so she wanted to reach out and feel it for herself. . .

Feel what?

It was gone, whatever this burning tension had been; even as he saw her eyes widen at it, fascinated — dangerous to him — he forced himself back under the iron self-control that was fast becoming his only shield against her. He dared not let her past it.

'You will have thought of it for yourself by now, Allegra. Cuthbert is Lord FitzCarlin's heir. His only family. Cuthbert has lived as his son since he was a baby. And Cuthbert has ever been indiscreet. . .'

Allegra could barely believe he could be saying it. What kind of world did he move in to make him so cynical as this?

'You want me to. . .*spy* on Cuthbert? To ask him things, make him betray his uncle? Knowing he will tell me anything because he cares for me!'

Luc did not need her to tell him how ugly it was. But war was even uglier, treason the worst of all.

'This is treason we are dealing with!' he spat back, lashed by self-disgust as he saw himself through her contemptuous eyes and needing to hurt her for showing it to him. 'I am trying to save this newborn peace of ours! Have you even the first idea what a fragile thing it is, how many lives depend on its being made to last? Your father's being one of them!'

'Oh, but you. . .you *bastard*, Luc Fleetwood! You—oh, I cannot look at you! Get out of my room! *Get out*!'

Because it was true. They lived in a world so warped by war that he was right and all her instincts of fair play and loyalty to friends counted for nothing. And, for all she would die rather than marry Cuthbert, he said he loved her and she did not dislike him; he would never deserve anything so cruel as this.

'So you agree?' Luc's voice iced over with pain he was not prepared to recognise. She had meant it that she could not bear to look at him. Yet not ten seconds before she had clung to him and he had thought. . . Luc's eyes chilled to glass as he ruthlessly dismissed what he had thought.

'Yes, I agree! What choice have I got? Now get out! *Get out*!'

Luc left. There was nothing else he could do. He of all people could never calm her now. Allegra was left staring down at his peace offering of her favourite violets, stabbed to the heart by the scent she loved better than any in the world. Why had he had to ask it of her? Why?

Because she knew now what she had not known before. That however angry she made him, however much he held her aunt's morals in contempt, however much he wanted to resist her he was not able to—not always. He was not immune. She had heard it in his fight to command his breathing, and seen it in the pulse that beat so wildly in his throat.

If he had not said. . .if he had not asked her to use Cuthbert; if he had not used her!

Oh, God! Allegra clutched her arms about her to stifle the pain. I love him! I *have* to have him. Whatever! Whatever he does. . .I *need him*!

And I could have had him!

I *know* I could!

She had only one way to assuage her hurt and her loss. Revenge. If Luc wanted her to be monopolised by Cuthbert then let him watch! Let him suffer too!

She could not shake off the instinct that he would.

But he never showed it. Not for a minute over the half-week that followed, during which it could be no accident that he was invariably out of the house before she descended for breakfast and never there for luncheon or dinner unless the Honourable Cuthbert was with them too.

Meanwhile the Dowager Lady Hawkhurst was left with a most unwelcome dilemma. Should she or should she not be encouraging the deplorable Mr Nettlesham? Quite by accident she found herself in *loco parentis* for the Duke of Alderley's only daughter, and the Duke was not a man she knew well enough even to begin to judge what he would make of Cuthbert's reckless proposal. The best she could do was invite Cuthbert to be her guest as often as she might, to try, in fairness, to get to know him better — and to fend him off from visiting all hours between.

So she swallowed hard on a sliver of Algie's favoured treacle tart and turned benignly to Cuthbert as he sat at her dinner-table gazing across it at Allegra with all the avidity of a man who had struck gold. She did not dare to look at her grandson who commanded the head of the table as if he were carved from stone, as silent

and remote as he had been ever since his return from
London.

Really, she was almost annoyed at Allegra—except
it could never be the child's fault that she was so
impossibly lovely no man could stay sane in her orbit
for long.

'Mr Nettlesham——' the Dowager strained her smile
to its very limits '—do say that you are to come with us
to the celebration tomorrow evening. . .'

'Ah——' Cuthbert laid down his napkin and
wrenched his gaze from Allegra just long enough to
allow his victim to snatch a bite of the food his
relentless ogling had quite prevented her from eating
'—for our new Duke of Wellington!' Uttered with the
utmost unction.

For it had been announced to all the world—who
had expected nothing less and were getting restless
waiting for it to happen—that as of two days since, the
third of May, Arthur Wellesley, hero of the Peninsula
and Bonaparte's Nemesis, was raised to the highest
honours in the land. The whole of Bath had been
buzzing with the news, old colonels in retirement
gruffly 'delighted, such a sound fellow', their ladies
quite shamelessly enumerating his new Grace's
heroic—amorous—conquests. Tomorrow night there
was to be a ball in Wellington's honour, held in the
Upper Assembly Rooms—inconveniently perched on
the slope above Milsom Street—which all day had
been a ferment of preparations for the occasion.

'Just so, sir——' Lady Hawkhurst wrestled her smile
back into place, wondering how it was she had not yet

strangled the maddening creature '—for we are all to go, except young Algie, of course——'

'Which I think particularly unjust seeing that his Grace is a *particular* friend of our papa's!'

It was the first time Luc had spoken throughout the entire evening. 'Oh, and you *want* to be surrounded by twittering females, do you, to be obliged to dance with the things, and all on only the most unspeakable tepid tea to drink and——?'

'Well, of course I don't!' Algie was visibly sickened. 'I just think——'

'I agree, it is unfair you should be left out. So we'll have a celebration of our own, if you like.'

Algie dropped his treacle tart in stunned surprise and for the first time, it seemed in her whole life, Allegra looked at Luc and thought, How can he be so kind to Algie, so much fun, and be so cold and manipulating with me?

'*Really*? What can we do? Something that will make a grand old noise because——'

'People don't make noises in Bath——' Luc smiled at him '—least of all your kind of noises, still less at Tiffy's dinner-table! But perhaps we can go and be rowdy somewhere else. Let me think about it.'

'Yes. . .thank *you*, and I'm sorry if I made a noise. . .'

Allegra found that her hands were tangling into her napkin beneath the table; If only Luc would smile at *me*! she thought.

Her eyes accidentally caught his. She knew before he did it that he would turn his coldly away. So she turned at once to Cuthbert. 'It will be the greatest thing, to go to a ball at last! I have not been anywhere that bears speaking of since I was sent from London because you and. . .'

She caught herself up. One presumably did not mention duelling at dinner-tables either.

Cuthbert, pink to the gills and clashing horribly with the lemon and lime splendour of his latest waistcoat, reached out a hand and patted her adoringly on the fingers until they were quite pulped to a throbbing ache.

'But who else should I take to the ball but you, my *Dearest* Lady Allegra? Why else in this World should I Assent to Go?'

With a scrape of his chair that all but struck sparks from the woodwork Luc Fleetwood, with the barest token of a bow to excuse his inexcusable behaviour, got to his feet and, emanating unadulterated fury, coldly—and he would never know how awe-inspiringly—left the room.

If anything his demeanour was even more arctic the next evening as he handed Allegra up into the grandest of the Hawkhurst carriages. She had spent quite five hours in her efforts to make herself look her very best, what with first pouncing on, then dismissing every gown that Sorcha patiently brought out for her and finally declaring frantically that she had not a thing to wear.

She had only half admitted to herself as she stood before her glass bedecked in the finest of ivory satin, soft with its cloud of silver-sewn gauze, that it was for Luc she was doing it all. Because he would not respond to her attempts to make him jealous of Cuthbert. She

had all bar concussed herself with boredom spending
every waking minute in Cuthbert's infuriating company
but Luc had not shown for even one second that he
minded.

Allegra had taken in the perfect arrangement of her
curls, twisted into ribbons glowing with tiny fresh-
water pearls from her father's own estates in Ireland,
and the heavy collar of great Indian pearls about the
pale slenderness of her neck. Taken in everything and
thought, Maybe he does not find me pretty? Maybe. . .
maybe I am not really pretty at all! Maybe it has only
ever been my fortune made people say so.

Chasing away yet another inexplicable threat of tears
with a proud toss of her head, she had dug her gloved
fingers into her palms. *Please* let him look at me. . .let
him be kind, as he was the night we met, she'd pleaded
silently. Please let something happen tonight to end
this aching, painful silence that has grown into a wall
of resentment between us.

But, as the carriage door slammed shut and Mr
Fleetwood took his place opposite her where she sat
drained by her efforts not to look at him and hope
again, Allegra knew that he had not even seen her. He
never would.

She knew it was deliberate. It was as if the very air
of the carriage throbbed with some gathering tension,
most of it emanating tangibly from Luc.

For the first time in her life Allegra was actually glad
to see Cuthbert, even though he stood so conspicuously
beneath the flaring torches of a phalanx of liveried
running boys, preening in the flattering glow of carriage
lanterns, encased in a collar and coat so tight that his

elaborate bow was almost certain to maim him; that coat so tight, indeed, that Allegra — and Lady Hawkhurst — began to suspect a corset.

Allegra flinched at the very thought. . .because it was a thought that led so inevitably to Luc. Luc, running like the wind, every muscle of his body at ease with his efforts, taut, hard. . .

Allegra was blushing so hotly by the time Cuthbert captured her unwilling fingers that she knew that the whole of Bath would take it that she was quite besotted with the wretched creature! Flushed with maidenly delight at the prospect of their future marriage.

Luc! So close behind them as they forced their way through the abominable crush that she could feel the heat of his body fusing with hers, feel when her shoulder was momentarily trapped against his chest. Felt, just before she was swept away by the crowing Cuthbert, the unmistakable lurch of his heart as he sensed her touch.

'What we are doing in this appalling place I cannot think! It is the most pitiful——'

'Tiffy, do keep your voice down! Not everywhere can be Versailles!'

'Oh, but you repulsive boy! As if I am even remotely old enough to remember Vers——'

'Yes, you are, Tiffy!' Luc took her arm and led her to the notorious gossip factory of the dowagers' benches where he knew she planned to take root all evening. 'Born and brought up in the vulgar great warren, and what a hell-hole of vice and tedium it must have been!'

'Well, I suppose it was, when I think about it. . .

and, by the by, have a care for your language; there is
the *shockable* variety of lady present! But—oh, Luc,
just *look* at the people here! I shall expire of boredom!'

Allegra, walking just behind them with Cuthbert so
inescapably in tow, was thinking very much the same.
Bath. Old ladies, even older gentlemen, determined
spinsters and a few implausibly demure schoolgirls out
for an unexpected treat. Of the few girls her own age
not one was a person she had met in London.

She knew what that meant and her heart sank. She
could not cling all evening to Lady Hawkhurst's skirts
and had no other acquaintance to turn to. Luc would
never rescue her. It meant the whole of the evening
spent listening to Cuthbert; it mean the waste of what
might—just—have been a perfectly good ball.

Far from the faded glitter of the Assembly Rooms the
Most Honourable the Marquess of Stonyhurst was
anticipating an evening of quite another nature.

Having taken himself off to bed, he watched at his
window until the very last carriage was gone from the
clamour of Pulteney Street and all was quiet but the
Watch on the prowl from his post at the entrance to
Sydney Gardens. Herr Kraftstein had long since vanished to continue his definitive translation of Virgil's
more obscure works into his native German.

Algie found his coat and, pushing into the pocket a
tinder-box, a notebook and pencil, he hauled his great
deerhound out of its comfortable slumbers.

'Come on, Brandy. We're going searching for that
bird which makes all the noise all night. . .come, boy,
come *on*!'

It was cold outside for all it was the beginning of May. Algie shivered and wondered perhaps if he might not prefer a night reading about pirates instead. He was still debating the issue when he saw the light.

Nothing but a peeling away of darkness from a window, a painting of the glass with momentary gold then blackness again. It was enough to see him running as fast as his treacle-fed bulk would allow him, Brandy struggling manfully at his heels.

The light was in Aunt Lydia's house and he was the only one here to do anything about it.

# CHAPTER EIGHT

'CUTHBERT——' Allegra removed the Honourable Mr
Nettlesham's hand from where she felt certain it ought
not to be '—*truly* I shall die if I remain on my feet a
second longer!'

Let alone with you! she longed to add, for each time
she had been on the brink of rescue by one eager
gentleman or another Cuthbert had smugly announced
himself her fiancé—which he was not until Papa said
he might be—and thus entitled to dance with her the
entire evening if he so desired it. All about them
huddles of dowagers were sighing at the impetuosity of
his romantic jealousy. There must have been something
very unexpected lurking in the otherwise unexceptionable fruit cup, for Cuthbert had so far threatened three
young military men and a parson with a duel should
they look in Such a Manner at his Beloved Allegra
again. His Allegra, meanwhile, was beginning to take
back every unkind thing she had thought of poor
Freddie Limmersham. Cuthbert—a Cuthbert three-
quarters the way towards intoxication—was a Cuthbert
girded and hungry for war.

'*Please*, Cuthbert!'

Cuthbert relented. But just as she felt the shackles
falling from her he clutched hold of her arm and smiled
deeply into her exhausted eyes. 'Then let me procure

for us a Secluded Corner and a Plate of Supper. Let us find a Place where we may be Alone!'

Allegra only just held in her groan! And, look frantically about her as she might, she could see no sign of the cavalry racing to her assistance. God knew, even the infantry would do! But they had taken the measure of the Honourable Cuthbert and none was prepared for the embarrassment of trying it.

Alone with Cuthbert. . .

'Ought we not to find Lady Hawkhurst and invite her to join us?' It was her last stand and she knew it for a hopeless one.

'Not tonight, my Dearest, Adored one! Tonight let us Send the Whole World away ——!'

The voice came out of nowhere, penetrating as a sword and ten times more effective.

'I think not, Nettlesham. No, I very much think not.'

Had Cuthbert been a little less fond of fruit cup he might have noticed a startling change in the heretofore amenable Mr Fleetwood, for Luc was towering over him in a fashion that could only be described as menacing.

Cuthbert, flinging one arm possessively — and most improperly — about Allegra's shoulders, was just one fraction too foxed to perceive the message. Until Luc's eyes hardened to such an intensity of warning that Cuthbert let go of his victim as if she had just slapped him and — mulishly, it had to be said — acceded.

'Well, I suppose ——'

'That you are placing my grandmother in a most invidious position, Nettlesham. Until Lady Allegra's aunt returns to Bath my grandmother has the care of her and you cannot think that she would wish it said that she allowed you to make so reckless a spectacle of the innocent child.'

Allegra, stunned with relief, stumbled for freedom like a man twenty years in chains. She took Luc's arm automatically—and felt his hand cover hers with a powerful grip of reassurance. Innocent child, indeed! Really, how many characters could Luc play? she mused, dizzy with admiration; he had skilfully taken on the guise of outraged uncle.

Certainly Cuthbert, nerves tugging at his brain through the fog of spirits, began to look at the matter anew.

'See your point, old fellow. . .'

'Of course you do, there's a good man,' soothed Luc mendaciously. 'What say you but you take yourself off and keep my grandmother company over supper? It would only be politic, after all. . .'

'Would it? Um. . .yes. . .'spose it might be.'

But Cuthbert was not so easily parted from his Treasure. With a movement somewhere between a dive and a lurch he made to take Allegra's hand to kiss it—only to find it firmly recovered from his clasp before he even realised it had been there.

Cuthbert had the vaguest feeling that the Divine Fingers ought not to be in Mr Fleetwood's treacherous clutches but he could not quite think up what to do about it. Couldn't start a mill, after all. . .not and upset the Dowager who would be reporting to the Duke of Alderley on his every move.

Cuthbert worked out that his best plan was to vanish and, with a sway in his step replacing the usual peacock swagger, vanish he did, leaving Allegra all but falling against Luc's chest in her gratitude.

He did not draw away. Indeed he was laughing so hard, if so absolutely silently, that she could feel it shaking through her entire body.

'Let that serve as a warning to you as to the evils of brandy, my child!'

'Oh, it will, it *will*! Oh, *Luc*!'

'Oh, dear! So bad?'

'Terrible! I was just at the point where the only way out I could see for myself was vicious assassination with the nearest fruit-knife!'

And she found that they were looking at each other at last, really looking; it was as if her eyes would never leave his again and she knew that, by a miracle, both were smiling, his with the utmost wickedness.

'That would have caused a stir, my lady!' He said it so severely that she found she was laughing out loud at him.

'Oh, I know! Think of it. . .' And she looked almost longingly about her at the glum gathering of revellers.

'And these could do with a little shaking, you think?' Luc's eyes were almost black with purpose now. 'So how say you that you and I be the talk of the town instead?'

He would, she knew it. But would she?

'What are we going to do?'

'Why, find a Place where we can be Absolutely Alone in the Whole Wide World, of course!'

'I——'

'Can't do with letting Nettlesham become so complacent!' Then he exploded with indignation, 'Really,

Allegra, you all but had the creature in your lap half
the evening; could you not at least have danced with
*one* other poor fool?'

'I couldn't! Cuthbert would not let them near me!
That one over there, the handsome colonel with the so
very grand moustaches, *he* tried, but. . .'

'*What* handsome colonel?'

'There. . .' Then Allegra's voice tailed away.

He was jealous. *He* was jealous! It was the one thing
she had seen enough of in her short reign as the toast
of London. Luc was absolutely seething with it.

Allegra had just gone to heaven.

He mistook the look in her eyes and returned
furiously, 'It seems I was just in time! Must you be up
to all your London games even in the provinces?'

And Allegra allowed him to fume as he towed her
ruthlessly towards his grandmother to whom he nodded
his outrageous intentions—and before Lady
Hawkhurst could spring to her indolent feet to deal a
death-blow to the incipient scandal Allegra found
herself in quite the last isolated spot she could have
expected. . .outside the Assembly Rooms where the
starlight rained down on her glittering silver sandals
and Luc Fleetwood sent a footman running for the
Hawkhurst carriage.

Then he changed his mind. Without another word
he took Allegra's hand and with not so much as a
glance at the astonished faces of the servants all about
him tugged her out into the relative peace of Bennett
Street, heading towards the singularly ill-lit Circus.

'Luc!' Even he could not go this far. Even she
couldn't!

Luc ignored her, simply taking off his coat and throwing it about her moon-silvered shoulders.

Allegra went with him. The man had no morals at all! He had not the least care that he was here alone with her—and in his shirt-sleeves too! She cast a glance at his shoulders, making the most of her first chance really to look at him, as the shadows of the exquisite cloth moved against the powerful muscles of his back and she wondered what it would feel like to brush aside his hair and——

'Stop dawdling! I'm causing a scandal, not planning to die from the cold!'

'Sorry!' Allegra's eyes roamed to where his hair fell so rakishly across his brow.

'You look a shocking mess,' she pointed out, unaware of the awe in her childish whisper.

He stopped short then and looked down at her. And smiled. 'And so do you!' Then he added quite out of the blue, 'What is it like to be the most beautiful girl in the universe?'

It was Allegra stopped dead then. She was never going to be able to move again in her life.

'I. . .*me*?'

'Well, who else is here?' And she heard something behind his laughter then that was dizzyingly exciting. She felt it in the blood that began to beat less steadily in his palm as she curled her ungloved fingers into his without even knowing that she did so.

'I—I don't know. . .I mean. . .'

'Not knowing what it is like to be the ugliest! Poor Allegra! I thought you were to be eaten alive in that place. Your handsome moustaches looked so exactly like a hungry lion!'

The Circus was not quite dark, but it was deserted at the moment for everyone was gone to the ball. Glazed in moonlight, an immaculate classical circle of the most expensively simple houses, Allegra thought it must be the most beautiful place on earth. And yet she was just a little frightened of the dark at the heart of it, being alone in it. . .with Luc. Who was saying things she did not quite understand.

She tried to change the subject. 'Is this the prettiest place ever, do you think?'

But he would not be deflected. The laugh was still warm in his voice, but it was little more than the softest breath of amusement, burning the blood to her cheeks as he bent towards her and whispered, 'It is now.'

'Luc. . .Luc, what are you doing?'

Because he did not even know himself he kissed her. And Allegra, swayed right off her feet, found herself caught against him as she had never been meant to be . . .as he had never meant to hold her. All he had meant was to take her away from that crawling lizard Nettlesham, from where a creature as vital and as exciting as she was should never be. He had watched them all evening until he felt he would suffocate in his anger at the waste of her. He had only wanted to get her away. Only meant to tease her a little ——

Only wanted to have her to himself for a while. The last chance he was ever going to get. For things were happening in London now so far out of his control.

Luc pulled her so hard into his arms then that Allegra clung to his neck, sobbing for the breath that was driven out of her. If she could have dissolved into him then she would have done it gladly.

Something was happening to her tonight, to both of them, and she was wild with joy at it.

'Luc!'

He had to let her go, he knew. But he did not. Not even when, it seemed a lifetime later, he lifted his mouth from hers and buried his face in her hair. Not wanting to. . .

But if he never could again. . .

'No! Not now, Allegra. No questions! Don't ask me anything tonight! Don't talk!'

Of course they did. And it seemed about everything and nothing, as if they had known each other so long, they knew every last thing there was to know about each other anyway—and yet greedy for answers as if nothing were known and had to be learned now. As if there was only now.

Allegra walked with him down the steepness of a near-deserted Milsom Street towards the abbey and the river and home knowing that everything she was doing was wrong. And that everything was right.

Betrothed to Cuthbert. . .irretrievably in love with Luc Fleetwood. She no longer cared if he guessed it.

He was not certain that he had. Because he would never want it to be true. It *must* not be true! And yet the reason he did not believe was because he *did* want it. Now he saw her like this, as he had always known she could be, untame and untamable—by anybody. And yet she must be one day, by the man she married.

No one could ever do it!

Unless that man were he.

Luc broke into a run as if he could leave the thought behind him where it belonged, unthought, unfelt, and Allegra ran with him, never able to keep up and yet not afraid of anything, not while he was here. Not while she could see him ahead of her, waiting. Laughing at her. Wild as a god, just as she had always known him to be, and she felt such a longing to belong to him, with him — be like him — she could only laugh out loud. It was too much. She did not know what was happening. Nor what he wanted, what he meant by it. Only that as she reached him where he leaned against a wall in the silent shadows of the abbey churchyard she was caught by the waist, hard against him, and that her whole being melted into his. Knowing so well how they should be closer. . .wondering if they never would be.

'Allegra. . .' He sounded as if all the breath had been punched from his powerful body, as if he had been running hard for hours.

'Yes?' She barely made a sound at all.

'I have to leave England. . .maybe tomorrow. They want me to go to Wellington. There is a letter only I can take.' He was within a breath of saying, Come with me. To her father, of course, where she would be safe, away from all that must happen here in Bath. But he knew what he really ached to say was, Come with *me*.

Away from all of it, everything — so she would never have to know the truth. . .

'Go?' Allegra was stunned. He could not go, not now. '*No*!'

'I *have* to — and while I am gone I want you away from Bath, do you understand? Tomorrow you go with Tiffy to Fleetwood. I ——'

'Luc——'

His hand smothered her to silence; she had to let him finish. 'I want you safe!'

Safe! Without him? Nothing would ever feel as secure again now she knew what it was to be held by him, like this — against his will, because he just could not fight it.

'But——'

He kissed her to silence this time. And somewhere in her dazed mind Allegra thought, How can we be like this and at war with one another? How can we be like this, as if a real war is about to break above our heads? Wild with the need to live while we can. It felt like that. As if everything in the world that mattered was here, now, and they were going to lose it. Fingers tangling into his hair as if she would never let go, Allegra met his kiss so urgently that she knew at last that it was truly dangerous.

Luc, of the ice-cool control — now he was just a soldier with an unknown fate ahead of him. She was just his girl. She had seen this so often, as wives clung to husbands, lovers to lovers, regardless of watching eyes and whispers, as the troopships made ready to pull out from home port into war. She had seen her own parents. . . .

Yet there was no war. It was over. They had no excuse. No excuse for the fact that his searching lips had found a hollow just beneath her ear that left her shuddering with the need to stay with him like this forever. Closer. And as he followed the trembling path of her pulse to where her heart raced urgently from her control and her skin burned his lips beneath the immaculate iciness of her pearls she thought, He does not even like me. He does not care for me. But he *wants* me. He wants *me*!

She felt the tears on her cheeks even before he lifted a hand to dash them away, then with a furious curse kissed them away instead, following each salt line of them so intimately that she could not bear it a second longer.

Allegra knew that she wanted him.

He had misread her tears—how could he do otherwise?

'It will be well, Allegra, haven't I promised all along? I'll make it come right, *everything*. Faron, Lydia, I swear I'll make everything all right!'

Faron? Lydia? Allegra barely knew who he meant. But she craved the comfort he was offering. It was as if there had never been any barrier between them. As if all in one kiss they had both said that they were sorry, made final peace. That they believed in each other. . . and what harm came next they did not care.

'I'm not frightened, not any more!'

And suddenly he was laughing again, that dangerous, intoxicating laughter. 'No, just betrothed to that insufferable clod Nettlesham and kissing me instead! Now what on earth are you going to about that, my kitten?'

'Me. . .?'

'Yes, you! *I* can do nothing——'

It came out in an agony of longing. 'But *do* you want me to, Luc? *Do you want me to*?'

And she felt the ground fall away from her feet as he answered, 'I don't know anything at all, Allegra.

Except that I want you.' He meant he wanted her—forever. He had no doubt at all as he held her in this moment he had never let himself believe would come. He said, 'I want you *now!*' He might have won her too; he knew it the moment he lost her because he added, 'It's all the time we've got!'

Sanity returned to Allegra as she had never thought it could again, as if she had forgotten what it was. She had almost believed—that he loved her and that that was what he meant. And, if it *had* been, the words he had just spoken could never matter. But they did.

Want, not love. Dear God, but she would have thrown herself into anything he asked of her for even the smallest hope that he might love her! But it was nothing more than desire and it could not last.

Two seconds ago she would have said that was enough. Now the moonlight chilled through her skin as she knew that it never could be.

'Luc. . .'

And he damned himself for a fool because he knew he would never touch her again. Never be able to say what he believed in this moment she wanted to hear. He could not say it because he knew what must come next. He knew what he had done in London.

'Yes, kitten, I'll take you home.'

It was all that was left to do

'Luc!'

But he had already seen it. The great deerhound scraping in urgent fear at Lady Hawkhurst's front door.

'Brandy!' Allegra began to run. 'Brandy should not

be out alone! He will not go anywhere without one of us; he. . .'

She knew already, with that instinct only truly understood by those who had felt the same — *Algie*. Something was wrong!

Luc was ahead of her, crouched beside the great dog, calming it. Even as she watched fascinated as he soothed the trembling beast and took its collar, watched every movement of the body she had been held against so closely just seconds ago, still feeling the heat of him in her own skin, he was on his feet again and the hound was leading him, just as she had dreaded, out of Laura Place, racing the length of Pulteney Street for Aunt Lydia's house.

It was locked. Yet Allegra knew as she caught up with Luc that Algie must be inside. Knew it beyond doubt. And he would not lock himself in. . .

She had never had to speak her fears out loud to Luc; he always sensed them. Any other man would have hesitated then, not knowing what to do. Luc, with the most economical thrust of his powerful shoulders, had the door open before Allegra could catch her breath. Not that she could, for she knew by his actions that he too felt the urgency.

'Algie! *Algie!*'

Nothing.

'Go, Brandy, find your master!' She urged the dog towards the stairs where it was hanging back, whimpering.

Oh, dear God! What could have happened to have frightened the animal so? It was as if it feared to look into a grave. Allegra was ahead of them both on the stairs; she had to find her brother.

She stumbled and all but fell over him as she at last reached her old bedroom door.

'Luc — here!' He was on his knees beside her before she finished calling for him.

Algie lay between them, white as death in a slab of moonlight; it was Allegra who first noticed the stain soaking into the satin of her gown and reached out, her hand to the boy's head. It came back sticky and black with blood and Algie felt as cold as if he had never breathed at all.

'Don't move him, Allegra. Not yet.' Even now, incredibly, it was possible that Luc could soothe her; just the sound of his voice and she felt, It cannot be as bad as it appears; Luc is here. . .Luc who was even now so competently feeling Algie's limbs for signs of further damage.

He saw her hypnotised eyes and shook his head at once to reassure her. 'Nothing is broken, but he has been here a long time. We must get him home at once.'

Even as Allegra rose to her feet ready to run for Lady Hawkhurst's and the menservants Luc had caught Algie's still form up into his arms and, as easily as if he carried a baby, was making his way down the stairs, moving with instinctive care through the shadows.

'Go ahead, Allegra; take Brandy with you and, if anyone tries to stop you, scream.' He even smiled. 'You can certainly manage that!'

'The Last Trump!' She smiled back at him, remembering out of nowhere what her maid had said. Already she was halfway across the road to Laura Place. When she reached it she fell against the door so hard that the footman primed to open it at any moment his employer should choose was almost obliged to pick her off the flagstones.

'Hurry!' she rapped out. 'Send my maid to my brother's room this instant! I want water and bandages; tear up a sheet if you have to!'

The footman did not work for Lady Hawkhurst for nothing; he was only ever issued orders fired at him as if from a barrage of artillery.

'Yes, ma'am!' And he was gone towards the back stairs and Sorcha so fast that Allegra could only be grateful for it — and for the almost instant appearance on the scene of Algie's tutor in his dressing-gown, his face as white as his charge's with alarm at the noise that she was making.

'Is anything amiss? *My lady*!' He had seen the blood. 'But what has happened?'

Allegra told him, hurrying up the stairs as she did so as they both headed towards Algie's room where the tutor competently built up the fire.

Luc was not a second behind them. In the fire's comforting glow Algie looked if possible even worse than he had done in the moonlight. But Luc was smiling at her.

'Just an ugly bump on the head; he'll be as right as rain by morning.'

She almost believed him. It was funny, she thought later, how she never ceased to trust him when it counted. How she never would. Whatever he had done in London.

Now her only concern was her brother. As she

moved close to him, edging aside the tutor, she had the most fleeting impression of cold; cold as if Herr Kraftstein was really afraid of something. Chill, almost as if it came from the clothes he wore beneath his dressing-gown. The clean, ice scent of night air.

It must have been Luc, as he leaned close and she realised she still had his coat about her shoulders. His shirt was a mass of blood.

'Luc! He has lost so very much blood!'

Still calm, almost unnaturally so, aware of so many watching eyes, Luc replied, 'You must keep him warm, kitten, I have sent a footman for a physician. He will say the same, I promise you. Keep Algie warm and he will suffer no lasting harm from this.'

But somebody would. Allegra watched the tightening of Luc's jaw as he gazed down at the injured boy and thought, Someone is going to pay dearly for this. Does Luc know who?

The physician, fat, panting and disgruntled, only forgave them for hauling him from his slumbers when he saw the age and condition of his patient.

'Tch! What has the young fool been about to get himself in such a state?'

'Looking for owls!' Allegra and Luc invented in unison, and smiled.

The doctor approved of this. 'Well, I've seen worse. Much worse. Owls, you say? Well, can't say I haven't done the same myself in my time.' And with a briskness belied by his lazy countenance he attended to Algie's wounds as if they had been no more brutal than a scraped knee. He departed with the instruction that

Algie was to be fed only if he asked to be, and then only hot beef broth or gruel, and divesting himself of the opinion that it was good to see that not all young lads these days had lost their stuffing.

Allegra could not have said how grateful she was for his calmly dismissive disdain for the damage. Algie really was all right. He looked terrible! Almost as bleached as the pillow against which he lay, swaddled in more bandages than he would ever need to be bragging about them forever to his cronies; he had not stirred in all the time since they had found him but he was warm beneath her touch at last.

'Set your maid to stay with him tonight, Allegra.'

But she shook her head. 'No, Luc, if he wakes he will want me.'

Luc nodded — then had to look away from her. What she had been through tonight! Tomorrow she would feel the shock of it.

'Then I'll have some chocolate sent in to you.'

'Yes, thank you.' Then, because she realised she sounded almost dismissive in her concern for Algie, she repeated, '*Thank* you! I think you may have saved his life.'

Luc knew that he had. If some wild need to defy his own feelings, to defy his knowledge of himself, defy what he knew could never be, had not led him to sweep Allegra from the ball, if they had lingered by the abbey, not come home when they did. . . Yes, left a whole night in the freezing cold and losing blood, Algie could well have died.

A good thing, he thought as he looked at Allegra

again and ached to take her cares away, that she had only said it; she did not yet know that she believed it.

Herr Kraftstein could not be consoled—if anything he was in far worse case than Allegra, who was holding her own so bravely, and Luc had no time for him. Never had, least of all now.

'It was no one's fault, Herr Kraftstein; we have all of us been children once.'

'But——'

'We have all of us been very, very stupid.'

Allegra looked up then, shaken out of her daze by words that seemed to mean so much more than they said. And yet again she saw Luc and the tutor exchanging glances. Yet again she felt the flare of animosity between them. She could make no sense of it at all, except that Luc blamed Herr Kraftstein for letting Algie slip his leash in such a disastrous fashion. . . What else could Luc mean?

She was too exhausted to care. She was so exhausted that she did not even notice when Luc left the room.

Not even though he had told her they might never meet again.

Yet he was the very first person she saw the next morning as he crept into Algie's room from where he had stood guard on the stairs for most of the night to prevent his grandmother's bursting through the door and seeing off the invalid with fright. He was followed by a much subdued Lady Hawkhurst, who did not even raise a reproving eyebrow as Luc reached out and flicked a finger against Allegra's cheek to wake her without causing her alarm. Luc was all Allegra saw as

she opened her eyes, it felt quite naturally, and began
to take in where she was and what had happened.

The next thing she realised was that Algie was
stirring. She was on her knees beside him even before
he moved his head a second time.

'Algie!'

His eyes flickered open and she could have wept with
relief. She felt an arm about her shoulders and instinctively curled into the warmth it offered her. Luc.

'I told you. Now there will be no holding him! How
much will you wager me, Tiffy, that the young lout
milks this vicious beating for all advantage he can get?'

'Oh, my dears!' Lady Hawkhurst was past laughing
with him or being soothed. But then this was the first
time she had seen Algie since last evening when he had
been bounding up the stairs, his usual hulking picture
of health. 'We cannot stay here, Luc. You were right
when you told me that. We must go to Fleetwood. . .
and, Luc, you cannot leave for Paris now. You *can't*!'

Allegra found that she had stopped breathing, and
only began again when he said, 'Don't worry, Tiffy,
I'm not going anywhere! Not now.'

Allegra's rush of relief was interrupted by the dramatic statement, 'Aunt Lydia.'

'Algie?'

'Aunt Lydia,' the invalid repeated.

'What does he mean by that?' Lady Hawkhurst had
turned as white as paste. 'Luc, what is going on here?'

Algie's eyes opened completely then. He said simply,
'I saw Aunt Lydia. Then someone hit me!'

# CHAPTER NINE

WHICH was all the Algie had to say in the matter, as he made infinitely clear not a second after this heart-stopping pronouncement by fainting away again in such a dramatic fashion that Allegra was properly frightened. Luc knew better. Taking in the slow but steady return of colour to the young victim's uncharacteristically innocent countenance, he took Allegra gently by the hand.

'Don't worry—no, look closely; Algie is going to be perfectly well in a day or so if we allow him to get plenty of rest.'

'But—you heard what he said!'

As Mr Fleetwood steered Allegra from the room she heard him say, beneath his breath and more than grimly, 'I heard.'

Safely out of earshot of an Algie now dozing peacefully under the competent eye of Lady Hawkhurst, Allegra rounded on Luc, unable to control her horror and disbelief a moment longer.

'He cannot have meant what he said! He cannot have meant that Aunt Lydia struck him!'

Luc, whose slow, purposeful pacing to the morning-room window to look so intently down into the everyday bustle of Laura Place was making Allegra more than apprehensive, smiled then, and it was not the kind of smile Allegra could like. Hard, cynical, as if he was amused at something she would never see; yet his voice was quite as usual.

'He did not precisely say that, Allegra. What he said was that he saw Lydia and *then* somebody hit him.'

'Yes. . .but — oh, yes, I see. You're right, of course; Algie is not half so bean-witted as he looks. If he sensed a second person then there was one. . .'

And suddenly Allegra remembered all the circumstances. . .and thought she knew. If it had been Aunt Lydia then who else could her companion have been but Luc's brother?

There was no one else it could logically be.

At the very moment she thought it, and her very real shock blanked out her all too expressive eyes, Luc turned back to her, wondering what he could say to comfort her, to make better what could not be made better until it could be explained; knowing he could never explain it. . .even if he knew. . .

Already he knew too much, but not enough. But he had to say something for Allegra's sake. Then he saw her eyes.

'I see.' He said it very slowly, and as if the whole of her body were draining inexorably of blood Allegra understood; somehow she had given her most damning fears away. He had seen that she still suspected his brother and he froze at it. Luc, to whom she had been so close — so close it did not bear thinking about. . .she would never be able to bear it, not now she had killed everything they might ever have had and they could never be close again.

She *had* to save it, whatever their closeness had

been, however much she knew it meant so little to him. It meant everything to her. It meant so much it did not matter what she believed of his brother. . .or of Luc himself.

'*No*! I know what you think but you don't see anything, Luc! Of course I do not think it is——'

Still more calmly, terrifying in his coldness, he returned, 'Yes, you do.' And most frightening of all was the fact that he sounded so reasonable, so politely aloof. Only doing his job—she could see it in the freezing over of his eyes as he withdrew into himself again, into the private man she was never meant to see; Luc the spy, and everyone his potential enemy. 'It is not so surprising that you would think so. . .'

And then he was Luc again—her Luc—wild with that ungovernable passion of his, towering over her until she was pinned hard against the back of her chair, so close she could feel his breath stinging against her burning cheeks as he spat back, so very finally, 'But it is unforgivable!'

Allegra half woke, struggling from her dreams as she had struggled away from Luc while she was in them; she fought vainly with herself for wanting to stay held so close against him, knowing him intimately, being known. She physically ached with the effort to be free from the hunger to give everything she had to him. In her dreams she would. In her dreams she had.

Allegra's eyes flew open as she woke completely to the stinging flood of heat into her cheeks and to a world that was stirring beneath her in a bewildering yet familiar fashion. Where could she be that the light should be so bright one moment, so softly, coolly darkening the next?

'I'm glad you have had a little sleep, *mignonne*, for it is quite a journey to Fleetwood when we cannot give the horses their heads. . .'

Lady Hawkhurst. At last Allegra remembered. Algie. They were taking Algie to Fleetwood. Quickly she turned to the miserably hunched figure of her brother held comfortably in the Dowager's arms to save him from bumping his head as the carriage swung over what were now but rough country lanes.

'Have we far to go?' Allegra's voice shocked her. She sounded so weak, so completely defeated. . . because they had only been dreams and she had had to wake up. She had wanted to flee them—but even more she had wanted to stay! Safe in Luc's arms where nothing mattered and nothing could ever reach past the shield of his protection to harm her. Safe from facing the waking world in which she and Luc really lived; in which she and Luc must face one another, remembering how they had been only last evening, what might have happened. . .remembering how it had all been destroyed.

Allegra huddled into the reassuring silver softness of her velvet travelling cloak although she knew the day was warm and she did not really need it. Lady Hawkhurst smiled gently at her, suddenly and not at all surprisingly so very calming a presence now they were faced with a real crisis. Lady Hawkhurst knew shock when she saw it. She simply would never in her life guess its true origins.

'We are perhaps two miles from Fleetwood now.

Look.' And she drew back the muslin hangings that shaded the opened carriage windows from the dust and flies beyond, and Allegra felt as if she would never breathe again.

The scent — the sight! As if she had not woken at all, it was so impossibly beautiful. They were passing between trees so ancient, so eternal they must always have been here, their roots sure and deep beneath the rivulets of bluebells and violets, where late snowdrops hung like pearls above the velvet moss, and everywhere the filigree curlicues of the ferns, translucent in the sun. It seemed that the wildness of it must go on forever.

'*Oh!*'

'Indeed, oh!' laughed her companion. 'Even to me it is beautiful and as you know I do *not* at all like the countryside! This is Hawkhurst land now. Passing through this woodland always tells me I am nearly home. I remember when I first came here with my husband. . .' She did not say more. Allegra did not need her to.

All she said herself was, 'You must have been so happy here, madam.' And let the Dowager's smile of serene remembrance be her reply.

Allegra lay back against the squabs and thought, If only I were so happy at this moment, if only I knew what it is to feel what she is recalling so sweetly now! If only I were coming home with Luc. . .

Then it struck her coldly — of course this was not Luc's home at all. Or at least it would not be once his brother Faron was married. What would Luc do then; where would he go? She knew by all the instincts that

had understood Luc so intimately from the first
moment they had met that he must love this place, that
it must draw him back with an urgent promise of peace
that he could never resist, from wherever he might be,
however wonderful and exciting the place. She knew
without thought that it was his longing to come home
to Fleetwood that had sustained him through the
nightmare years in Spain.

What would become of Luc if his brother and Aunt
Lydia married?

But she could not let such dismal thoughts last, not
on a day such as this, vivid and reassuring as spring
blossomed into early summer, not as the carriage at
last glided out of the woods and its perfectly sprung
wheels touched upon the first crumblings of a gravelled
carriageway. Not as she at last resolved, I have lost
him, but I *will* survive it, and understood that the only
way to surmount it in this moment was to forget. Never
let herself think of it for a moment. She would think
only of the sun and the scent of the wild violets — live
only in the moment and for the day. . .

Allegra suddenly found that she was leaning forward,
all but hanging from the window, she was so eager to
see what lay ahead of them. A deep, slow excitement
that she only half understood stirred in her blood
because she had faced her first adult hurdle, and with
real courage. Fleetwood was ahead, unknown, and the
unknown had always been intriguing to her. Fleetwood
did not let her down.

Brought up in the brooding gloom of a great border
fortress on the Marches of Wales, Allegra had only
ever dreamed of houses such as this. Pale gold stone

soaking up the promise of real heat to come as the early afternoon sun began to gild the lush, surrounding valley, the purity of the great mansion's classical structure echoed in the geometric beauty of the Italian gardens that stepped in terrace after terrace towards lawns even now being scythed to the sheen of velvet by a line of gardeners working in timeless rhythm and accompanying themselves with an equally timeless song. Beyond the lawns a vast, glittering lake at the misty centre of which lay an island crowned with a perfect little Grecian temple — and a very tumbledown tree-house indeed.

'Ah, but that is when I know I am back! Regard, Algie!' Lady Hawkhurst nudged her patient to wakefulness. 'See, the boys' tree-house? Quite the most excellent place to go spying on your owls!'

'Owls?' murmured Algie, then suddenly he blinked his lashes open on eyes rounded with awe. 'Oh, may I really? Is it for *me*?'

Lady Hawkhurst smiled and hugged him. It was a measure of Algie's very real pain and fright that for the first time ever Allegra saw her undemonstrative brother hug someone back. As she looked at his unravelling mess of bandages and understood at last just how easily she could have lost him, Allegra — as anyone would have done she told herself — burst into a flood of utterly senseless tears.

Algie was better, no doubt of it. 'Well, it's no good bawling your head off, Sis, 'cos you know you cannot go climbing up trees any more; Papa said so after the last time when. . .well, *you* know what happened. It ain't proper!'

Allegra blew her nose furiously into her very much mangled lace handkerchief and thought, He will be more than fortunate if I don't put him straight back in the need for a surgeon once he is well enough for me to slaughter him!

It was on to this scene of glowering sibling hostility, as the carriage drew gently to a halt in the shadow of the vast Palladian façade, that Luc opened the door and remarked, so blandly, as if nothing had ever gone wrong in their lives for as much as a moment, least of all what had gone wrong between him and Allegra last night, 'Repaired to rude health, I see, Algie, and terrorising your elders as repulsively as ever! How do you feel about a late luncheon scrambled in with a very early dinner? After all, condemned men are always granted a hearty breakfast, but I really don't think your sister plans to leave you alive that long!'

Algie, grinning even though it caused him the acutest pain in the jaw, tried his very best to leap from the carriage. It was only because it was Luc that he did not mind when he found that he was unable to walk. Swung very inelegantly up on to Luc's shoulder, he was in heaven at the thought of sustenance.

'Oh, never mind Allegra; she's just sulking because she can't go up trees! But I'm going. The minute I have eaten my——'

'The only thing you are climbing until I say otherwise is the staircase to bed!'

Because it was Luc, Algie did not even think to argue.

It was Pythagoras, swaying uninvited from Mr Fleetwood's other shoulder, who managed the words Allegra was too stunned to utter. 'Vile Conspiracy!'

Then let her down by adding, vulgarly, and with quite gratuitous irrelevance, 'Wimmin!'

Allegra stamped up the steps behind them wondering how it was that Luc could continue to do this to her. As if this morning's final misunderstanding had never been, here he was, just as infuriating as ever, treating her if anything even more like a child than usual; and here was she — she was obliged to face it — too helplessly besotted to mind it. She always would be. She was even grateful to be so light-heartedly cross with him again, so patronised and so thoroughly ignored. And grateful because she guessed that Luc, so long the man of the world when she was only just beginning to find her place in it, had known all along exactly how she must be feeling. He must know she loved him; he might never forgive her suspicions of his brother but he was going to do his best to make the shattering of her every last dream less impossible to bear.

He *meant* to carry on as if nothing had occurred. And, as she watched him spare his back by sliding a hallooing Algie and parrot up the marble banister of a very imposing central staircase, she found that she was smiling. The tears still stung her eyes but she was laughing.

Growing up was not easy; the next part of it — letting go of all hope of Luc — would be agonising indeed. But Luc, because he was Luc, was going to help her.

She knew they would never talk of what happened. Never talk as they had in the past, so intimately, so passionately, or even so angrily again. But she knew as she watched him disappear round a corner, Pythagoras flapping wildly to hang on, that while he was here she could not mind it. She had grown up so much, she knew that she could be, if not happy, glad of the little she had of him. Glad to have what she knew to be her very short time left of knowing him.

Pushing aside the thought that threatened to upset all this adult wisdom — What if his brother marries my aunt and I shall have to see him, maybe even with his own wife and children one day and never once let anyone see how it matters? — Allegra, with a laugh that was not quite so convincing as she thought, raced recklessly up the stairs in their rioting wake.

'The Yellow Salon!' called Lady Hawkhurst, pausing for breath on her hectic way up behind them. 'Left, right, then left again, and straight on!'

Lady Hawkhurst watched Allegra, trying so hard to be courageous, disappear around the same corner as her brother and Luc and found that she too seemed to be in need of her handkerchief.

Children, she sniffed maternally, could be so exasperating at times. The only thing was, Luc was rather too *big* a child to be given the talking-to his grandmother was so determinedly planning. He could be so towering and intractable. Spoilt, she mused, blaming not herself, of course, but her over-indulgent and now selfishly departed daughter-in-law. Too independent. Too used to his own way. Too stubborn and far, far too proud.

And dangerously close to breaking a very vulnerable young heart indeed.

Lady Hawkhurst pulled herself smartly together. Luc — well, Luc was going to have to listen to her and like it!

'*Gorringe!*'

And behind her she heard the reassuring scramble of her maid's booted feet as the servant sprinted to see what her mistress would be demanding for refreshment.

'Eat it slowly, Algie!' Allegra could not believe the amount of gingerbread Algie had managed to gobble down despite the protestations of his aching jaw.

'But it's lovely——'

'And you——' Luc removed a tray of honeyed sandwiches from his locust-like vicinity '——are meant to be confined to gruel!'

'I—you *wouldn't*!'

Allegra felt her treacherous heart tip over as she saw Luc smile. 'No, you're right, you young ruffian, I wouldn't. Somewhere in my mounting years I've turned as soft as butter!'

Algie took this as a hint that he might take another slice of plum cake. Allegra very hastily had to flee the room. Luc knew then that he had left it perhaps far too late ever to say that he was sorry. But he was going to try it. Nothing that had happened had been Allegra's fault; all she had ever thought or said had been understandable and fair; least of all had he the right to take out his frustration over this impossible mission on someone who had only ever tried to help him.

Damn him for a fool for ever letting himself become so responsible for her!

That did not stop him leaving the room straight after her, leaving Algie to look at Lady Hawkhurst, round-eyed, concerned and his cheeks bulging far too much with cake for him to comment.

Pythagoras did it for him. 'Oh, Gawd!'

The last thing in the world Allegra wanted was that Luc should follow her.

He caught her so easily and somehow she found that whether she had planned it or not he had turned their steps out beneath the great portico, winding between the clipped box hedges of the Italian gardens, heading once more for the magical tranquillity of the woodland beyond the lawns.

They walked a good half-mile in silence as Allegra rapidly passed through many deeply unsettling sensations. I cannot have him here. . .I want to run and run and be where I don't ever have to look at him! I don't want to be alone with him again. . .until I am stronger. Stronger in my defences against him. I don't want to be alone with him ever! But as he opened the parasol he had, with his usual absent-minded thoughtfulness, snatched from the hands of a very startled Sorcha as they set out, she thought, I would not mind now if he were not so *close*. If he did not make me want to be closer. She found she had to keep moving herself away, as if every time she relaxed her guard she was inexorably drawn nearer.

But as the sun showered down and at last she felt the first snap and tangle of the woodland path beneath her feet she began to feel calm. Quiet. Because he was calmed. . . She felt — as she had never thought possible again — serene.

She knew why the moment she looked up at him. Luc was standing very quietly, eyes seemingly fixed on something very distant, some time perhaps, a smile softening the corners of his mouth, whatever expression warmed his unsettling eyes hidden by the comforting shadows.

She spoke without thinking. 'I knew the moment I saw this place that you must love it.'

For a terrible moment, as Luc's skin drained of all colour, she thought, I should not have said it! It was too personal. . .such intimacy for us is finished.

Then he smiled and she knew that, for this moment, it was not.

'Of course I do.' He did not even express surprise that she had guessed it. 'Can you imagine anything better for a boy than this, and a big brother with whom to spend endless, unspoiled days fishing, exploring? Fighting, of course. Playing bandits. Have you seen our tree-house on the lake?'

'Yes. . .' And she knew the moment she spoke that her wistfulness was umistakable.

Luc certainly heard it. He turned to her then, laughing openly, totally relaxed. He sounded—she *knew* he was—completely happy. Just being back at Fleetwood had done this for him. It was catching.

He caught her hand and smiled wryly at her. 'And you would like to climb up to it?'

'Could I——? Oh, but you *brute*, you are only teasing!'

'No, I'm not.' He touched a finger to her lips to silence any interruption. 'I thought that might be Algie's treat. Remember I promised him a celebration in honour of Wellington? I thought we might have a picnic on the island. We could even light a firework— the blacksmith in the village has quite a way with them, if I remember. Set three acres on fire on my eleventh birthday!'

Allegra was dazzled. It was childish, it was idiotic, and never had she wanted to do anything so much in all her life.

'Oh, yes, Luc!' She found she was clinging to his hand with both of hers in delight. 'Algie would love it better than anything in the world. When?'

And when he smiled and murmured, 'Impetuous kitten!' she felt utterly at peace. 'Soon,' he added. When they started walking again he did not let go of her hand and she did not try to take it away—until she saw the bluebells so thickly clustering about her feet that she could barely walk through them. Her first thought was Lady Hawkhurst.

'Luc, would it be all right to pick some for your grandmother? Would anyone mind?' Then she anticipated his laughter, and said, 'No—it would take an army to make even the smallest inroad on this; it is magnificent!' So saying, she started to gather up her booty.

It was almost, as she knelt quite careless of moss stains to her muslin, that she had forgotten Luc was there. And yet not forgotten. She was no longer afraid of what he might think or say or do. Only aware that he was near, her awareness but a gentle warming of her skin as she threw off her cloak the better to acquire her posies. Luc dutifully bent to pick it up and promptly found his pockets stuffed full of bluebells.

'Well, what else can I put them in?' Allegra defended, seeing his eyebrow lift in what threatened to be protest.

'I suppose if you must — so long as you don't expect me to clutch them between my teeth like some serenading Continental suitor!' Then he added drily, 'You might always use your bonnet.'

Which of course made an excellent basket and before Allegra knew it half an hour had passed and another mile and they were deep into the woods where the violets grew safe in the shelter of the medieval oaks and she was utterly worn out with racing about like a three-year-old after this delicate bloom or that.

It was Luc who collapsed first, having the good sense to toss her cloak over the dampness of the grass before falling on to it in theatrical exhaustion. . .the better to watch her as she stood in front of him, her cheeks glowing and her eyes ablaze with happiness.

Disarmed, off guard, he held out a hand to her and Allegra took it, falling to her knees beside him. Looking at him. For a long moment their eyes locked. Spoke so much that words never could. Things Allegra almost understood now.

She broke their silence, but there was no nervousness any longer in her hectic, 'Thank you!'

'Thank my brother when you see him.' Luc smiled. Just for the briefest second Allegra saw something flash into his eyes, hot, angry. . .worried. But it was gone as quickly as it came and Luc was saying, 'You act as if you had never seen a bluebell in your life. Where can you live that is so rugged and inhospitable? I had not quite pictured you marooned on some rocky ocean outcrop.'

'It might just as well be!' Allegra's sigh was heartfelt. 'It is very grand, of course; Edward the First built it

. . .obviously not by himself. . .it's a castle. A big one. Where the Black Mountains of Wales meet England. It was put there to stop the ——'

'Natives revolting?'

'Idiot! The only trouble is it is the castle that is revolting. To live in, I mean. You cannot have the least notion, Luc, having a home as beautiful as this. Some of our walls are so dripping with damp they are *green* with fungus! Algie scrapes it off and keeps it in little dishes. Herr Kraftstein moved to stop him when he tried to make it grow on breadcrumbs.'

'That really is a repulsive child you have there.'

'I know,' she sighed, and thinking of brothers let her ask, 'Luc, where will you live? I mean, if—if your brother were to marry my aunt? How can you bear to have to leave?'

And at last she understood the light of contentment in his eyes. 'I never shall. Come and see!'

This time as they walked his arm was about her waist where it had been from the moment he swung her to her feet, and again she felt so secure with him that she did not draw away.

'There.'

At the far edge of the woods, beyond a tumbling stream, reached by a tiny stone bridge only just wide enough for a carriage to pass, as far as the eye could see until they blended with the soft Somersetshire hills, lay meadows, wild with grasses and hot with mass upon mass of poppies where the corn still grew in what had once been cultivated fields.

'Here. This is where I shall live.'

And Allegra found she had tucked herself closer

beneath his shoulder, just because she needed to be part of his contentment.

He allowed her to be. 'It was once a thriving estate but has long been derelict. Not long before my father died he bought it for me. I think he hoped it would bring me out of the army, out of the war. After Faron was hurt it was almost more than Papa could bear to have me in Spain, he was so certain I would never return. But—well, I knew this would always be here, waiting. I wasn't ready, I was too young, I wanted to fight. I suppose I was selfish, but my father understood. . .'

'I think he must have been very proud of you. I think you know he was.' She felt his arm tighten and knew that, somehow, just those few words from her had dissolved for him long years of guilt.

'Yes. And now I can do what he really wanted—be near to Faron; look after Fleetwood. My brother really *is* quite useless, you know!' And suddenly his mood lightened and he was tugging Allegra across the bridge, out into the centre of the meadow to where a vast oak stood alone, from where she could at last see where an ancient manor house had been.

'Destroyed in a fire. Deliberately, of course.' She heard the anger sear into his voice. 'It was mortgaged to the hilt but well-insured.'

It was not the first time she had heard such a story. England was littered with small estates crippled by the war where the owners had found their own way out of bankruptcy, fleeing to the Indies with the insurance money, leaving their labourers and servants destitute to fend for themselves.

'I'm going to make it work again. It has only been seven years; nothing is irreparable.' Then suddenly Allegra felt he was looking at her. 'Nothing has to be lost forever. Nothing!'

And she was looking at him. 'No. . .'

It was not over! As he bent to kiss her Allegra's arms were already about his neck. They were both laughing. It felt to Allegra very much as if she had drowned in brandy. . . Certainly she could not stand. Even though he barely held her, barely touched her, even though each kiss was but the softest grazing of his lips across hers, she was shaking so much she was helpless. Her arms tightened about him and she felt his laughter mingling with hers as they both fought vainly for a steadying breath.

It was the sun, it was the summer. It was the second chance. Allegra felt she would die from the happiness of it.

A third party, however, felt otherwise.

'Awk! Lay orf the laidy!' Pythagoras — in his ripest Cockney. 'Guv'na!' he added when he saw who it was he was talking to.

'I — *Pythagoras*!' Allegra was still too dizzy to think, but slowly she was beginning to realise. Pythagoras, swinging beadily in the branches above them.

'Oh — oh, dear God, but he's run away *again*! Algie will never forgive me! I — what on earth do you find to amuse you so, Luc Fleetwood?' For she had been so very abruptly set free. Mr Fleetwood needed both his arms to hug himself as he all but doubled up in hysterics. Allegra, bewildered, shaken, her lips still tender, tingling from his touch, scowled — and lost her very fragile temper. 'Well, is that not just typical of a man? Just when you are most needed you must be so helpless as to be *useless*!'

Which disabled her victim so much, he had to sit down, he was laughing so painfully. Until he saw what it was Allegra was intending.

She was halfway up the tree to recapture her parrot before he was on his feet to stop her. Allegra found herself clasped uncompromisingly by the ankle, and Pythagoras even more ruthlessly by the beak.

'Ow!' Allegra.

'Aww!' The startled parrot.

'Let go of me, Luc, do you *want* me to lose him?'

'Just at this moment I should be happy to lose the both of you! Get down this instant, you infernal child!'

'I. . .*what* did you just call me?'

'Infernal! But let go the bird's beak and see what he comes up with! Will you get down or do I have to pull you——?'

'You wouldn't!'

He did. Pythagoras flapped to the ground, disaffected with his taste of freedom. Allegra fell heavily into Luc's arms and right into a situation she was never for a moment going to be able to handle.

Luc was blazingly, raging angry.

'Ye gods, can you think of no simpler a means of killing yourself?'

'I——'

'Will *never* do that again, do you understand me, Allegra?'

'You——'

Luc kissed her so hard then, with a violence so

shocking, that Allegra stumbled back against the tree, clinging to it for support, too stunned to cling to him.

This was different. This was new. And it was in both of them. It was frightening.

Luc's mouth never left hers for a second as, one hand each side of her, he trapped her so completely that the oak bark cut into her back. . .and she felt herself move against him, understanding why she did. . .even as he pinned her hard against the oak trunk with one fierce thrust of his hips, and held her there. . .until she was nothing but the blood beating so frantically as it cried out to his, nothing but an engulfing, burning darkness as he blotted out the sun and she felt at last her hands, weak, instinctive, reaching out for him, pulling him closer. Deep into his hair, curling about his shoulders as she listened as if from a great distance to their breathing — broken, desperate, hungry. . .

It was like that for her, as if she would starve to death if she could not touch him. Without even knowing it, as she felt at last the rhythm of his kisses alter, deepen, as she felt it penetrate every last nerve until its echo began to pulse at the very core of her, she found she had slipped her hands beneath his loose country coat, urgent for the heat of his skin through the soft linen of his shirt, awed by the feel of it burning into her palms. Moving without knowing how or why, as his fingers lifted to her throat and began a gentle, stroking caress until her neck was so weak with her need for him that she could not hold up her head and it fell back into his urgent hands, her hair tumbling from its pins, and Allegra caught her arms about his waist to keep herself from falling.

Cold, metallic, terrifying, the pistol met her questing fingers.

Pistol? Just an idea, a long-distant thought, as she was pulled hard into Luc's body and she knew that there was to be no turning back. . . .

Pistol!

The truth burst over her like a storm of lightning. Allegra thrust him away, panting with a fear so primitive she could not express it.

He misunderstood. She knew it even as she watched him smile — gentle, reassuring, his eyes black with the promise that he would love her as no one could ever love her again. Here. Beneath the sun among the poppies.

She tried to speak. She couldn't. How could she explain that he had done the impossible? He had reminded her that there was danger even at Fleetwood. He had brought all her misery and fear into this magical, inviolate world.

Even as she realised he carried the pistol only to protect her, because the people they were ranged against were dangerous, the stakes too high to take the slightest risk. . .even as she knew all that Allegra could not bear it.

Without a word, without looking back, she ran faster than she had ever run in her life towards the safety of the house.

Away from the danger in Luc Fleetwood.

Of course he would come after her. She had expected him to catch her before she even reached the woods. The fact that he had not was the most disturbing thing of all. Allegra hunched miserably on a window-seat in the Yellow Salon wishing to heaven that Lady Hawkhurst had not taken Algie off to bed. Wondering if she should not flee to her own bed herself. Only she knew he would come for her even there. Because she knew that Luc had never been so angry.

He was. It was the way he shut the door so quietly that disturbed her the most. He was so controlled again. So determined that she would explain the impossible. . .

She had not run from him!

Or had she?

For the first time ever she was grateful for the sight of Pythagoras, recaptured and glad to be indoors again. He could always make Luc laugh.

'Here comes trouble!' Pythagoras blurted.

Luc failed singularly to be amused. His mouth was set in unremitting fury.

'If you are not silent, Pythagoras. . .!' he all but hissed at the bird.

The parrot's beak dropped upon in astonishment. 'Eh?'

'*Silence!*'

Pythagoras was silent.

Allegra, desperate now to escape the coming confrontation any way she could, attempted flippancy. 'I had never thought to see you bully a dumb animal——'

'*Dumb!*'

It wasn't working but she floundered on. 'Well, helpless, then. You ought not to shout at poor Pythagoras——'

'You would rather I yelled at you, ma'am?' And at last he was standing over her with real menace. 'Good—because I much prefer it to have my victim's permission!'

Allegra tried to get to her feet. She was peremptorily pushed off them again. 'Sit down!'

Now what should she do?

The very worst happened. She knew it. . .it was always going to. Because—well, he looked so very wonderful when he was angry.

'Do not even *think* to smile your way out of this, my lady!'

It was inevitable. Allegra—because she was shocked and scared and so hopelessly in love with him—burst into gales of laughter.

Luc was utterly astounded. She had run from him—*afraid* of him! *Now*, after all they had been through! After the exquisite peace of this afternoon when they had been so truly friends.

When they had been meant to be lovers.

He knew he had been in the wrong. But he knew that knowing it would not have stopped him. They had gone beyond that; now he *had* to have her. Whatever the cost. And she was laughing at it. . .

And then, miraculously, he knew that she was not the only one who had to grow up. He saw himself through her newly adult eyes——spoilt, moody. . . ridiculous.

Allegra could not believe it, but she acted on what she thought were the beginnings of a rueful smile.

'You really are quite magnificent——'

'If you say I look wonderful when I'm angry I will—

slowly, and very, *very* painfully — tear you limb from limb!'

'I'll defend you!' cried Pythagoras.

Then just as they began to laugh together, tentatively, almost shyly, new people, treading new ground, friends who had come a very long way in a very short time, they both heard the crumbling on the gravel. A spanking new curricle driven with anything but spanking style.

And Luc replied to the parrot drily, 'Put up your sword, Pythagoras; here comes one with prior claim to disembowel me!'

'Good gracious!' Allegra knelt dramatically on the window-seat. 'It's *Cuthbert*!'

'Breathing fire, from which I take it your St George has come to rescue you from my loathsome clutches.'

'It was the dragon breathed the fire, not St G——'

'You know, it is absolutely beyond me——' and suddenly Luc began to laugh quite helplessly again '—what any man can want with a wife even half so pedantic as you are!'

He was not to know that to Allegra, ashamed, with not the first clue how to escape her ludicrous engagement, such a crushing remark was not the least bit funny at all. Because she was angry, and hurt — after all he *could* have sounded a little more aggrieved that she was still betrothed to Cuthbert — she turned and glared at him stonily. 'Why is he here, Luc?'

Still laughing, for once the observant Mr Fleetwood failed to see the warning signs.

'Well, why do you think? Employ that pea-sized

brain of yours for once, my kitten. . .where else should I want Cuthbert to be but under my eye until——?'

'You—you *invited* him? You——'

And, not at all sure what he had done wrong—therefore righteously convinced it was nothing—Luc began to lose his equally ungovernable temper. 'Of course I did, dammit! Allegra, this is not a game——'

'I know it is not a game, you. . .you *worm*! It was my brother was nearly killed! I——'

'I know it! Why do you think you are here but that Algie swears your own aunt involved in it and nothing will shake his story? By God, have you *anything* rattling inside that skull of yours——?'

'*Naw!*'

'That's it! That bird goes out! I——'

'You leave Pythagoras alone, you great bully!' Allegra flew at once to stand shoulder to shoulder with her parrot. Luc saw them both looking at him with unequalled hauteur and completely exploded.

'Now—no, do not even *think* to interrupt, Allegra, because believe me you will not enjoy it if you do!'

Allegra fought the treacherous thought that she probably would enjoy it, very much, and glared even more hotly back. She did not quite dare speak.

'Good! Now, if you can ignite just one spark of life into that brain of yours, it might just occur to you that we cannot overlook the fact that the Divine Cuthbert may play quite the greatest part in this mystery. I am even beginning to wonder if your removal from London was not engineered——'

Allegra froze. 'I. . .are you saying that—that Cuthbert fought Freddie knowing Papa would have me sent to Aunt Lydia?' She was too stunned with hurt to ask *why*.

He told her. 'It would make sense of the fact that Lydia wrote to you, that she knew you were already set out to visit her. She *did* know to expect you. It also makes sense that your London house should be so conveniently empty for a while.'

Ice-cold with pain, she managed, 'Whatever for?'

'Think, Allegra; it is your father these people most need to discredit. Think if something incriminating were to be planted among his papers. . .yes, I *was* deliberately set on the wrong track in coming to Bath. No. . .no, that still makes no sense. . .'

He was so taken up with his theories that he did not even see what he had done. Allegra watched him and thought, Maybe it is true and even Cuthbert does not care for me. Maybe Luc is right and I am nothing any man would fight for. Not without another secret motive. After all, why should anyone want me that badly?

The door blew open to reveal a hot and panting Cuthbert; a Cuthbert with the gleam of battle in his eye. And suddenly Allegra thought, Is it all an act? Am I only being used? Even by Cuthbert? And by Luc?

She was glad for Cuthbert's ringing, 'Sir, a word, if you would be so civil!' She desperately needed an excuse to flee the room.

Flee to where? She did not know the house and so she wandered disconsolately until she found a picture gallery full of tough and quelling ancestors, all looking so disconcertingly like Luc.

She had nearly given herself to him — her skin burned with the horror, the shame of it; she knew it was true. She could not have stopped him. She had not wanted to stop herself. She had had no thought of anything at all but her love for him.

And now maybe, maybe even *that*, that blind, reckless passion she had felt shattering all his ruthless self-control to nothing, maybe it had all been untrue!

Plainly it made sense to Luc that Cuthbert did not really want her. He saw nothing odd in it that she might just be an unwanted pawn in this game of treachery. He could not see that to Cuthbert she might be special. Or to Freddie, or to any of the others who had so convincingly declared their love for her. . .

Even Luc had done that. . .with his body if nothing more he had declared a need of her that saturated his blood, an absolute need to be part of her. . .

Maybe none of it was true.

Allegra pressed her head to the glass of the gallery window and took a long, deep breath. This had to stop. Now. She had to stop herself, and this stupid, childish longing for what could never be. From now on she would smile at him, be civil to him, even laugh and joke with him if she must for Lady Hawkhurst and for Algie's sake. But she would never be vulnerable to him again. Never disarmed. Not now.

Now she would never completely trust him again.

She was ice-calm with grief and shock as she ruthlessly forced herself to let go her hopes and so she turned quite casually to greet the footsteps; probably a servant come to show her the way to her chambers.

It was a stranger. Or would have been, had he not

been standing at that moment beneath a portrait so unmistakably an ancestor. So like Luc!

'Hello,' said the Earl of Hawkhurst. 'You must be the heartless creature my brother is even now fighting over in the library.'

She was so astonished, not least by his lack of astonishment, that all she could find to say was, 'They *were* in the Yellow Salon. . .oh, *no!*'

Lord Hawkhurst had the most friendly, the most comforting laughter. '*Were*, yes, but I wanted that; just got home and all that, you know. Couldn't have them barging about when I'm so exhausted. . .besides, I have a fondness for my furniture. . .'

'You are. . .' Allegra checked very carefully for the glint in his vivid blue eyes that would tell her this was only jesting '. . .only *roasting* me, sir. They are not *actually*. . .'

And something in her own eyes told her new companion the truth. Certainly he said very gently, 'I was only teasing. Now, how do you say that you and I return to the salon and send for a pot of lemon tea?'

Allegra found she was laughing quite genuinely. 'Not brandy? It usually is with your family!'

There was a real silkiness to Lord Hawkhurst's still damaged voice that quite startled her then. 'No, I think that should be saved for what is left of Mr Nettlesham, don't you? Now come along and tell me how you shall like it having me to be your uncle!'

Allegra went back to the salon with him, dazedly wondering if she would ever in her life begin to fathom this bizarre family out.

## CHAPTER TEN

A WHOLE hour later, and Lady Hawkhurst, in full Gallic flow, still berating the errant Faron for his quite staggering lack of remorse at having disappeared on them without one word of warning, Mr Fleetwood sauntered back into the room. His expression was grim, until he saw that Allegra was watching him, and then, instantly, that impenetrable mask of well-bred insouciance came down, erasing every last trace of expression from his eyes but the lazy, sardonic laughter she could no longer trust in any more. His manner was so deliberately his most nonchalantly ironic that it hurt.

'It pains me to have to say this, Allegra, but you really are the most perilous female to have for an acquaintance. Mr Nettlesham has just challenged me to pistols at dawn, in my own home, no less!'

'To — *what*? In this house? But that is *scandalous*!' Two could play at this frivolously aristocratic unconcern.

'Yes, isn't it? And I'm most touched by your concern for my person — comforting to know in one's final moments that the social delicacies have not passed everyone by!' There was nothing at all in his expression but humour, yet Allegra scented real anger in his words.

At her playing his own sophisticated game? She *had* to, now she had begun; Allegra smiled her most brittle débutante's smile and replied, though the words were like lead in her throat,

'Oh. . .well, I beg your pardon. Of course I shouldn't like you to be killed! But. . .Luc, what are you going to do with poor Cuthbert?'

He smiled then, taking in his whole admiring audience — grandmother, brother, Algie and parrot — then grinned. 'I limped regretfully across the library, bravely waving aside all offers of assistance, and contrived. . . just in time. . .to collapse on to the nearest sofa. I think you will find your Cuthbert most fastidiously embarrassed.'

'Oh, Luc, but what a *scurvy* ——'

'Yes, cowardly, wasn't it? But I did not feel I could burden my brother with the disposal of one of your suitors ——'

'Can't see why not; plenty of compost needs gingering up,' put in Lord Hawkhurst, so plainly used to playing up to his brother's fooling, so obviously, even paternally fond of him.

He got what he deserved. 'Ah, *Faron*, now we are all here and my Honourable nemesis is safely taking a cooling stroll around the lily ponds, contrive, if you can possibly begin to make me believe it ——' then he exploded completely ' — to tell me where the sweet *Hades* you have *been*! You had us worried *senseless*! I ——'

'Sound like a bleating nursemaid to me,' flattened his brother with unexpected firmness. 'Sit down and rest your limp and I'll tell you all what happened. Not that I understand it myself. Thing is. . .' he nudged a fallen log on to the early evening fire with the toe of his boot '. . .had a *most* peculiar note from Lydia, saying she was in trouble. Can't have that, you know!'

Aunt Lydia again? But. . .it made no sense! Allegra looked swiftly at Luc and saw that it made no sense to him either.

'Wait on it,' he demanded of his brother. 'You say that Lydia sent a note calling you away from Bath?'

'That's right.'

'Yet she sent one to Lady Allegra to let her know she was *in* Bath and expecting her any moment at Pulteney Street! From where was your note from Lydia sent?'

'London. Can't say I made much of it, just that it was even more of a scramble than usual even for Lydia so I thought I'd better see to it at once. . .'

'You're sure it was from Lydia?'

'Positive. Always getting them. . .notes I mean. Do this, do that, help, help, and all that. That aunt of yours needs taking in hand, if I may say so.' Lord Hawkhurst turned sternly to Allegra as if it were in some way her fault that Aunt Lydia was such a thorough-going menace.

She fought vainly not to laugh, because he was just as Luc had said he would be. He seemed such fun, so good-natured. . .and rather endearingly silly. And without any doubt at all deeply in love with the undeserving Lydia. It twisted Allegra's heart to see it. Faron Hawkhurst did not even know the damage such a match might do, and if he did he would never care.

So very like his brother.

To bury that far too tender and undermining thought

she put in, 'We had all supposed you must have. . . well——'

'Bolted for the border? Lydia! Good gad, the gel's *far* too lazy! Come to think on it, so am I.'

'Yes. . .' Allegra turned her choke of laughter into a most unconvincing sneeze. 'Excuse me. I can see that now.' Meaning never had any couple born been half so well, if disastrously, suited! 'Only, we were *half* right — you *had* vanished because of Aunt Lydia. Only you were called *to* London, which makes a nonsense of Luc's theory that my family were to be lured *away*.'

'Not entirely.' Luc's voice had a definite edge to it now. 'After all, Lydia was not there when Faron arrived.'

'And never had been! So I asked about a few of her friends and acquaintances, but no one had seen her; besides, the only servant left at Alderley House would insist upon it that you and young Algie had been sent to Pulteney Street. So I came back to Bath and found you'd all gone from there and the only thing left to think was that you must all have been invited here by Tiffy.' The quite towering unlikelihood of this notion seemed not in the least to unsettle him. 'You know what, Luc, there's something dashed peculiar about this whole business. . .hadn't we ought to be doing something about it?'

Unbelievably, Allegra found her laughing eyes had met Luc's and that, before they could help themselves, they smiled.

She had less to smile about, however, when she realised that her part in his plans for the immediate future was to keep the Honourable Mr Nettlesham occupied. The thought of drifting through the bluebells borne along by the soft breezes of his abominable poetry put her quite finally off any thought of being gracious at dinner. The next few days were going to be the most appalling struggle.

Just how much of a struggle even she could never have imagined, although she had had from the very first an inkling that the greater part of her battle would be keeping her fingers from Luc's throat.

Luc, who knew her far better than she liked, consequently seemed to be taking the most careful precautions never to be caught with her alone. But, late one evening, searching yet again for her hated embroidery that had been pilfered as usual by the parrot, Allegra came upon Luc alone and unguarded, and suddenly, however much she wanted to turn and run from him, she knew that she would never forgive herself if she did. He looked weary too. But she was far too hurt and angry to care about it.

'Luc, I want to talk to you.' She astonished herself with the cool, unwavering command in her voice.

His response was all too masculine and predictable. He groaned, 'Not now, Allegra, I'm tired. Besides, I am in the middle of——'

'Staring out of the window doing absolutely nothing so far as I can see!' she retorted, ruthlessly ignoring his exhausted gesture in the direction of a table littered with maps and papers. 'Certainly not telling me what is happening!'

'Probably because, since you are now quite safe at Fleetwood, it is no longer any of your——'

'Not my concern!' Allegra had not realised she had

the energy left in her to explode. But she had, and she
did, and it felt wonderful! 'Oh, no, of course not. I'm
a *female*! And I must leave everything up to the men —
who as far as I can see have not the slightest
notion — '

'I might, if I could get a minute's peace!'

'Ah, yes. Peace! So meanwhile I am condemned to
day after *day* of Cuthbert. While you are sitting about
trying to make use of your *minuscule* brain, Cuthbert
is writing me odes — and I am having to listen to them!'

It was because he nearly laughed, because even
though he felt his bones had turned to dust with
weariness as he struggled to make sense of this plot
that could bring the country to its knees today,
tomorrow. . .perhaps it was already too late. . .one
look at Allegra, tense and hostile as a wild cat, and all
sense of danger and urgency was gone in a flood of
pride and laughter. And need. . .

It was because he needed her that he was behaving
so badly. Because he needed her to see he was tired
and confused and not some great Romantic hero
capable of righting the whole insane world with just
one finger. . .

It was because she was glaring at him as if she had
never in her life seen anything less like a hero. And
even in his relief he resented it.

It was because *she* confused him. *She* was the heart
of his problem. She had been from the very beginning.
Just as from the very beginning he had determined she
must not be.

Luc wanted to take her in his arms and feel that
instinctive awe of the hunger in him, her helpless,

urgent response; so even more badly did he want her to get out of the room, out of his sight, so that he could try to get her out of his mind where he had never planned for anyone to be. Least of all a girl so young that she lacked all restraint, so impulsive that she. . .

He turned on her so savagely because he would not think of what had almost happened. Or her.

'You are the one agreed to marry Nettlesham, my lady; no one did it for you. *You* said yes, now live with it!' He spoke so cruelly because the very thought of her with any other man ripped his insides to pieces.

She never had a hope of understanding, of course. Allegra watched as Luc swung more abruptly than ever between irony and anger and thought, That is cruel! He knows how I feel; he knows I never meant to agree to Cuthbert. . .he knows because I cried so stupidly in his arms and he comforted me. I thought he understood. It was cruel; Luc, who had not a cruel bone in his body. . .except when he was faced with her. Did he hate the sight of her so badly? Even though he wanted her even more, she knew that.

Yes. It was possible. It was more likely than anything that his anger was because he wanted her even while he could not find even a shred of respect for her. She began to understand a little that he was raging at himself for his weakness in wanting what he could only despise.

Hurt stung through her. Because she would not bear the force of his self-disgust. . .because she could not . . .she hurt him back.

'What I shall never be able to understand is how such a family as yours, which has such wonderful

people as your brother and your grandmother in it,
ever came to produce a monster like you! I cannot
believe someone as kind and generous as Lord
Hawkhurst is related to — '

'No?' She would never begin to know how badly that
cut him. Nor how deeply. He cut back, even deeper.
'Well, don't look to Faron to rescue you from
Cuthbert, my lady. . .one of your family already has
my brother in her toils!'

He could not have said it! Allegra's cheeks flared
with humiliation and pain. He saw it and he knew he
must undo it.

But Allegra gave him no chance. She turned and left
the room so silently, it was as if he could reach out and
feel it like a wall of ice between them. Completely
shutting him out, as he deserved. As he wanted. . .
*must* want!

Allegra made her way blindly to her chamber thinking, He despises me that much! To imagine I might. . .
what?. . .try to entrap his brother? Just because Faron
has all the lightness of spirit Luc has lost. What she
would not admit to herself was that her tears, when
they came, hot and silent, were for Luc in that moment.
She knew she had been the witness to a bitter jealousy,
born out of guilt for his brother's hurt in the war when
he had only been in Spain to look after Luc for their
father; she knew Luc would never forgive himself for
not protecting Faron. She cried because it was such a
waste that he should feel so alone and tainted, because
he was haunted by inner shadows he did not deserve.
She cried because he envied his brother his innocence,
because he was not even surprised she should say that

Faron was the better man. She cried because she had never meant it; it was not true.

Luc thought, just for a moment, that he must follow her — then he felt it again, like a kick to the stomach, the sick, brutal ugliness of jealousy that had engulfed him when she spoke of his brother, that burned like acid deep inside him now.

He hated it, and her for making him feel it. And most of all himself. Because the thought of her admiring any other man was intolerable. . .

Yet he was meant to want it.

Luc laughed at himself then, with bitter mockery. Had he been his brother or any other man he would have now got spectacularly drunk. But he was the controlled one, the one everybody always leaned on, the one who expected the impossible of himself because so did everyone else. Luc threw aside the brandy Faron had left on the table where he had been struggling to make sense of instructions come from London this morning and hooking a chair towards him with his boot, Luc sat down and did what he had always done: lost himself in work. That way he did not have to imagine that Allegra was crying. Least of all because of him.

Of the two of them it was Allegra awoke next morning knowing that this could not be allowed to go on, who determined that if it was the last thing she did she would not quarrel with him again.

The next time they met she smiled quite calmly at him. 'Good morning.'

Luc was left to watch her as she strolled away on Cuthbert's arm, playing her part although it was killing her, and to understand something he had not before: maturity had nothing to do with age. Just in this moment Allegra might have been a hundred years wiser than he was.

He should have fought the knowledge, his unwanted pride in her courage, but he found that he was smiling as he watched her.

And for a whole two days they were so impeccably civil to one another that Lord Hawkhurst was moved to remark to Algie that one or other of their siblings must be seriously unwell, leaving Algie with a vague but nagging puzzlement at her incomprehensibly good behaviour.

But just as it really began to worry him he discovered to his greatest relief that it could never last.

Algernon, Marquess Stonyhurst, did not enjoy his lessons. Maintaining only the most distant relationship with his intellect, he would attend the things, if he must, occasionally spraying down a note or two with an ill-mended pen, then leaning his elbow in large blots upon his efforts while making little doodles in the sand tray. He had long since been designated 'stony ground' by his exasperated, even despairing tutor.

Algie sighed at the prospect of a morning of mathematics ahead. It really wasn't on for a fellow to have to use his head when it still sported lumps on it the size of duck eggs nearly a week after its brush with the Grim Reaper. He sighed again; his new passion was bugs; the bigger, the uglier, the more repulsive the bug the better. And he had just found one.

'Damned if I've seen one of those before!' remarked

his companion as they lay side by side, heads poked under the sideboard.

'Ain't too amusin', is it?' remarked his second confederate, sliding under to join them. 'Not before *breakfast* and all that.'

'Well, don't poke at it with that eye-glass!' Then Algie remembered to whom he was speaking. 'Sir.'

Allegra, after two more days of Cuthbert, two days of viewing Luc Fleetwood only at so cautious a distance that invective and murder were rendered so frustratingly impossible that she was obliged to be good, descended wanly to breakfast to be met by three pairs of top-booted legs blocking her way to her anticipated refreshment.

She had been waiting for her chance; but she had never hoped to be blessed with one as good as this. So she remarked sweetly, 'Whatever it is, Lord Hawkhurst, please do not let Algie put it in his pocket. It will only climb out again and I really could not face it blinking at me from the marmalade. Since I cannot trust your brother. . .' At which point she accidentally and with painful purpose, stood on the leg that looked the most familiar.

'Ouch! Dammit!' The Honourable Mr Fleetwood sat up in his haste to wring her smug little neck and banged his head on the sideboard.

'Not,' reproved Algie and his brother, 'in front of a lady!'

'That,' growled Luc, to Allegra's deepest satisfaction, 'is not a lady!'

Allegra pounced. 'In that case I cannot see that I must continue to be excluded from whatever it is you have all been whispering about these past few days. And *don't* say you haven't. . .' Then the plea broke into her voice because one more morning of Cuthbert would break her. '*Please!*'

She looked and sounded so much like a child who was not allowed out to play with the bigger children that Luc, in at last relenting, began to be honest with himself about what it was he had been doing to her: punishing her with Cuthbert. Punishing her for rejecting him, for so obviously preferring his brother. For running away from what she knew had happened between them. For letting him run. For no longer trusting him.

Not for one moment able to imagine the reason why — that he had so deeply wounded her — her rejection had hurt him as nothing had ever done before. For days now she had been so exquisitely polite that she might just as well not have been Allegra at all. Not his Allegra, the one who fought and scratched as mercilessly as the kitten she had always seemed to him. He had punished her for that too — for taking his so vulnerable, so trusting kitten away.

He did not like himself for it. Because he knew now how selfish he was being; knew that before his eyes a child had turned into a woman, a woman who had always had a mind of her own and an independence of spirit more than the equal of his. Just because he had taken one look at her and wanted to keep her warm and safe — curled in a basket with an endless supply of milk and caresses! he mocked himself — just because he wanted her to be helpless, to need him, it did not mean she ever would.

Luc rubbed the imprint of her heel from his thigh and saw her at last as she really was: beautiful, funny, angry—and resolutely strong. She did not need anyone. Least of all did she need him.

That was the moment he knew he was going to make her.

Allegra met his gaze steadily, beginning to understand. . .that he believed she had escaped from her love of him and he did not like it. Why did he not?

Did she dare let herself be drawn back? His smile alone could make her. After all, they had always been meant to be friends.

'We were only keeping it a secret because you'd tell Algie and ruin the surprise,' he explained.

'I——'

'Yes, you would!' put in Algie, bug forgotten as his eyes blinked at the words he liked best—'Algie' and 'surprise'. 'I'd have sat on you and made you talk! *What* secret?'

It was Lord Hawkhurst, deftly ducking aside as Algie tossed down his hapless beetle, who told him, 'We thought we'd have a picnic.'

'Picnics are for girls!'

'One more word out of you, you ungrateful little toad, and you won't be getting anything!' Never had Algie heard Luc Fleetwood so stern.

'Sorry!' He meant it.

'That's better. Moreover, picnic is all you are going to know until we get where we are going. You will have to wait and see. . .'

They waited and saw.

Even Cuthbert Nettlesham exclaimed in delighted

astonishment. On a gentle rise above the lake, in the shade of a giant cedar, the grass had been spread with a host of ancient Persian rugs, piled high with the most luxurious of cushions. Boxes and baskets of luncheon — and the inevitable cakes — had been transported to the shade of the trees by Allegra's own footman and Sorcha who were even now bending to cool bottles of lemonade and wine in a pool of rushes. Behind them, in a sunlit clearing in the woods, was pitched a very creditable campaign headquarters made up of what must be the remnants of Luc and Faron's military exploits. To wit: one sorry tent — leaky — two blankets — disgustingly mangled — and on a battered old campaign chest stood a lantern, a telescope, a cobwebbed bottle of rum — empty — a pistol — broken — and a map of the lake weighted down by a very pock-marked cannon ball indeed.

But best of all, their makeshift sails painted brightly in the colours of the British Union and of France, two rowing boats hugged the shore of the lake, and Algie was transported to heaven.

'Oh. . .I. . .!'

'Trafalgar! Then luncheon. We're the French.' Luc and Faron suddenly managed to look monstrously Gallic and threatening.

'And I'm Nelson?'

'Of course.'

Allegra was enchanted; she could barely believe it. All this time she had been so angry with Luc for deserting her and — she saw it now — having Cuthbert under the strictest orders to steer her away from any activity that looked remotely interesting — and all the

time they had been plotting this wondrous treat for
Algie. It must have taken them hours of clandestine
effort to manage it. They had even painted the word
*Victory* along the side of Algie's flagship in very wobbly
lettering indeed.

'Luc, Lord Hawkhurst. . .and *you*, Cuthbert!'
Allegra rounded on them, not even beginning to know
what to say.

Cuthbert blushed with happiness. 'Well, *had* to keep
you out of the way, what? Fleetwood explained. But
they would not tell me *quite* what they were about in
case, well. . .tongue runs away and all that. . .and I
must say. . .' For the first time ever Allegra realised
that Cuthbert was human. A little boy as lonely and as
entranced as Algie now gazed out of those longing
eyes.

Algie saw it. 'You had better be the English with
me, Mr Nettlesham.' Then he explained rather shyly,
'Thing is, I've never been allowed to sail before. . .'

Everyone looked at Cuthbert then, at Cuthbert's
painfully contricting fashionability. . .and saw a new
man. Cuthbert was struggling out of his coat like a
migrating salmon. 'It has been a very long time, young
Algie, but. . .well, I always liked boats best of all,
don't you know!'

Allegra and Lady Hawkhurst, knowing better than
to insist on joining them on the water, waved them off
in suitable adulatory fashion. Algie hummed what
appeared to be the 'Marseillaise' until he remembered
he wasn't the French and tried for 'Heart of Oak'
instead.

They were to do battle for the island and Algie roared with delight when he saw what with.

'Oh, may I *really* throw them at you?'

'You can throw,' taunted Luc, 'but you won't hit!' And with that he carefully divided a very large stock of missiles indeed, made — and the washermaids were *not* going to like this — almost entirely from a loathsomely sticky mess of oatmeal and water. Allegra crowed with laughter when Algie tried one out, just when Luc was not expecting it.

Mr Fleetwood wiped his eye and returned with very Napoleonic menace, 'This means war!'

The battle was on, and for an hour missiles rained furiously down, some flung so carelessly that the civilians on shore were in very real danger of being annihilated. Herr Kraftstein stared in stunned disbelief as at last he understood that all the things he had ever been warned to watch out for in the English were true, and Pythagoras — who had once been to sea for real and had not taken to it in the slightest — retreated to the safety of a very interesting dish of sweetmeats indeed. The dogs barked highly partisan encouragement and Lady Hawkhurst forgot herself and yelled, '*Vive l'empereur! Vive Napoléon!*'

Allegra ducked a very badly aimed shot from Cuthbert and complained, 'Algie, will you please tell your henchman I am on your side?'

The boats rocked perilously but she knew her brother was safe. Cuthbert really did know boats, his cleanly dipping oars tacking the *Victory* in lively fashion just out of Luc and Faron's reach, racing for landfall on the island. Algie swayed precariously in the stern, standard — painted hand-towel — in hand ready to leap out and plant it in triumph at the top of the tree-house.

It was — Allegra caught her breath — the most magical, the most ridicuous of days, with the most magical, the most ridiculous of families. The lump in her throat tightened. If only it could always be like this! Never had she seen her lonely little brother half so much at home, let alone a fraction as happy. Never had she seen anyone do so much just to please a child as Luc.

She knew it was all for Algie, for she knew that Luc did not want her; he was not being kind to her brother in the hope of winning favour in her eyes. She stood uncaring of the wash of the boats lapping over her delicate slippers and thought, He is the kindest man who ever lived; I shall die of love for him! I'll never stop. She felt it so fiercely, as if every last feeling in her body and soul were laid bare in her desperate eyes, and Luc felt it. Felt his whole body struck as by a lightning bolt as he turned instinctively and caught her gaze.

Fatal.

'Luc!' warned Faron but it was too late. Algie felled him with one cracking blow to the ear and Luc was overboard, laughing and striking out for shore even as Algie jumped for dry land, the victor, and raised his standard.

'We won! We won!' yelled Algie.

'No sense of the dignities of victory and defeat, your little brother!' Luc surfaced at Allegra's feet, coughing and picking a large frond of pond weed from his hair. She retrieved another from his shoulder without thinking. Just as she hugged him because she could not help it, wet though he was, until the bodice of her muslin clung to her skin with the ice-chill of the water. 'Oh, Luc, thank you, *thank you*! It's the best day. . .' she was going to say for Algie, then she told the truth '. . .the best day I ever had!'

She never knew why he broke away from her, not sharply, just firmly, until she heard the rasp in his voice as he tried to laugh. 'Has not anyone told Algie he is meant to be the *late* Lord Nelson?'

And looking into his eyes Allegra realised she had quite forgotten all about Trafalgar, and Nelson, and who beat whom. He held her gaze too long. . .she *must* turn away. . .

It was Luc who found the sense to haul himself from the water to the derisive catcalls of his loving grandmother, and take himself back into the house to change.

Allegra retreated in a daze to her silken cushions. It is happening again, she thought. I am letting it happen all over again! I just don't seem able to resist him. Even knowing. . .

Even knowing he did not really want her—the bother of her, the responsibilty of her immature love for him—a little voice nagged and nagged at her, He cannot really resist me!

Luncheon was all Algie's—in the most literal sense, for by the time he had chewed his way through what he saw as his fair share of the celebration feast there was little left for anybody else to choose from. The afternoon sun was hot now as Allegra gazed up through the branches of the cedar into the cloudless sky. Not long till June. Soon Papa would be home and all this would be just a wonderful, heartbreaking dream. All gone.

She curled into her cushions and let herself drift into half-sleep, soothed by the softly dramatic tone of Luc relating to Algie one of Ulysses' least credible adventures. If she kept her eyes closed, if she stayed silent and never stirred again, maybe this day could go on forever. She wished with her whole being that it would.

Through her fragile muslin the heat of the sun-warmed rug soaked deeper beneath the shade and soothed her as the sleepy shimmer of the first real heat of summer cast its languid spell and a soft breeze cooled in the mists of the lake stroked away all pain and she was comforted. But most of all by Luc.

And, letting herself do what she'd sworn she would never do again, Allegra let herself dream.

It was a dream rudely shattered by Algie.

'Can we have another battle now?'

His victims groaned. Sated by wine and good food and the soft lure of the sunlit grass, not one of them felt like moving ever again.

'Not even a *tiny* one?' Algie did nothing to keep the childish wheedle out of his voice. . .because it always worked on someone who did not know better.

Lord Hawkhurst. 'Very well. . .' And he tried, not immediately successfully, to sit up.

Luc did not even bother. Resting an arm across his eyes to shield them from the sun, he looked up and said, 'We could just about manage a dignified surrender. . .'

Algie brightened. 'Yes, that would be capital! I shall be his Grace of Wellington and you can be Boney——'

'Boney didn't surrender to Wellington.'

'Well——' Algie had him cornered '—Nelson did not *quite* win at Trafalgar either. . .'

Hoist with his own petard, Luc gave in.

'How *does* one surrender, if one is Boney, by the by?'

Without even thinking Allegra said, 'With this. . .'

She had brought her sewing box, but never opened it. It was also her most private treasure trove and in it she had. . .or at least she thought she had. . .'Yes, here it is!' Pale blue-grey paper. Her letter from Napoleon.

Luc had snatched it from her hand before she even realised he was upright. He was more than that, he was kneeling over her, eyes blazing, and she sat up at once, realising. . .

'No, Luc, of course it is not the same one! How could it be? *You* took that.'

'Then how in God's name. . .?'

'Well—but did I not tell you? That is how I knew what you had found before. My aunt sent it to me——'

'Your *aunt*!' He had inevitably misunderstood again. 'Not Aunt *Lydia*, Aunt *Dido*.'

Luc stared at her as if she had just spoken a language from another planet; she had never seen him so remote, nor one whit so astounded. For a whole half-minute he was speechless. Then, 'Dido?' It was not a question. Just spoken very, very thoughtfully.

'Yes, she married a Frenchman years ago and that is how she received this letter. She knew how I liked to collect such things and so she sent it to me.'

Tension flared between them so fiercely now that it

was as if there were but the two of them in the whole world, so much so that Allegra jumped when Lord Hawkhurst interjected, 'Well, is that not just like Lydia? She did not even tell me she had a sister! Other than your mama, of course. . .'

'Well——' Allegra was suddenly very unsure of her ground '—I don't think she *does* have. Nobody has heard from Aunt Dido since. . .yes, my birthday, in 1808. She was an even worse correspondent than Aunt Lydia, if you can imagine it, but she never forgot our birthdays. When she did, Papa said we must prepare ourselves for the discovery that she had died. He made enquiries but it was very difficult, in France, you see, what with the war. But anyway, it fell out that she *was* dead, so I expect that is why Aunt Lydia did not tell you.'

It was Lady Hawkhurst's turn. 'But of course, I remember the three of them now, your mama, Lydia and Dido—such pretty things. And Dido did marry abroad; her mother made a shocking fuss about it. Anyway, *I* had heard that she and her husband the *vicomte* succumbed to an outbreak of the smallpox. It is very sad.' And she flapped her fan distractedly, puzzled as to why Luc seemed to be suddenly so disturbed.

Certainly he pocketed Allegra's precious letter before she could stop him and Allegra knew as she felt his eyes burn his warning into hers not to speak of it again in front of anyone outside their respective families.

There was no need to worry. Of all the picnickers it was Cuthbert who dreamed on, dozing off a large helping of apple tart and victory. Herr Kraftstein was well out of earshot, scribbling more abstruse notes on Virgil by the lakeside.

Luc got to his feet. 'Algie, do you mind if Lord Hawkhurst surrenders without me?'

Algie did. Without Luc the game would never be quite the same fun. But Luc already had his sister by the elbow and, inexorably, was propelling her away for what looked ominously like another quarrel. Algie decided not to let that spoil his day.

'So — I've won the war!' He turned on the hapless Lord Hawkhurst. 'What have you to say to that, you Corsican —— ?'

'Upstart!' obliged the parrot.

'Why in God's name did you not tell me about this sooner, Allegra? My God, but I could —— '

'You could what?' She was cold now in the shadow of the trees, having been dragged ruthlessly from dreams of paradise to the real live Luc all but shaking her with pent-up fury.

'It will keep! First you are going to tell me everything you know!'

'But I don't know anything!'

'You know you have aunts dotted about any old place bar Outer Mongolia and you have not the sense to tell me of it!'

'I just did — and I don't!'

'Try being *really* incoherent!'

'You *bastard*!'

'That's better! Now —— '

'I talk better if I am not having the life squeezed out

of me. . .' Allegra rubbed her wrist in well-justified fury. 'I cannot say that I like your methods of interrogation, sir!'

'You are not supposed to!'

Allegra glared. 'Very well. For those too flea-witted to comprehend even the simplest of his Majesty's English let me repeat: my aunt *Dido*, who was married to a *Frenchman*, sent me that letter as a souvenir when I was a *very little girl*. I do not remember my aunt Dido except that she sent the prettiest presents. I was very sad when I heard that she had died.'

'You are sure?'

'Well, of course I'm sure I was sorry; she was my aunt——!'

'That she is dead, you *impossible* little idiot!'

'Yes. . .*yes*, and damn you, Luc, now see what you have done to my sleeve!' His grip was so ruthless he had badly torn the lace of her cuff. *He* was so ruthless he saw not the least cause to apologise.

'Be damned your frills and flounces, Allegra! How do you know your aunt is dead?'

'Because—because Napoleon himself apprised my father of the fact, that's why!'

It sounded terrible. It sounded so like what Luc had so long been suspecting! But it had only been courtesy; a civilised gesture of condolence from one enemy to another. It had come to the Imperial ear that the Duke of Alderley was concerned that he had not heard from his sister-in-law; the Emperor, knowing the facts of the matter, had spared His Grace the trouble of endless expensive enquiry. Her father would have done the same for Bonaparte. It was only decent. Only humane.

She began to say all these things but Luc was never going to listen, she could see it. His quick brain had already ressessed everything he knew, rearranged it. She misunderstood the look of enlightenment that suddenly flared into his eyes.

'Oh, but I hate you. I *loathe* you, Luc Fleetwood! How can you *dare* to think my father. . .? Oh, you are *intolerable*; I shall not speak to you any more!'

She was gone, storming back to the party by the lakeside before Luc even realised what she had said.

He started after her. She was the most unmitigated little brat, but he would have to explain. Only not now. No time now. . . Time only to get this fresh information to London. If Dido had loved her Frenchman, had loved France, and Lydia loved her dead sister as Luc loved his brother. . .yes, he could see at last how the plot against Allegra's father was meant to be sprung.

London. And tonight.

He arrived at the lake to find that Algie had inadvertently surrendered to a startled Lady Hawkhurst, who thanked him very nicely, before inexplicably knighting him with a parasol.

Pythagoras had other things on his mind. 'More tea?'

# CHAPTER ELEVEN

SOMETHING would not allow Allegra to sleep. Round and round it went in her brain as she struggled for oblivion, but she could not catch up with it. . .not even in her dreams would this one small fact which she knew to be so desperately important resolve itself into anything she could understand. Unhelpfully, she dreamed of Luc, and woke, hot and very cross-tempered indeed . . .and stayed awake, staring into useless space for answers that were not to be found there.

Two hours later, maybe three, she trudged her insomniac way to the window; never had she so desperately craved fresh air. Outside the night was cold and calming. . . Allegra took the long, deep breaths her father always upheld were the best thing to send one into deep, untrammelled slumber and took in the beauty of the scene before her as the Italian gardens cast their shadow-patterns in the moonlight and the clock above the stables rang out its soothing quarter-hour.

Which hour Allegra no longer cared. Fleetwood was so beautiful and she had always loved the moonlight.

*That* was not the moon! Moonbeams were not yellow and did not dodge about the woods at night in such a furtive manner that she knew at once they were not wanting to be seen. Indeed they were so soon extinguished that for a long moment she thought she must have dreamt them.

Then, in a chilling twist to the very core of her spine, she knew she had not. Someone was out in the woods tonight where nobody should be. Fleetwood had been, as Luc had so expressively put it, sewn up as tight as a sack of gold — he had men posted everywhere.

Everywhere but in the woods, just at the bounds of the estate. . .

Allegra, schooled by long years of creeping about dark castles in the dead of night on bug-hunts with Algie, snatched up her darkest cloak from her travelling trunk, the better not to be seen, then with only the moonlight to guide her she let herself out of her room. She had to find Luc.

She knew which was his room and without a thought for how it might appear to anyone wakeful at this hour she tapped softly and listened. No answer. Tapped a little harder. Nothing.

Allegra, her mind only on the lights in the woods and the unmistakable chill of danger in her blood, flung open the door and — he was not there!

Her first sensation was relief, flooding through her just at the thought that Luc was up and about and must have seen the lights himself and gone already to investigate. Then she realised — his rooms were on the wrong side of the house.

Maybe the lights *were* Luc?

One of them anyway. Only — who was it held the other?

\* \* \*

The night air was bitter as the ice-breath of mist coiled up from the lake and snapped Allegra's cloak around her with the crack of a mainsail in the wind. She huddled the cloak around her, wishing passionately that Luc had not confiscated her pistol and forgotten to return it. Then she saw him.

Rather, she heard him first. Them. Luc and his brother, Faron already mounted on a powerful roan, both man and beast fretting to be gone.

For one stark moment Allegra stared and thought, Have I got it all wrong still? Is it Faron is the traitor? *Is* it Luc? Then she followed every aching instinct of her heart and raced out across the stableyard to catch them.

'Luc!' Just an urgent whisper hissed into the gathering wind but he heard her and was running towards her.

They ran so fast they had to catch hold of one another to stop themselves, to stand, breathless, Allegra panting with the importance of her errand, and just a little from the exquisite gentleness of Luc's touch as he stroked the back of his hand down her cheek and said so calmly, 'Tell me.'

'The woods! Someone is there. And do not tell me it is poachers bec——'

'I wasn't going to! Did you hear that, Faron?'

'Yes—do you want me to stay?'

'No—no, it is even more important now that you go. You know exactly what to do. I have horses stabled all along the route; just go—and don't stop until you get there!'

Briefly the brothers clasped hands and Allegra felt a

lump rise in her throat that threatened to stifle her. She
could all but smell their fear, for each other, not
themselves. Faron did not want to leave Luc—Luc was
not sure it was safe to let the far from capable Faron
go alone. But they trusted each other just enough.

'Go!'

And Faron was gone. Allegra watched as he raced
the roan so silently out across the lawns and heard Luc
laugh behind her, 'Don't worry, he won't touch the
road until he is beyond the village; no one will hear
him. Now——' and suddenly she had all his attention
'—where were these lights of yours?'

'Where we had our picnic. . .a little beyond, but not
quite so far as the stream with the bridge. . .'

'Excellent! Now, back into the house with you.'

'*No*!'

Allegra found herself seized so ferociously by the
shoulders that she quite literally bit her tongue.

'*Yes*! One member of your family in bandages is
quite enough for me! Don't be tiresome, there's a good
girl——'

Allegra, tasting blood and knowing just who to
blame, stood her ground and spat furiously, 'Don't you
*dare*, Luc Fleetwood,' then, unconsciously using his
habitual threat, 'Don't you even *think* about treating
me like a baby now!'

'I had rather that than be tending you as a corpse!'

'Two are better than one—and don't tell me you
mean to call up your men to come with you because
you don't! You know that would frighten whoever is in
the woods away and then you would be no nearer
knowing who they are than—— I. . .*why* are you

laughing at me like that? If you are not the most *obnoxious* man——'

'Oh, ye gods! I surrender! Jupiter, but you are the most appalling little fishwife! I never met a woman who could *nag* at a man so——'

'I have not even started!'

'No?' Then his voice altered and she heard the dry amusement of real authority in his tone. 'But you have finished!'

Allegra nodded. . .because she had come to know Luc so very well now and she knew it was quite pointless to argue. And anyway, she had won!

Taking her hand—less to comfort or help her, she felt, than to keep her well under his remorseless control—Luc ran at a pace that spared his victim nothing until they reached the edge of the woods. Here he paused, listening, as if he was used to scenting danger in the dark.

Allegra was used to stalking animals with Algie. She heard the movement first.

'Luc—I think there is someone in Algie's tent!'

Luc knew that there was. Allegra felt rather than saw his hand slip beneath his coat and shuddered. The arm that went about her then was anything but comforting, given that the hand at the end of it contained a very purposeful-looking pistol indeed. He did not have to tell her to stay where she was while he moved so silently into the clearing.

The tent stood, still surrounded by the paraphernalia of this afternoon's sport, in a dangerously bright arena of moonlight. Allegra watched as Luc circled until he was behind the rather haphazard opening. . .watched

as he went closer. . .went in. . . And heard a voice
that stunned her with its robust familiarity.

'Don't move another step or I shall. . .shoot you!'
Then it amended in the interests of honesty, 'Well, I
shall kill you with *something*, just see if I don't, you
. . .you villain!'

She did not know whether she was laughing or crying
as she raced towards the tent. She had only a few
seconds in which to haul Luc from the jaws of certain
death. . .

He—just—succeeded in extricating himself, and a
very bullish Algie whom he had held ruthlessly by the
collar. Algie—the unmitigated lunatic!—was armed
only with his shrimping net.

'Algie!' Allegra saw his bandages slip dashingly over
one eye and just managed to control herself from
smacking him within an inch of his short existence.

Luc had no such inhibitions. Since the Marquess
Stonyhurst's left ear was already injured Luc cuffed
him very briskly round the right one instead. He was
incandescent with rage.

Never had Allegra and Algie admired him so much.
And if anything their wide-eyed veneration only
poured fuel on his anger.

'If you are not the most stupid brat who ever was
born! In fact I begin to doubt that you were born at all!
The gods alone know how you got here! What in the
name of all that is sacred do you think you are
*doing*——?' He was so infuriated he just could not go
on.

Allegra knew why. Fear for Algie—and he had lost
his quarry. They all heard it, just as Algie ducked his

second cuffing—the sound of a horse cutting very swiftly through the woodland towards the stream and freedom. Then nothing.

Which made no sense of the words Algie elected upon to save himself. 'I saw them! I mean, I *sort* of saw them and I definitely really did *hear* them! Only——'

'Them?' Luc demanded. There had been only one horse. One person flying for safety.

Allegra was just as puzzled, because Algie was right. 'Yes, Luc, there were two lights; I saw——'

'There you are!' Algie was suddenly and most unusually grateful he had an older sister. 'And I'm telling you I saw them!'

'*Who*?'

Algie had known this was coming, and it posed a rather troublesome dilemma. He shuffled his feet, then felt the full force of two sets of very angry eyes upon him and thought he had better try for an explanation.

'Thing is, I came out because, well, I *so* wanted to see what it is like to sleep in a tent, just like Papa——'

'Your father never slept in a tent in his life!' snapped Luc heartlessly. 'He commandeered the nearest peasant shack for a billet or he slept in the snow just like the rest of us!'

'Oh!' It was the first time Algie had ever really understood what it was his father had suffered. And Luc too. 'Sorry! But—well, I like to study animals, and I thought. . .well, in the woods there would be *bound* to be foxes and badgers and rabbits and. . .'

'Get on with it!'

'*Sorry*!' Algie had a nice way with mutiny. Even so,

he continued more coherently, 'Well, because I was waiting for animals I had to be really, really quiet. . . and so when they came — the people, I mean — I could hear them. I — well, I can't explain exactly but ——' and he shuddered at the memory ' — but I knew it wasn't you. . .'

And Luc, sensing the child's fear, probed more kindly, 'So who was it?'

'Well, that's just it. I *know* I know them, only I don't know who——'

'*Algie*!' Allegra glared at him as if trying to decide which bandage the better to strangle him with.

'Well, *I* can't help it if I can't think very well at the moment! I *have* got a bump on the head, you know!' And she sensed at last that her brave little brother was very close to tears. 'I can't hear very well either. I tried, really I did! I even thought to come out of the tent but they had lanterns. . .'

Luc saw the tears too and felt his stomach twist in pain. He felt so responsible. He had nearly allowed Algie to get hurt again. 'Can't you tell us anything?'

'I. . .well, the thing is. . .I can't because it *can't* have been who I thought. . . I mean it wouldn't have been a *female*, would it?'

Aunt Lydia?

Impossible, of course! Impossible because it would only make sense if her confederate were Lord Hawkhurst and Allegra herself had seen him riding in the opposite direction. Hadn't she?

The most important thing was to get Algie back to the house at once.

He walked between them, keeping very close to

Luc's side because he felt so much better that way, and struggled all the while to remember. 'I thought it was a woman because she was so much shorter than the man. And I know he was a man because. . .well, he was so tall. . .'

'And?' Luc encouraged him.

'And I thought it was a female because of the voice. I couldn't make out anything it said but I could hear *it*. Oh, dear. . .'

'You're making perfect sense, Algie,' Allegra coaxed from his other side. 'Go on.'

'Thing is, it was a high sort of voice, but it whispered most of the time so I couldn't be sure. Except that it wasn't *really* deep, not like the man's. . .'

'And you could hear nothing of what the man said?'

'No. . .I only know that I thought——'

What he thought they never did find out because at that exact moment the woods erupted into life from all directions as at one and the same time came from the left Herr Kraftstein, plainly on the tail of his errant charge, and from the right, of all the unlikeliest people in the world, Cuthbert Nettlesham. Both were fully dressed, as if neither had yet been to bed and yet it must be three if not four o'clock in the morning.

Allegra stared helplessly as the two men met in a tumble of limbs and fastidious apology. One short, one so tall. One voice so light and affected, the other so deeply correct.

Helpless was far too faint a word for what Allegra felt then as she just gazed at Luc and let him do the talking. . .when he could get in a word between Cuthbert and Herr Kraftstein.

'Oh, but thank goodness! I could not think what it might be,' panted Cuthbert.

'Algernon, I shall be having a very serious talk with you in the morning!' Herr Kraftstein, plainly furious with relief.

The calming of the mêlée was not assisted by the fact that one or other of these gentlemen had come armed with Brandy and the deerhound was now capering about as if this whole expedition had been planned especially to please him.

It was Allegra's nerve that snapped first. 'Oh, be *quiet!*' She clapped her hands over her ears just to make certain that they all understood her. 'All of you! Now——' and she levelled a look at Cuthbert that turned his bones to jelly '—you, Cuthbert! Explain yourself, if you would be so civil!'

It was Luc who was on the end of her next, one hundred times more blistering stare because, in spite of everything, and the fact that his eyes never left the faces of the other men even for a second, his air of competent watchfulness never faltering, he was laughing at her—and, the heartless animal, at the quaking Cuthbert.

'*Well*?' she demanded, and could have sworn she heard from Luc's direction one whispered word:

'Fishwife!'

Cuthbert almost forgot his capital letters as he stammered, 'The—the lights. Saw 'em, you see? Well, couldn't think what they could be——'

'You did not think to come to me or to my brother?' Luc asked it so courteously that it was chilling.

Cuthbert's innocence was palpable. Almost too

much so. 'Course I did, old fellow! Weren't there, was you? As for Hawkhurst—well, he'd trotted off too. I have to say I thought it most——'

'*Cuthbert!*'

'Sorry, my Angel!' And for once Allegra saw that he was truly Abject. 'Well, couldn't *not* investigate, could I? Might have been somethin' it oughtn't to have been, if you follow. Couldn't have that.'

'Indeed not!' stepped in Herr Kraftstein and Allegra could feel the anger banked down beind his ever careful manner. He had always displayed the strongest sense of justice and plainly thought her to be picking on poor Cuthbert. Since she had been, and quite deliberately so, Allegra had the grace to feel chastened. When he was satisfied that she was genuinely repentant Algie's tutor went on, 'I saw Mr Nettlesham hurrying outside and I thought, *Ach*, something is very wrong here and I must investigate. The first thing I investigated——' and he swivelled the gaze of a Gorgon on Algie '—was Algernon! Needless to say——'

And Luc had had enough. Allegra could feel the tension building to exploding point inside him, building between all three men, until it chilled her even more than the dew-drenched moonlight.

'So, we all saw the lights and came to investigate!'

Allegra had never heard his tone so sardonic and yet she knew it was only she who detected it, or was meant to. Just as she and Algie were the only ones who felt the warning in Luc's tone as he continued, 'And what we found was this *malevolent* young reprobate determined to keep us from our sleep by hunting *badgers*, if you will believe it!'

'I believe it!' Herr Kraftstein's tone managed to convey to his charge that the talk he was planning for the morrow had just grown a great deal longer.

Cuthbert seemed oblivious to everything. Too oblivious? 'Badgers?' I say, haven't seen a badger in years——'

Luc's already fractured temper gave at the seams. 'Largely,' he scathed, 'because badgers don't hang about doing the pretty to the dowagers at Almack's! Now, I don't know about anybody else but I am cold and I am tired and I am going to bed! When, Herr Kraftstein, you have finished with this loathsome little reptile in the morning, please deliver what is left of him to me!'

Algie almost believed him. Enough to look very much bedraggled and subdued, just as Luc needed him to be.

Luc threw a look at Allegra that said, When you reach the house wait for me. . .

Allegra consequently — and with great difficulty — shed the grovelling Cuthbert, hurried in to the library and waited. Luc was a very, very long time. She was shaking with cold by the time he came, bringing with him the chill scent of dawn on his clothing and stirring up yet another elusive memory. . .of the night Algie was attacked. Elusive and gone. . .

And so very, very important, she knew it.

Luc saw the pinched, exhausted pallor of her face and went to her at once, pulling her down on to the nearest sofa and holding he gently within his arms while he explained. 'No need to tell you that one or other of those so impressive performances out there was a fraud.'

'Maybe both?'

'You saw it too, did you? Yes, of course you did! Why do I think that in your family you got the lion's share of the brains?'

'Oh, that's not fair, Luc, besides which without Algie we would not even have reason to suspect——'

'That because your tutor is so tall and so gruff, and your betrothed so short and so——'

'Don't you dare say Cuthbert squeaks!' Allegra squirmed in his arms at the terrible word 'betrothed'. 'He has been so very good to Algie lately, and it was very wrong of me to be so surprised at it. Oh, Luc, I— oh, I know I cannot bear it that I must marry him but I don't want the traitor to be Cuthbert!'

Luc's voice was hard as ice then. 'None of us wants any of this,' he grated. 'And none of us has everything we want in this life!'

Now what had she said, done? She had only defended Cuthbert. . . Allegra, without a clue as to why she was yet again in his blackest books, hurried on, 'If it is so intolerable, Luc, can it not be left up to London?' Meaning, whoever it was he was working for; fighting down the treacherous voice that said, He might be working for himself and against Papa. . .

Luc shook his head, preoccupied and immune to being softened. 'No. No—because, well, for the life of me I am *damned* if I can see where Kraftstein could ever fit in with Cuthbert!' And with that gesture she so loved he ran both hands into his already wildly

dishevelled hair in real fury. 'Gods, Allegra, the more
we know, the less it is possible to understand it!'

Algie did not enjoy his breakfast, Herr Kraftstein saw
quite resolutely to that, and nothing Allegra or Luc
could do for him the rest of the morning could soothe
his ruffled temper.

'After all—well, I came so very near to solving
*everything* and *he* must prate on and *on* about pro-
prieties and how I should comport myself in other
people's houses and——'

Allegra and Luc rushed in to offer their wounded
hero another currant bun. Anything to stem the flow
of these injustices.

They were still sitting with him, confined by earlier
rain as much as a very stern edict from his tutor that he
was not to leave his room for the next twenty-four
hours, muddling their not too competent way through
the Latin comprehension he had been set for punish-
ment. The afternoon had cooled to the enticing haze of
an early summer evening and Algie looked longingly
out of the window as Luc cursed, 'I detested Virgil at
school and I cannot say I like him any better now! How
anyone can be supposed to care——'

'I think I have this bit wrong. . .' Allegra handed
him her efforts and was rewarded by a very unkind
choke of laughter indeed. 'Well, it is not *my* fault I was
never allowed to go to school because Aunt Lydia said
that schools are only for provincial females. I should
have liked to go—besides, my governesses were all
quite hopeless!'

'All of them?' Luc was perched cross-legged on

Algie's bed correcting Allegra's shocking spelling. Allegra tugged her eyes away from the quite fascinating lure of his muscles, taut beneath the tightest of riding breeches, and tried to concentrate on the question. . .

'Oh, yes, every one of them. They all said *I* was the problem, that I was. . .um. . .well, not very clever, but that was grossly unfair! I was just so very bored and Aunt——'

'*Lydia*!'

For a moment, Algie's interjection being so well-timed, neither of his companions realised what it was he was saying. And then they did.

Luc surged to his feet hauling Allegra bodily from her chair and all three of them glued their noses to the window.

'It is, look! It is Aunt Lydia's carriage, see, Allegra! Who else but Aunt Lydia would ever have bought that——?'

'The bay! Yes, oh, Luc, it *is* Aunt Lydia! She does not like her carriage teams to match like everyone else's so. . .the black and the grey, the roan and the bay. . .'

Then Allegra froze.

Aunt Lydia. So close on the heels of all that had been happening. . .

But, even worse, Aunt Lydia had come to take them both away.

Allegra cast a glance at Luc as his eyes followed the carriage as if he could burn some answers from its occupant, and thought, I cannot bear it! It has been such fun. It has been *agony* but I love him and I never want to leave! I never want to go away from Fleetwood because if I do I am never going to see him again.

He must have felt her looking at him. Allegra was too stunned with pain to understand what happened next. Luc's hand reached out and, more reassuring than he had been since the very first night, caught hers safely into the comfort of his own.

Allegra stared straight ahead and thought, The very last time. And twisted her suddenly ice-cold fingers into the warm protection of his.

Luc smiled so enigmatically as they at last made their way into the Yellow Salon to greet her errant aunt, but then Allegra was not to know that Luc had been expecting this development — if not quite so soon — and had his grandmother well-primed as to how to deal with it. Luc knew what Allegra did not: that he was never going to let her be taken away from Fleetwood.

Not until everything was safely over. And then, when she was no longer afraid, she would no longer need him. Allegra would not want him any more.

Luc's hand tightened painfully on hers as he thought, If I let her go now the next time I see her she will be married to Cuthbert Nettlesham.

That was not going to happen either!

He could never keep her himself, he knew that. But if it killed him she would not throw herself away on an idiot like Cuthbert.

Allegra mistook his tension, even though it felt to her so very like her own. She hung back for a moment by the door, knowing that one more step and she must let go of him forever, and so it was Algie who plunged forward to greet their aunt before her. And raced, as usual, right into trouble.

'Algie, but I cannot have you charging about in such an unseemly fashion; what is Lady Hawkhurst to think? Especially when she has so kindly offered to let you stay here at Fleetwood until you are quite better. Now I see you for myself, well—' and here Aunt Lydia turned to Lady Hawkhurst, who was waiting for this '—I really do not feel we can impose upon your kindness one moment longer.'

Algie was not the only one who stared. Allegra's mouth only just stayed shut on an exclamation of utter astonishment; then she understood. Of course Aunt Lydia was being good; she was sitting beside the woman whose grandson she was proposing to marry. Lord Hawkhurst had never made a secret of the fact that such was his and Aunt Lydia's intention. Had Allegra not understood she might have thought her aunt a visitor from another planet.

It was almost funny. Certainly it brought a quirk of cynical amusement to Luc's ever-expressive mouth and Allegra whispered, 'Heavens, but poor Algie does not know where to place himself! He has never been reprimanded by Aunt Lydia before!'

'It is called ingratiating oneself with one's future grandmama-in-law!' Luc laughed in a manner that completely bewildered her, then he added more teasingly still, 'Come, let us see what she is going to do with you!'

What Aunt Lydia did as Allegra came rather nervously forward, not sure how best to behave the better to help Lydia's suit in the Hawkhurst household, was—

well, going much too far! Surely *this* was not remotely necessary!

'Ah, there you are, my pet! What is this I hear about you, clever child? To have netted Cuthbert *Nettlesham*, no less!'

So it came about that the very first thing Allegra said to the aunt whose disappearance had all but scared her to pieces with worry was, 'You mean. . .' Oh, dear God, no! 'You — you mean you are. . .*pleased* about Mr Nettlesham, Aunt Lydia?'

And her aunt looked in her turn as if it were Allegra who had just run mad. 'Well, of course I am pleased, besides that it quite disposes of the scandal of his having fought a duel over you with——'

'Freddie, but——'

'Well, I must say, my sweet, you are behaving very oddly for a girl has just hauled in the richest catch in England! What an ungrateful little thing you are!'

Now *that* was just Aunt Lydia! And in a rush of relief she had never expected to feel in her life Allegra flung herself into her aunt's open arms, and remembered all over again how she had always loathed the scent of Aunt Lydia's favourite perfume.

Aunt Lydia, whose excuse for having gone missing was all too plausibly confusing, involving among other things a trip to Budleigh Salterton, was all for their leaving to return to Bath that very evening, but Luc had a contigency plan to put a stop to anything like that.

'Algie, I want you to do something or me. . .'

'Is it *important*?'

'Vital! The future of Europe is at stake!' How was the boy ever to know that he meant it?

'Oh, count on me!'

'I do. Now, listen. . .'

So it was that, just before the Alderley offspring were sent about their packing, Algie, with great aplomb, fainted flat to the Caucasian carpet, and stayed there just long enough for his aunt to have no option but to exclaim, 'Oh, Algie! But oh, he *cannot* travel like this!'

Luc stepped in with the innocence of an angel. 'Of course he can't, Lydia. I shall carry him to bed at once. . .'

Allegra was left staring after the departing conspirators wondering how in the name of heaven Luc's blandly expressionless face could have so eloquently conveyed a wink.

She should have slept like a pile of logs after the disrupted nights she had been suffering but she could not; because Algie could not keep this invalidism up forever and she had no doubt at all that tonight was her very last at Fleetwood.

How she was going to miss it! And how she refused even to begin to think of how she would miss Luc.

Sending away her maid with the promise that she was quite able to undress herself and get into bed, Allegra sat by the fire now lit in her grate and stared unseeing into the flames. It was the smoke made her eyes run with tears, of course. . .

That was when she determined that she take her last look at Fleetwood.

Someone was still up in the room the gentlemen had

set aside for whatever it was gentlemen must do when they had managed to shake off the females of the party. Allegra had long since learned not to be curious about such matters. The social habits of gentlemen were best left to the darker corners of the imagination.

Outside, Luc's men were spending yet another freezing night pacing about the grounds, patrolling the gardens, keeping her safe. She was grateful for it. After last night she knew just how dangerous this was become. Because last night had no explanation. There was no reason at all why any part of the conspiracy should not be centred on Fleetwood. It made no sense at all that something had happened here just as inexpeclicable as all that had happened to them in Bath.

And was happening again! She could not believe her eyes as she caught a flash of light on the far side of the rising woodland while she made her way sadly through the picture gallery. . .not even Algie would be so foolhardy again!

No. Not Algie.

For the second night running as the clock struck two Allegra found herself running for Luc's chambers. This time she went straight in, and he was there. But she could not wake him.

She was ruthless — and terrified. He was breathing so strangely and when she tried to lift his shoulders to shake him to wakefulness his head fell back so heavily, it was as if he were dead.

She was frightening herself; Allegra pulled herself sharply together. He was only asleep. And yet. . .it was not like Luc. Luc, with the instincts of a cat in the

night, Luc by nature and training should have woken
at the very first sound.

Allegra understood then. Someone had seen to it
that he should not wake up tonight. . . .

She had to get him to his feet because they must find
out why. And who.

Or should she risk it alone? There was no one else
she could turn to. She was just resolved to set out for
the woods alone when he stirred, this time without the
aid of her tugging quite frantically at his lapels. For the
first time she noticed what she should have seen at
once. Luc had not undressed either. He had been
expecting something to happen. Somebody had
guessed as much and made certain he could not be part
of it.

'Luc! *Luc*!' She dared not shout, because she did not
know who else might hear her.

He was coming round. At least she could have sworn
he murmured her name.

He did. And in a manner that set her whole being
on fire.

He moved then, and she found herself caught against
his chest, until all she could feel was the racing of his
heart beneath her own and she struggled to remember
why she had really come here.

'*Luc*!'

He said it quite clearly. 'No, kitten — don't go. Stay
with me!'

Allegra was shaking so much at his words, at the
passionate way he said them, she almost failed to see
. . .and then she did. He was sleeping still, and yet he
knew she was here. If he was dreaming then it was of

her. And he dreamed of the two of them, together,
they way she did.

She was frantic to wake him now. She became quite
angry with it. 'Oh, *will* you wake up?'

'Virago!' And at last she knew he had woken. He
still would not let her go. Of course he could not be
held responsible, she tried to tell herself. He did not
know what he was doing. . .

He didn't. But he did it anyway. Without even
knowing how it happened Allegra found herself beside
him. . .beneath him. . .all breath stilled in her body as
she listened to the clamouring of her heart and watched
his eyes. . .felt her love for him steal so helplessly into
her own.

In all the times they had been close, all the times he
had kissed her, it had never been like this. Never so
tender, so gentle. . .never so complete. Allegra could
not have freed herself if she had tried.

But she did not try. She could not. Nothing in the
world would make her end this.

She knew he did not really know what he was
doing. . . Oh, but dear God, if felt as if he did! And it
was not just the remnants of the opiate that slurred his
speech now as he bent so close to her ear and murmured, 'You are mine, kitten. *Do* you know that, *do
you*?'

And she stirred so restlessly beneath him as she
heard herself whisper, without hesitation, 'Oh, yes!'
Yours, she thought, if she was really thinking at all any
more, always. *Always*.

Now.

This time there was nothing to stop them, . .no one

to know. It was her very last chance to keep him and she was going to take it.

She was almost laughing with disbelief as he bent his head again and began to kiss her throat, teasing the swell of her breast beneath the fragile muslin; she felt an echo of laughter thrill through him as he pressed her deeper into the softness of his bed. . .and she reached up and drew his mouth back to hers because she had to let him know. She had to make him know and want it to be true; want *her*, and not just the body he held so plainly now between his questing hands. She would make it impossible for him to leave her. . . She knew for certain in that moment that she could. So she told the truth. She could not help it. She was never to know if he heard her, 'Oh, Luc, I love you so *much!*'

And suddenly all about them there was light, disturbing, lights and sounds that were alien and could never belong here, and she heard a rasp of laughter that was not his. . .

Aunt Lydia! A candle in her hand and a look of coolest amusement on her immaculate features.

'Well, so one is not enough for you, my angel! You really *are* taking after me, after ——' Her voice snapped off as Lady Hawkhurst, drawn by the sound, appeared behind her, her face as white as ice in her absolute distress.

Allegra sat up, knowing there was nothing she could do to hide what she had meant to happen. Not just Luc had meant, *she*. More so. For Luc was still slow with the influence of his drugging. . .

But not that slow. For as she opened her mouth to speak she felt his hand snap about her wrist warning her to silence. All she could do was stare in agony at her aunt and rage, Why now? *Why*? Why could I not even have tonight? Then, What is she going to do? Aunt Lydia is going to murder me! But Luc first. For all her laxness, Aunt Lydia had always been the strictest of chaperons. Aunt Lydia would never countenance such abandoned behaviour as this.

Then through her daze, as she watched Luc's coolly sardonic gaze settle on her aunt even while she felt burning in his touch the absolute ferocity of his frustration, she realised. . .

Aunt Lydia *laughed*. She laughed that I was just like her!

Disgusted, appalled — because her love for Luc could never be anything like Aunt Lydia's mindless liaisons — Allegra only half realised she was thinking, Aunt Lydia should not have laughed. She *cannot* be amused.

So when Luc said, very gently, 'Leave us, Allegra. . .' and she got obediently to her feet to go she was already bewildered and wary.

But not half so much as when she saw her aunt look Luc almost mockingly in the eye and say, oh, so softly, 'Oh, yes, she will be leaving you, Luc, depend on it! We shall all of us be leaving in the morning.'

And she thought, She does not sound surprised to have found me here. Was it so obvious that I am in love with Luc! How could Aunt Lydia imagine that this would happen when I never meant it to?

How was it that Luc and Aunt Lydia smiled at each other then in a manner that was half conspiratorial, and half — she felt it as a shudder deep inside her — the cold salute of duellists?

How was it that, even deeper inside, she began to wonder—just how well it was Luc knew Aunt Lydia. And she began to doubt again.

Most terrible of all, doubt Luc.

## CHAPTER TWELVE

NATURALLY Algie was not given the true reason why they were leaving at what felt like daybreak the following morning, but he guessed that something very serious had happened. Allegra sat in the carriage as pale as if she were ill; she had hardly been able to respond to the pointedly reassuring warmth of Lady Hawkhurst's kiss to her cheek and had refused to look at Luc at all. In fact it had been only to Cuthbert she had shown any life at all — Cuthbert, still in the dark about what had happened and who Aunt Lydia so plainly determined never would find out at all, Allegra had just made up her mind she had to tell him.

After all, as Aunt Lydia made so painfully and finally plain the very moment the door of the Pulteney Street house closed behind them, Cuthbert was the only person Allegra could expect to be permitted to see in Bath, or anywhere until her father came home.

Allegra took it very quietly because she had been expecting it, and because Aunt Lydia was right. But everything else in the whole wide world was wrong.

Algie found her leaning back in her favourite silk bergère in her little silver-grey sitting-room too drained for tears and suddenly feeling far too old. She had grown far beyond tears in Luc's arms last night, for all nothing had really happened between then. They both meant it to and she found the courage to say that she loved him.

If he cared, if he had heard, if he wanted her, he would come for her and then—well, Aunt Lydia could do nothing. If not. . .

Aunt Lydia, however, proved a great deal more enterprising than Allegra could ever have supposed; she locked the door, having given her orders to Allegra's bewildered servants that it was only to be opened for Allegra to receive her meals and for her to visit with her brother. She might only leave her rooms when Cuthbert came to see her.

Never would Allegra have believed she could long for Cuthbert's maddening presence!

'Oh, hello, Algie.' She roused herself because it was not fair to frighten Algie by behaving so out of character and she could see he was very disturbed.

'Allegra, please, you've got to tell me what happened.' And she found she was looking at her brother and thinking, So you too have just grown up. She had the most unsettling feeling that he understood a great deal more than he was prepared to tell anyone.

'Luc.' It was all she needed to say.

Algie did not crow or laugh or utter any of his easy vulgarities; he just sat at her feet, his bandaged head against her knees, and said, 'I always knew you *did* like him really.'

'Did you, Algie?'

'He likes you.'

'Does he?' She was too tired even to begin to believe it.

Algie was so changed, so calm. 'Of course he does. . .'

So sure. Allegra asked, 'How on earth can you know that?'

It was very simple really. 'He told me.'

Two days, three, and no Luc. Proving once and for all that Algie had misunderstood what Luc had said to him. For Allegra knew Luc to be back in Laura Place; she had watched from her window as he rode into town alongside the Hawkhurst carriage the very same day she had returned, surprised he should be here when he knew that there was danger, surprised most of all that he had brought his grandmother from the safety of Fleetwood.

He looked so far away! Only one, two hundred yards but it might have been a lifetime. Not once did he glance down the street towards Aunt Lydia's.

Algie was wrong.

Allegra, leaden inside with grief and yet still half mad with boredom, gazed helplessly out at the Hawkhurst residence longing for a second sight of him, but it might as well have been that he was not there. Longing too, as if her life depended upon it, for Algie and his tutor to come home from Duffield's Library with the novels that were all that stood between her and going completely demented.

Then, just as she turned away, worn out with waiting and close to tears, she saw a familiar figure. Cuthbert!

As if he had felt the sudden lift to her spirits Mr Nettlesham looked up and saw her, high as she was above the street, and he smiled, and Allegra found a little grief to spare for what she must do to Cuthbert.

He had known anyway.

'I know I am not a clever man, Allegra, and not. . . well, I suppose it was vain and stupid to imagine anyone like you could ever want to marry me. . .but I am not so dull I cannot see that you love Fleetwood.'

And as Allegra took his hand, so grateful for his sparing her the most unpalatable task, he saw that his eyes had clouded over so sadly and she knew much more was troubling him than that she did not want him.

'Cuthbert, what is it, what is wrong? I can see it is something. . .'

At first Cuthbert was stubborn. 'It is nothing.' Then, because he had to tell someone, because it had been nagging at him for days, 'Nothin' I can put my *finger* on, if you see. . .'

'Yes. . .' She had been feeling very much the same as the days went by; maybe he could do better than she. '*Try*, Cuthbert. I cannot tell you everything that is happening but, well, I am so closely involved in it I cannot see clearly at all. Maybe you——'

'Well, that's the thing. Mean to say, *my* involvement. I mean, it was all very civil of Lady Hawkhurst to invite me to Fleetwood but to tell the truth, Allegra, I came because. . .well, wanted to see you, of course, but. . . well, was *worried*, if you follow? Somethin' very odd . . .had a feelin' someone wanted me to be there who wasn't you, only made no sense, you follow?'

'Yes. . .?'

'Well, what I really cannot understand is your aunt.

Mean to say, you know as well as I, Allegra, she never thought me half fit to sweep the ground you're walkin' over and yet here she is greetin' me at the door as if I were the prodigal returnin'. Somethin' not right, don't you see. . .'

Just as she was feeling — half understanding, teased by fleeting sensations of unease, the feeling that something that they were looking at was not what it appeared to be. But she was no more clear about it than Cuthbert.

But Allegra was clear about one thing now. So clear, she took the greatest risk of her life. She made up her mind to confide in Cuthbert.

'Cuthbert. . .I need your help, and you're the only one I can trust!'

'Course you can, with your life!' He had quite forgotten his affected capital letters and she knew undoubtedly to believe him.

'Aunt Lydia has me locked in!'

'I — *no*! She would not do anythin' so. . .well, it ain't civilised!'

'I cannot blame her, Cuthbert, and I cannot really explain because. . .well, it involves someone else and. . .'

'Fleetwood?'

'Yes. . .oh, Cuthbert, I know it is the most terrible thing to ask you of all people but, please, could you go to him and tell him that I am being treated like a prisoner? I — I just need to be sure that he knows it.'

'He can't do,' asserted Cuthbert robustly. 'Would have done somethin' about it if he did. Not one to sit about star-gazin' when a lady's in trouble — besides. . .'

She never heard what else Cuthbert was going to say because she could not help herself. . . . Allegra kissed a very startled Mr Nettlesham on one burning crimson cheek and clung so gratefully to his hand that he almost fainted.

'I don't know how to thank you, Cuthbert; you're a real friend!'

And a real man, she saw it now, behind his silly affectations. Calm and accepting, easygoing and sincere. 'Then don't try Allegra, because what else is it that your friends are for?'

He left not a minute later and Allegra felt her heart soaring with hope—until Aunt Lydia came into the room, her inevitable vague and forgetful self, never remembering for one moment to the next where anything was kept, always running into the furniture, and announced, 'I have made up my mind, Allegra. We go to London tomorrow to await your father there.'

'*No!*'

Aunt Lydia froze. 'Do you mean to challenge my authority, Allegra?'

And this time it was Allegra who froze. Yet again she felt something to be very, very wrong here, if only she could stand far enough back to see it.

It was worse than she had supposed. Algie burst into her room wielding a tray of supper and quite plainly fighting hard not to show a very real confusion that was bordering on fear.

'Where's Sorcha?' For the maid had always brought her meals.

'Gone.' Then Algie set down the tray with a thump

that sent her glass of chocolate flying across her counterpane. 'They've all gone!'

'*Who*, Algie?'

'Our servants. There's a man of Aunt Lydia's here
that I've never seen before, that's all, and that new
maid she took on in London——'

'Our servants have *gone*!' Allegra knew there was
something very important in the fact, but what could it
be?

'Yes, to open up Alderley House, Aunt says,
because Papa will be home any day now——'

'Oh, nonsense, Algie! Papa is either coming at a
particular time which he had expressly told us or he is
not coming at all! When have you ever known Papa be
anything but quite military in his arrangements?'

'Well, that's what *I* thought; why hasn't he written
to *us*? Allegra, what's going on? This isn't like Aunt
Lydia at all.'

No, thought Allegra, still stumbling in the dark. Not
like Aunt at all.

What was going on was that they were set to do their
own packing. They would be leaving at first light
tomorrow morning.

It was Algie who remembered the parrot. Poor
Pythagoras had been banished as usual to the morning-
room next to late Uncle Barnaby's study. He had a
cloth thrown over his cage but he was nevertheless
wide awake and, Algie could tell at a glance, quite
bursting with something to say about his abandonment.

Algie, terrified for reasons he could not explain that
Pythagoras should make a noise and he be caught
where he was not meant to be, kept the cage well-

covered as he sneaked back up to his bedroom by the servants' stairs, for it was well after midnight and Herr Kraftstein had been on the prowl in a most officious manner all evening. Algie shut his door and, without thinking why he did so, locked himself in. Then he took off the cloth the better to feed his cross and resentful parrot. Pythagoras ruffled his feathers huffily and deigned to accept a handful of raisins. Then he tucked down his head as if about to doze off to sleep. He was sulking and Algie smiled.

But what he had to say became too much for the parrot. Algie had just nodded into fitful sleep when he was woken by a very loud squawk indeed.

'Dido,' said Pythagoras. 'Dido, *liebchen!*'

Algie was out of his bed and rooting through his pencil box within a second—it was as if a firework had gone off in his head. He had the answer! He and Pythagoras had solved the riddle! Without the help of any of the grown-ups!

Now he only hoped he had something with which to break into her rooms so that he could share his revelation with his sister.

He was caught, of course. He had expected it. After all it was not an easy thing to pick a lock with only the contents of one's pencil case, least of all with Allegra hissing infuriating encouragement from the far side of the keyhole.

Algie turned to find his aunt standing over him, his tutor at her side. He was nothing if not courageous.

'I know who you really are!' He needed Allegra to hear before the door was opened. 'And I know everything you are planning! You're not Aunt Lydia at all, you are Aunt Dido. My parrot said so!'

Dido. Yes, of course! Allegra stood suddenly icy calm and studied her aunt more closely. Not Lydia. But only just failing to be exactly like her. It had been the most brilliant impersonation. Identical in every way to her third triplet as she had been to their own mother, she had only made one really serious error. . .the one that had made Allegra feel even at the time that she was in the presence of a stranger. Aunt Lydia, whatever her own reputaion for immorality, would never have laughed to find her in the arms of Luc Fleetwood—least of all when he was her own lover's brother.

Strangely, now everything was at its most dangerous Allegra was no longer scared. But not because she thought that her aunt would not harm them—she would never forget what had happened to Algie. That had been Herr Kraftstein, of course. . .though he must have hated it he had still done it. Herr Kraftstein who had called Aunt Dido his darling in his native German . . .right under the beak of the ever-inquisitive parrot!

Darling Pythagoras! Both Algie and Allegra stood guarding their hero's cage and were mocked for their childlike solidarity.

'As if I care what your foolish bird does now! As if there is anything anyone can do to stop me! It is too late. Much, much too late!' And Dido broke into the most disturbing laughter.

Allegra had never seen anything like it before but she understood; and she faced it out because she had every faith in Cuthbert. He would have told Luc. . .

Dear God, but she knew now that she had every reason for her faith in Luc! And she behaved as if she had — coldly, haughtily, as if her aunt were nothing even so elevated as the dust beneath her feet.

'You are a fanatic! You are obsessed with Bonaparte——'

It was true. Her aunt's eyes flashed with a fire that was horrifying. 'Yes, the *Emperor*! He will return. His enemies will be broken. I shall see to that!'

'*You*!' Allegra fought to keep her scornful tones steady in the face of something so unnatural. 'With your trivial little plot to harm my father, who was only ever a friend to you! Do you really think you can discredit the Duke of Wellington? See, we know all about it! I even know who it is you are in league with at the Foreign Office!'

'So Fleetwood told you! Well, well. Of all men in the world I should not have expected him to take a female into his confidence, least of all if she warms his bed for him——'

'Enough!' It was Herr Kraftstein who spoke then, and Aunt Dido fell unnervingly silent. 'Not in front of the boy! I have told you before——'

'*You* have told *me*!' Aunt Dido burst into a peal of contemptuous laughter so disconcertingly like Aunt Lydia's that Allegra felt quite sick.

But the tutor stood his ground. He had always been the only one who had come anywhere near to taming Algie. Allegra looked at him and acknowledged the depth of her hurt. They had all trusted him; they liked him. . .

'I just don't understand. . .what is your part in this?'

He answered very simply. 'My country. I do it for *my* emperor, for Austria, because you British are become too powerful in our alliance against the French. Because Wellington and your father are too strong a force for us ever to gain what we must from the peace talks if they are allowed to be there.'

Of course. Everything explained. Now what was to happen?

Aunt Dido already had her mind on leaving. Allegra knew it, just as she sensed that once again the house was empty, except for the four of them. . .

What now?

'To the attics with them, I think. The servants' rooms at the back of the house. Long enough to give us the time we need. . .'

And as Allegra, Algie and the parrot were bundled firmly up the stairs and locked into the smallest box-room Allegra thought, It is not too late. Someone can still stop them; someone has to stop them! And it has to be me. Somehow. I cannot rely on Luc to have guessed the real urgency of Cuthbert's message. He of all people has every reason to believe my aunt has justly banned him from the house because of. . .

She could not think of that right now.

As the door closed and the key ground in the lock she had only one final question. Banging on the door, she shouted after them, 'Aunt Lydia—what have you done with Aunt Lydia?'

She was met by a burst of ice-cold laughter, then silence.

\* \* \*

Trapped high at the back of the house, she never heard the rattle of stones against her bedroom window in the early hours of the morning, the moment Luc returned from his urgent trip to London. Nor did she see the letter, written in Cuthbert's unmistakable hand, pushed beneath the front door telling her that everything was well and to stay where she was until everything was safely over. Telling her not to be frightened of anything any more.

Luc had thought of everything, even down to guessing that Allegra would be allowed access to the harmless Cuthbert's missive; everything except that there was no one left in the house to give it to her. And that she was locked three floors up in a filthy attic.

'Try harder, Algie!'

'I *am* trying! Besides, how can I see what I am doing with you standing in the only scrap of moonlight?'

'Temper!' reproved the parrot.

And instantly Allegra had the answer. Pythagoras. Unlocking the attic door was hopeless, calling out even more pointless, but if they could only reach the tiny window near the ceiling. . .if they could only find a way of getting the bird to fly to Luc. . .if only they could find a way of making him give the right message. Then they would be rescued. Then Luc would still have time to stop Aunt Dido before it was too late and she escaped, as she was surely planning to do, to France and nobody would ever believe when the plot broke against her father, that Dido had not been Lydia all the time. The only person to swear the difference for sure — Lydia's lover — had never seen Dido. Dido had made very sure of that, meeting with Herr Kraftstein every night in the woods at Fleetwood, waiting until the tutor told her Faron was gone before she arrived in the guise of Lydia. It had been immaculately planned. But Allegra was not going to let that beat her!

'Algie, hold that chair for me!' Broken but sturdily made of solid oak. Allegra could just reach the window, stuck fast by years of unattended damp. No time to waste, she ruthlessly smashed it open with her shoe. Cold air swept in and her spirits soared with exitement. Now for the message. . .

'Algie, will Pythagoras repeat what we tell him to?'

'I don't *think* so; he never does anything he's supposed to.'

'No. . .then have you anything to write with?'

'Yes, but we have nothing to write *on*, nor any way to attach it to his leg even if we did.'

Allegra had the answer as if her whole brain were working at double speed. . .it felt as if it was, and she was exhilarated by it.

'Here — my hair ribbon!'

Pale ivory — just the thing for Algie to write neatly upon in the charcoal he always kept in his pockets for sketching rabbits.

Ten minutes later Pythagoras found himself coaxed, then threatened, the finally bribed, out on to the flat of the roof, his head positively ringing with instructions.

'House! Luc! *Help*!'

Anything to obtain some silence! Pythagoras flapped off into the night and was gone. Along with a message that read simply, 'Dido — tutor — A and A in attic!'

Three hours later — because Pythagoras was a

leisurely bird and savoured his little taste of freedom—Allegra heard what she had been waiting for. For the second time since she had known him Mr Fleetwood was breaking down a door.

Allegra and Algie sat down to a desperately needed breakfast in Laura Place as Cuthbert exclaimed again, 'But it is quite brilliant! Her plans cannot fail!'

And Luc knew that someone was going to have to tell him.

Cuthbert—to Luc's very real surprise but no longer Allegra's—took the fact of his uncle FitzCarlin's involvement stoically and without even a second's hesitation as to whose side he was on.

He sounded sad as he said, 'Wish you'd said somethin' before, Fleetwood. I could have told you my uncle would hand his whole fortune to the Devil—beggin' the ladies' pardon—for the chance to do Wellington ill. But to be party to so *wicked* a thing as this. . .'

'To have false papers planted upon Lady Allegra's father implicating him and Lydia Limington in plans to free Bonaparte from exile and set him on the throne of France again? No, how could you ever have thought of that? And you are right, Nettlesham, it *was* a plan of genius. It could still defeat us. . .'

Allegra could think of only one way out of it. 'Then we need to find the real Aunt Lydia and prove where she has been all this time!'

It seemed to her then that it had been a very long time since she had seen Luc smile. Least of all in a manner so patronising as he did at that moment when she met his eyes and flushed at the memory of how plainly she had been overjoyed to see him.

'We have not been sitting on our hands, Allegra.' How dared he and Cuthbert smirk at one another as if she were only some precocious schoolgirl? 'Whilst you were dithering about in your attic Nettlesham and I have been very busy. . .indeed you should have noticed the house to be singularly devoid of footmen.'

Which was true, and she would have noticed had she had eyes for anything but Luc. Allegra set down her cup, utterly disgusted with herself.

'Where are they?' she demanded suspiciously.

'Each one headed for any possible port of exit, riding, and well able to overtake Dido's carriage. Each one carrying orders signed by the Prime Minister himself — have I not told you I have spent the last three days well-occupied in London? — sealing the ports until Dido and her confederate have been captured.'

'I —'

'And Nettlesham here is this very moment to set out for London to apprise the Prime Minister of the latest developments.'

Cuthbert, the one who was truly going to suffer in all this, whether Dido won or failed, whose family would be forever tainted by association with a man who was all but traitor.

Allegra wanted to comfort him. 'Cuthbert, Lord FitzCarlin cannot have truly wanted to aid Bonaparte, he just craved more power at the Foreign Office, power Papa and Wellington would never have let him achieve. I think Aunt Dido only really involved him because he . . .well, he knew Aunt Lydia so closely once. . .and

she needed what he knew to help make her impersonation convincing to us. . .'

'Don't fret over me, my dearest Allegra. The world
will know my uncle for what he is—a fool, not an evil
man.'

'Is Herr Kraftstein evil?' Algie put in plaintively. 'He
hit me very hard on the head and I thought he liked
me.'

Luc looked at Allegra then and she knew what he
was thinking. Could it be explained to a child?

When that child was Algie it could. 'Not evil, Algie,
just caring dreadfully about his country, the way we
do. And, fatally for him, in love with Dido.'

'I see.'

He did. So much so that Allegra felt her heart turn
over and she could no longer bear this inaction.

'If Cuthbert goes to London what do we do? We
cannot do nothing——'

'You can, and you will! And keep Tiffy
company——'

'*Never*!' Allegra surged to her feet. Men! They were
going to leave her out of things again! Just when
everything had really become exciting, and after all she
and Algie had done. 'Where are *you* going, Luc?' she
demanded wrathfully.

'Portsmouth—and not with you!'

'Why Portsmouth? And——'

'Um. . .well, I'll be hoofin' off, Fleetwood, and don't
worry, I'll see everythin's set square in London. . .'

'Cuthbert,' wailed Allegra, 'I thought at least you
would plead my case! I am *so* very tired of being
treated like——'.

'A baby? Then don't behave like one!' Luc.

'*I am not!*'

And Cuthbert smiled. 'Thing is, well, won't loaf about to catch the outcome of the mill, y'see. Never could find the stomach for the spillin' of blood!'

Allegra was left glaring at Luc furiously in the cravat, thinking very seriously of standing on the settle the better really to incinerate him with her furious eyes, watched in awed fascination by her brother and the parrot.

'You are *not* coming with me!' repeated Luc doggedly. 'I have not the least intention of being hampered——'

'*Hampered!*'

'Yes, *hampered* by a female when——'

'I can ride just as well as you can!'

'I'm driving! You see, it so happens I am expecting to acquire a passenger. . .'

'Drive? What passenger?' Then she knew. 'You think you know where my real aunt Lydia has got to and you *still* think you can leave me behind!'

'I can and I will.'

And Algie quite forgot himself in his—very partisan—enjoyment. 'Thing is, well, you could do a great deal worse than take along Sis, because, well, she's the most cracking whip-hand I ever saw——'

'Keep silent, Algie!' Luc began to feel well and truly cornered.

Allegra knew she was going to win. 'I am! Freddie Limmersham taught me and he is a member of the Four Horse club so——'

'That self-congratulating mob of road-hogs! I——'

'You're only jealous because you're not!'

It worked, inevitably. Because—Allegra smiled almost indulgently at him—he was a man.

'You're saying I cannot drive as well as Limmersham, are you?'

If there was one nerve she knew how to touch now, and painfully, it was the one that led straight to his store of jealously.

'You couldn't possibly,' she countered haughtily.

Which was how, half an hour later, she found herself on the road west out of Bath, perched up on the seat of Cuthbert's smart new curricle, heading at a speed that almost terrified even her along the route that would lead them across the plains of Wiltshire and south until they reached the coast at Portsmouth.

Hanging desperately on to what was quite her favourite hat and in imminent danger of losing it forever, Allegra struck her wickedest blow.

'Well, after all you really *aren't* so bad a driver. . .

Allegra was told, most evocatively, to be silent.

Never had she seen anyone so determined; face set grimly into the wind, Luc kept up such a punishing pace that he would exhaust himself.

Halfway through the afternoon they stopped for their third change of horses—these seconded from their duties with the military courier service by the briskest of orders, Luc barely having to wave his official papers beneath their custodian's nose, so authoritative was his manner. Allegra watched, wondering if she would ever cease to find something new to marvel at in him, some new respect to hurt her all the more when she must let him go. They were together now. . .but only for now.

Already she could feel that Luc's mind was so much on the task in hand that he had all but forgotten she was with him. And that he had someone else who could take the reins so that he might rest.

She knew the moment she slipped the reins into her hands while he spurred on the ostlers that he was going to be impossible about it. Thus it was that Luc turned back to find her glaring at him so stubbornly he could not help himself. He did the most unforgivable thing and laughed at her even as he leapt up beside her and said most sternly, 'Now, you will give those to me?'

Allegra felt herself flushing even before his head brushed against hers—even before she felt his arm hard against her shoulder. Out of sheer self-defence she turned it into a flush of rage.

'Do you have to be such a fool, Luc? Why must you always be so obstinate? Why do you refuse to accept that I can help, I can be useful? I. . .' But her words were burned away by the intensity of his eyes—and the intensity of his words, though they were never so innocent.

'I have never refused anything from you, Allegra, though God knows I tried!'

She could not begin to imagine what he might mean, and so was more thankful than she could have said when, with just a rueful quirk of that dazzling smile, he set the reins back into her hands with the unforgivable, 'Please, take your turn. I shall sit quietly here, offending nobody, and treat you to my thoughts on female drivers!'

It served him right that she was better than even he had suspected—so fast, indeed, that he spent the next two hours just trying to keep his balance. Allegra fumed. When Luc next took up the reins they were — very pointedly — not speaking. And in the silence Allegra began to think.

One thing had not occurred to her as she'd bundled her things into a small valise and Algie had tied it up beside Luc's — fast though the curricle was, at least half a day faster than the carriage she knew Aunt Dido had taken, they were not going to reach the coast before at least one night intervened, and if the weather broke, as it looked very much as if it might, even two.

It dawned on Allegra, somewhere to the north of Romsey, that she had put herself in the most invidious position. But she was still so drunk with her excitement at the chase that she forgot it was not the least bit funny and laughed at it.

Luc, who was negotiating a particularly awkward bend, snarled at her, 'What you can find to laugh at — ?'

'Us. I mean. . .' And then she petered out, crimson with embarrassment.

It was not funny at all. It was all the things she never wanted to think about again, wanted to pretend had never happened. Like that one fatal moment in his arms when she had said she loved him. When he had not said a word in reply. When not once since had he shown anything towards her but his old, almost brotherly irritability. . . Because he had heard her foolish confession after all, and hoped that in the drama of it all it could be forgotten? Because he had never loved her.

It was her abrupt, flushing silence that told Luc what

she meant. And so sure of what he wanted, and that
he had heard her say she loved him so she must want it
too, he made the mistake of really laughing at her.

'Bowling about the shires without a chaperon? Yes,
I think you may safely say you no longer have one
shred of reputation!'

Reading his laughter as complete indifference,
Allegra flared back, 'I — why must it only be *me* who is
ruined?'

And Luc, slowing suddenly in the twilight behind a
particularly noisome farm cart, swept his eyes from the
road, pinned them on Allegra so fiercely that she could
no longer breathe and announced in the last place, at
the last moment he had ever intended, 'Nobody is
going to suffer for anything; why should we, seeing
that we are going to be married?'

# CHAPTER THIRTEEN

'WHAT? Stop this curricle this instant! I ——'

'We have stopped, in case you have not noticed it!' Luc's voice never lost its blandness but behind it she sensed he was suddenly wary, suddenly beginning to doubt something he had been very sure of. 'We are stuck behind a cartload of manure; besides, it is getting so late we must stop in the next village for the night!'

'I am not spending the night with you anywhere!' cried Allegra.

How could he ever understand — that he had said the very worst thing in the whole world? That he would marry her not because he loved her but because, through her own stubborn stupidity in coming with him, she was compromised.

Luc, who had not been planning to make his declaration in the middle of a rutted lane — least of all when he was no longer certain of its welcome — lost his equally beleaguered temper.

'You may remain right here if you like! God knows, I am damned if I spend my time with you nagging at ——'

'I do *not* nag!'

'You were the one who *would* come! I warned you I did not want you!'

'You didn't say I'd have to marry you!' she retorted

273

brokenly. And as simply as that Luc saw that it was hopeless.

'Have to marry you'. The words were like a blinding pain to his head. He had been wrong all along—wrong most of all that through that drugged haze of desire he had heard the words 'I love you so *much*'. His stomach tightened against a kick of real agony.

Allegra felt as if everything inside her had died.

And none of it was helped by the sudden onset of rain.

They reached the inn of the King's Head in quite the vilest of tempers, so much so that Luc had not the least difficulty in convincing the innkeeper's wife that they were really married.

'I am *not* having you anywhere near me!' Allegra could not bear it. Not now. She had never meant to do this to him, trap him into feeling obliged to offer for her. What if he thought she *had* meant to?

'I'm not having you!'

Luc savagely bespoke the two best rooms in the house, muttering under his breath that the further apart they were, the better he would like it.

The innkeeper's wife was all solicitude for the put-upon Allegra. She took a very dim view of the masculine half of the species and had not the least care who knew about it.

'Poor little thing!' She stood at Allegra's side like a dog on guard. 'I know precisely what has happened! Kept on the road all day, and the way that *gentlemen* drive these days—it is a mercy more people are not killed, so it is!'

Allegra tossed Luc a 'so there!' expression over her

shoulder, desperate to get away from his anger. Luc sank exhausted on to a seat in their private parlour and looked with bruised solidarity at the inn-keeper. Neither of them bothered to say it. Women!

So how come he was so hopelessly in love?

He knew, of course, looking at her as she stormed — the only word for it — into the parlour after availing herself of the opportunity to change into something a great deal warmer. She needed the comfort of the soft, midnight velvet, as if anything could warm the pain of her unhappiness away.

The look Luc cast at her as she entered the room all but sent her fleeing up the stairs again.

He is so angry with me, he must hate me! she cried silently. He looks — quite truthfully — as if he would kill me.

Luc was wondering when just the thought of her, let alone the sight and the sweet scent of her violet perfume, would stop all but annihilating him.

He had never wanted to fall in love. He had misspent most of his youth making absolutely certain he avoided it. How was he to guess that — quite off his guard and going about his legitimate business breaking into other people's houses — *she* would be there, aiming her pistol at him, backed up only by that idiot parrot?

He could not help it. He smiled. The memory was so sweet, it cut like the deepest wound, but he never wanted to forget it.

Tentatively — because she would do anything not to have him angry with her any more. . .even if he could not want her, just let him be kind! — Allegra smiled back.

Luc saw that smile and thought, She knows at last. She has been so very slow to see I love her. Absurdest child, when every other man who sets eyes on her adores her. . .

But not like this! *Never* like this!

She yelled at him, she hit him, she scared the life out of him wth her hare-brained exploits; she nagged at him, she had landed him with her impossible little brother, and still he needed but one look at her to want to scoop her up like the most fragile, the most vulnerable of orphans and carry her off to somewhere she would always be safe, always be warm. Always be so passionately loved.

Back to Fleetwood and the land that he had shown her that day. The home he would build. Had she really not understood he had been saying it was for her?

It was. He could never build it for anyone else, not now. There was never going to be anyone but her.

She could not spell, she had the education of a dormouse, she had picked up the most deplorable language from the parrot, and all he saw was a tumble of windswept curls — could the child never manage to stay tidy? — and her ice-pale skin against her midnight velvet. Pale because of him, eyes all bruised and huge because of him. Because of what he had said that had so appalled her.

She could never bear to marry him.

He wanted to explain why he had offered it. To explain what he felt. To say those words he had sworn to himself he had more common sense than ever to want to utter them at all. *I love you.*

What he said was, 'This is a very tolerable pie.'

Quite why that should make even a child as volatile as Allegra burst into a flood of tears he could never know, but he acted on it instinctively. He had caught her on to the wooden settle before the fire before he could think it might be the very last thing she needed, and was cradling her against him as if he could caress all her misery away.

When at last he could find the voice to speak he murmured brokenly, 'Oh, kitten, what in the world have you got to cry about?' As if he did not know. As if she could ever tell him!'

'You said it was a nice pie,' she sniffed helplessly into his shoulder.

He interpreted this—as he believed—correctly. 'Allegra, my sweet, silly angel, you do not have to marry me, not if you would hate it so!'

'I don't. . .' Then she heard what he had said. 'I— *what* did you just call me?'

He was so urgent to console her, he did not know.

'My most idiotic darling!' Then once more he reverted to his fatal reflex of defensive flippancy. 'Something to that humiliatingly besotted effect, at any rate.'

He needed that flippancy more than he had ever needed it before. Needed it so that she would never know as she turned his offer down how much it mattered. He would die rather than have her know how deeply she could hurt him. He had seen how badly she had felt over Cuthbert Nettlesham.

He was so far turned against inevitable rejection that he took a whole minute to realise she had said, 'Why?'

Why! And in that sad, lost tone of hers. . .so wary,

so afraid. . . At last he knew. That everything he had believed in their closet moments had been true. That everything he had thought he had destroyed survived. Because it could survive anything.

He was laughing when he said it, really laughing, just as he had been the very first moment she saw him. The very moment she had fallen in love.

'Oh, Allegra, I have the most powerful feeling we are quite the most stupid beings on the planet!'

'I don't see ——'

'Because I love you, and you love me. . .' Suddenly he swung her round to face him and never in her life had she seen such intensity, such passion in his gaze. 'You *do* don't you? And you always 'have! Just as I loved you from the very first moment ——'

'I — *what*?'

He *could* not have said that! Only, he was saying it again. 'I would probably have loved you even had you shot me!'

'I would never have done that!' Allegra was stunned, shaking; she did not know what she was saying or doing so she said the very first thing that came into her head. 'You looked far too *nice* a person to kill.' Then she said what she really meant. 'I thought you were my greatest friend. I did, Luc all the time, right from the start. Even when you were such a beast ——'

'And you were such a maddening little demon ——'

'I don't think *that's* fair; I only said *beast* — oh, Luc, did you *really* just say you loved me?'

'Wrong tense. . .'

'I ——'

'If you say "I — what?" even once more — well, don't even ——'

'*Think* about it!'

'No!' And suddenly he felt his arms tightening possessively about her. 'Think very, very carefully about marrying me instead.'

'I don't have to.'

'Yes, you do, Allegra. I very much doubt we should survive each other; one or other of us would be cold beneath the daisies before the first month was out. I've got the absolute devil of a ——'

'Temper, yes, you're *vile*, Luc: really you can be the most *hateful* man was ever born! But it is not as if I am not ——'

'The most tiresome female who ever had existence!'

Allegra looked at him then, and watched the firelight soften the hard, difficult lines of his face, and without thinking she lifted her hand to follow the shadows flickering across his cheek.

'We would have a terrible life together, wouldn't we?'

'Three squabbles a day, at the very least, and out-and-out fisticuffs once a fortnight.'

'I *throw* things. I thought I had better say.'

'That's all right — I duck!'

I was inevitable that Allegra should burst into another flood of tears, this time because she was so overwhelmed with happiness even while she was too terrified to believe. Yet she could see it in his eyes, *feel* it. She had *always* known it, hadn't she? Deep down, just as she knew it now. Yet she dared not *believe*. . .

Luc dealt with this outburst very practically.

Allegra's tears were kissed away in such a frenzy of passion that when she finally emerged trembling from his embrace she would never doubt him again.

There was only one thing left to be said. . .

'Luc. . .?'

'Mmm?'

'Do you suppose you could ask me to marry you again?'

'Whatever for?'

'Well. . . I did not *precisely* say yes.'

'Luc?'

The fire was dying and beyond the windows Allegra could hear the beginning of a thunderstorm, but she would never be cold again. Never afraid. Never alone. She curled still more contentedly against his side and felt him smile so softly against her hair.

'What is it?'

'Aunt Lydia? Papa? Is everything really going to be all right?' And she felt his arms tighten around her as he knew at last she could be told.

'Yes, it will be now, even though for a while. . .' Allegra felt the tension in him as he looked back on the very real dread and pain, and lifted her head to kiss the shadows away, glad to know she could always make him laugh at her. 'I must mope more often!' Then he was serious again. 'For a while I was so blind—for a while even though I was working for your father all along I thought it might be Lydia. . .'

How he must have felt, doubting the woman his own brother so loved.

'I didn't know about Dido then. Dear God, but it

only your idiot parent had told me there were three of them! Triplets! But of course he thought Dido to be dead.'

'Because Bonaparte told him and Papa. . . Papa believed it to be an act of kindness!'

'I know. Dido must have been working for his cause all along. And she is the best. . .the best I have ever come up against. . .'

'But she has not won?'

'No, thanks to you and Algie she cannot. Because I found out about her existence in time we shall be able to prove there are two sisters and save Lydia. Our being able to guess that truth was her greatest fear. The only thing she could not risk was being seen in her false guise by my brother.'

'But. . .if she wanted us out of London and at Bath, why was the house empty when we found it?'

'Because it *was* Lydia who sent you that letter. . .and was somehow herself tricked away just afterwards. Just as my brother was tricked safely out of the way on a wild-goose chase to London. It was so simple really. . . think of it — letters actually written by Bonaparte, planted on your father and on Lydia, and no one to believe Lydia had ever been away; whatever tale she told would be so impossible that it would be even harder to believe her. This was planned a long time ago, Allegra, before the war was ended. Bonaparte has been desperate for so long to bring Wellington down. But now so many people have suspicions, his case is hopeless. . .'

'Once we find Aunt Lydia. . .'

'Yes, once we find Lydia.'

And they sat for a long time in contented silence,

certain now that all their troubles were at an end. Every port was watched. Dido and Herr Kraftstein could never get away.

Allegra was still drowsing in his arms when a most unwelcome thought suddenly struck her.

'Luc. . . I have just this moment thought of it. Am I *allowed* to marry you if Aunt Lydia weds your brother and he is my uncle?'

'I — *what*?'

'Now you are saying it! But think, Luc. . .are there not a vast number of rules and laws about who may marry whose relations?'

'A whole thicket of the damned things, I should think, but it need not concern us.'

'Why not?'

'Because if it takes an Act of Parliament to make any marriage legal then it will be Faron and Lydia's! They will have to wait!'

'Why?'

'Because I *can't*!'

All of which was true and left the Honourable Luc Fleetwood with the most frustrating dilemma, the major part of which was retaining his hold on the claim to be called the *honourable* anything at all by the morning.

It was a very good thing, thought Allegra, as the moonlight stole so enticingly across the floor of her tiny chamber, that he could not bear it a second longer.

Because if he had not come to her, she would have gone to him.

\* \* \*

Allegra was handed the reins the following morning by a Luc who was fighting with every last breath not to pull her down from her perch on the curricle and go straight back into the inn, and to the devil with Bonaparte!

Allegra watched him, still suffused with awe, the soft smile in her eyes so private that only he could ever understand it. He who had put it there; he knew that if it killed him he would never let her lose it.

Allegra had not known how she would feel—would she be shy of him, awkward? But the moment she had woken to the laughter in his eyes she had known she could never be again. . . Instead she now found herself wondering if it would *really* matter so very much if Aunt Dido reached Portsmouth before them.

But of course it did. With the final shreds of the self-control that he had felt burned so finally away in the passion that had erupted between them through the night, Luc said—wondering how he managed to say anything at all when all he wanted to do was kiss her until she fainted— 'If you will be so good as to hand those reins to me. . .'

And Allegra tossed back her hair, her eyes alive with laughter at him. 'Just because you were so terrified when I drove yesterday——'

He sprang up beside her. 'I was not——'

'You *were*!'

It was probably because he kissed her so ruthlessly to silence then, much to the delight of the goggling ostlers, that made her whisper it.

'But, Luc, *I'm* not scared of anything any more! Nothing, ever! Not now!'

And he smiled so very seriously. 'No, not ever. Not now.' Before he urged the horses into motion and added very casually, 'Though there is the little matter of explaining our intentions to your father!'

Her father was waiting for them at Portsmouth, just that moment docked from France, and with him, of all people, Aunt Lydia!

Whose very first words were the exact match of Allegra's.

'Where in this world have you been?'

'Paris,' explained an Aunt Lydia as languid and as muddled as ever. 'It truly was the most vexing thing, for I had a message at Bath that because the war was ended you were to go to France to be with your papa instead.'

'But Aunt, the war was *not* ended when you wrote that letter, at least Papa's part in it was not, for all you knew of anything, at any rate, for you never in your life read the papers!'

'No, I realise that now, and I cannot say that anything was more infuriating! For there I was trying to get to Paris——'

'To join me and you and Algie, who were not there!' put in a so far silent, and very much amused, Duke of Alderley.

And at last Allegra realised it was finally over. Burned by the sun and scarred by war, yet so familiar and loved it was as if he had never been away——

'Oh, *Papa!*' And after a very long time when neither could say anything at all she managed, 'It is the most dreadful thing, I know, and you are sure to be most absolutely furious about it, but I am going to marry Mr Fleetwood!'

And so she did. With the utmost respectability at a very grand ceremony indeed in Hanover Square.

The elegant ball which followed at Alderley House would have been equally unexceptionable had not a certain party been eavesdropping on other people's conversations again.

Luc, wild with happiness and not caring who among their stiff-necked Society guests knew about it, drew Allegra urgently apart from the the congratulatory throng, and, impatient as ever with rules and regulations of conventional etiquette — let alone his need to have her to himself again — pulled her into his arms, laughing out loud that she came so willingly.

'I have said all manner of solemn things today before that pompous idiot of a bishop, all but what I really mean!'

'He is *not* pompous, he is Cousin Alberic — '

'Allegra. . .*be quiet!*'

'I — *what*?'

'So I may say how much I love you!'

And she flung her arms ecstatically about his neck, not caring in the world who saw it.

'I love you too!'

From out of a potted palm the hero of the hour, Pythagoras, opined, '*Gawd 'elp us!*'

# LEGACY *of* LOVE

## Coming next month

## SERENA
### *Sylvia Andrew*
#### Regency (West Indies/England)

Miss Serena Calvert, owner of Anse Chatelet on the West
Indian island of St. Just, was determined to give her young
niece Lucy a London Season, whatever the financial
privations. But their aunt's health would not permit her to
launch Lucy, and Serena was forced to go too, as chaperon.

Once in England, Serena met a delightful gentleman in
slightly scandalous circumstances, and both looked forward
to meeting again more formally in London. But that meeting
resulted in a massively public snub for Serena, and only then
did she become aware that *she* was the target of revenge...

## HOSTAGE OF LOVE
### *Valentina Luellen*
#### Scotland 1740

Rufus MacIan and Alistair Denune have feuded for years, but
now their children are grown. Michael Denune and Maura
MacIan want to marry, *must* marry, for Maura is pregnant.
But Rufus will only permit it if the Denunes will agree to a
hostage, to be held until Maura's child is born.

How can Cassandra refuse, when she loves her
brother—even if this does bring her into contact with Rufus's
adopted son, Adam MacIan? He, at least, seems to be
civilised...until Cassandra realises the feud hasn't died.

# LEGACY of LOVE

## Coming next month

# THE RELUCTANT BRIDE
### *Barbara Bretton*
#### Delaware 1887

The Pemberton Arms would have long since crumbled but for the optimism of Molly Hughes. She dreamed of a chance to restore the old seaside hotel, the only home she'd ever known. That chance was suddenly within her reach—depending on how she handled Nicholas St George, the Englishman who had just inherited her beloved "Pem"—and meant to sell it off! Nicholas had been appalled when he'd set eyes on the ramshackle nightmare he'd inherited. Nothing could save it. Not even the charm of Molly Hughes...

Before he weakened any further, he'd conclude his business and sail home—post-haste! Molly had a surprise in store for Nicholas...

# WICKED STRANGER
### *Louisa Rawlings*
#### France/New York 1817

Elizabeth Babcock had always been "just plain Bessie", overshadowed by her socialite sisters. Few suitors looked beyond her razor-sharp repartee—and temper to match—before leaving for less challenging opportunities. Until, that was, a night in Paris, when she crossed rapier wits with Noel Bouchard...

A gambler, a soldier, a man of the world, Noel Bouchard prayed never to be saddled with a dull domestic life. Marriage, if entered into at *all*, should be an adventure—tempestuous and lusty. He needed a woman with verve and spirit. With passion and wit. A woman like Elizabeth Babcock...

# FOUR HISTORICAL ROMANCES

# & TWO FREE GIFTS!